Books by Jeremy Hodgson

HISTORICAL ROMANCE
Dance on the Terrace

ADVENTURES IN RESEARCH
Curing Emily
Secret in the Seas

ROMANTIC AFRICAN ADVENTURES
Leap of a Lifetime

EGYPTIAN SAGA
Take Me Instead

AERIAL ADVENTURES
Breathe On Me

We Are One

Jeremy Hodgson

ISBN: 978-0-7961-5471-2
e-ISBN: 978-0-7961-5472-9

Jeremy William Hodgson
Villa 99, Tamarina Golf Estate
Black River, Mauritius
90922
jwhodgson42@gmail.com

This is a work of fiction. Names, characters, and some places and incidents are either products of the author's imagination or are used fictitiously, and any resemblance to persons living or dead, business establishments, events, or locales is entirely coincidental.

Structural evaluation by Wesley Thompson
Editing by Sharon Dell
Proofreading by the author
Cover by Nikki Meier
Maps by Louise van Wyk
Typesetting and ebook by Liquid Type Publishing Services

For my lifetime friend, John Siebert

Foreword

TO WRITE A FOREWORD TO THIS BOOK THAT GRABS MY HEART is complicated, for it describes a world that is a foreign country to most who will read it, a country so alien that it might be on another planet. So if the stories in this book appear mythical, impossible, or unbelievable, please accept them as fiction. To those who acknowledge they are authentic, I'll say they display the behaviour of cultures that have learnt to live together in peace and harmony, something this planet desperately needs. We can learn from them.

Let me describe the country where the events in this book take place.

Millions of years ago, the planet was far wetter than today. In Zimbabwe and Botswana, continuously flowing water once carved the broad rivers now filled with sand and an occasional trickle of water. The Congo equatorial basin that feeds moist air southwards brought heavy sustained rainfall to countries like Angola, Zimbabwe and Botswana.

Lakes, shallow but thousands of square kilometres in size, captured this rainfall and fed rivers that led to the sea.

Over millennia, the rainfall dropped, the lakes dried, and the Zambesi changed direction, leaving only the immense salt pans of the Makgadikgadi that drained, dried and sank.

One thing stopped all of Botswana from becoming an arid desert.

The Okavango River that flows from the Angolan highlands diverted, feeding water to keep the most northern lake areas flooded, but only just. Slowly, the lakes filled with reeds and became the enormous Okavango swamps, a paradise for birds and animals of every kind. The animals evolved, antelope like the Sitatunga developed splayed feet to run on beds of reeds and swim well, and the Lechwe marvellously adapted to running in shallow water, with longer hind legs and waterproof fur.

Fish from the Okavango filled the swamps and evolved into species not found elsewhere, and every living thing adapted to feed on what the Okavango provided.

But as the reducing rainfall created a new ecosystem, so did it become more seasonal, and, as in the Serengeti, the massive animal herds learned to migrate north to south and east to west. The Chobe River now linked the area. As in the Serengeti, the migrations supply data to those who study them.

But others come to see and marvel. Spread throughout the area are game lodges: Specialised hotels where trained staff can show and teach visitors about the ecosystem, striving to preserve the world's great wonders in the face of the growing needs of an encroaching population.

We who manage these reserves and welcome you to visit them want to preserve these parts of our planet, not as a zoo to look at, but as a shining example of how diverse cultures can live together in harmony.

Sam Daniels, Doctor of Zoology, Harper Adams University

Prelude

. . . .

Twenty-three years ago

SAM

FIVE-YEAR-OLD SAM DANIELS WAS QUITE SURE HE KNEW ALL about females. He lived happily with his parents in a small town in Buckinghamshire, England. His mind, a-little-bit-different-from-others' minds, had classified them, although Sam wouldn't learn that word for many years. Trying to make sense of his world from limited observations, he had three mental boxes under *Females*. Sam labelled the first, the most important, *Mothers*. A soft voice, a fluffy loose dress, and a warm lap qualified a member for that box, and if they hugged him and kissed him, that confirmed they were candidates. The second, labelled *Ladies*, contained the remaining tall ones, usually with smooth tight dresses and no lap to sit on, with either harsh voices or hands that sometimes patted him on the head. The third was *Girls*, all the shorter females he ignored, as most ignored him right back. The smallest ones played with dolls that didn't move, while his friends, the spiders, terrified them.

At first, babies with no apparent gender didn't fit into his system. He had no idea where they came from. Eventually, he established a logical link between his boxes. When the *Girls* with dolls grew, their dolls became babies, and the *Girls* became *Mothers*. The *Ladies* were *Girls* without dolls. He knew one with a rabbit; she would be a *Lady*.

Sam's rudimentary classification would change as the years passed.

He was still five when a woman came to fetch him from playschool. She was a *Lady*. Although he'd never seen her before, there was no doubt about it, for she patted him on the head and said, 'You must come with me, Sam.'

A *Mother* in the house she took him to was a Mrs Grundy. She continuously gave orders, like 'sit here' and 'play here', was busy-busy, and had five children of different ages to care for, all sent to her by the social welfare department. She didn't have time to loan her lap to any of them. Sam moved her to the *Lady* group. He didn't understand why he was there and didn't dare ask, so he withdrew into a corner and looked at the picture books she gave him. Sam ate and slept when told and said nothing, his fear of the unknown building with every hour and every day until it was overwhelming.

A week later, the other strange *Lady* returned, and Sam, sitting near the living room door, heard the conversation. 'Good morning, Mrs Grundy; I've come for Sam. How is he?'

'Healthy, but that's all I can say; he hasn't spoken since you brought him.'

'Have you told him?'

'No, not my job, Miss Jones; I expected one of your psychologists would come.'

'Oh dear, I suppose I must do it. Can you fetch Sam, please?'

Sam stood silently in front of her, expressionless. Miss Jones wanted to reach out and take him in her arms, but staying emotionally distant was part of her job. 'Sam, I must tell you something. Your parents had a car accident, and they won't return.'

Sam felt a terrible emptiness. If Anita Jones had taken him in her arms, had said 'Your Mummy and Daddy' instead of 'parents', and had said that they were dead, it wouldn't have been so hollow. He might have cried. He didn't; petrified by the overwhelming fear that had built, he said nothing.

'I'm taking you to a care home, Sam, where there are many other children, and they will look after you.'

At high school, a psychologist who came to evaluate the new students for curriculum guidance interviewed Sam. A kindly man, he never wrote anything in his reports that might dog a student for years, so he avoided any psychiatric definitions. Sam's report stated:

> Sam has a brilliant mind capable of honours in higher degrees in Zoology in his fields of interest. A social misfit due to his childhood, he has nevertheless learnt how to function in society when required, although his natural reaction is withdrawal. Team sports will be stressful for Sam and not recommended.

Sam remained withdrawn, and over the years, his withdrawal worsened until he earned the nickname *Silent* Sam. However, no boys bullied him. His obligatory high school sport was judo, and during the school holidays, he ran, a solitary runner on country roads.

MELISSA

She was four when her mother took her to the doctor.

'Good morning, Mrs Grouwer. What's the problem with Melissa?'

'She may have an ear infection, doctor; she keeps stuffing bits of cloth in her ears. It started ten days ago when she began attending nursery school.'

After finding no infection, her mother took her to a hearing specialist. The test results took three weeks.

'Mrs Grouwer, Melissa is both lucky and unlucky. She has perfect hearing. Too perfect. One in ten thousand people have perfect pitch, which I consider a gift, but she also has overly sensitive hearing. It is rare, and less than a hundred people worldwide have both. She doesn't hear things as we do. To you, background sound may seem like a low buzz; to her, it's painful, a gabble of different sounds. You said you noticed it when she started going to nursery school. I'm sure she's had it since birth, but hearing sensitivity really only develops once the brain learns to separate the frequencies. A horde of kids yelling and screaming is unbearable for her, just as someone playing music at a high volume can be painful to you or me.'

'But what can I do, doctor?'

'Here's a prescription. Take it to the hearing aid company mentioned. They will make earplugs to filter the noise, especially the higher frequencies.'

'Must she wear them all her life?'

'I hope not. The perfect pitch will, hopefully, remain throughout Melissa's life, but not the sensitivity. It usually diminishes from the onset of puberty, as it does for us all, but it will take ten to fifteen years. The earplugs will need adjustments, like spectacles, at least once a year. Please take care of her: psychological complications can develop as she tries to deal with it.'

Melissa's mother took good care of her for five years until she and her husband died in a plane crash. The consequences were enormous. The only relative willing to look after Melissa was her Aunt Jane Delvers, who was kind but busy with her business. Melissa already had a physical wall between her and the world – her earplugs. Without her mother at her side to help her, her father to hug her, and the haven of the warm cocoon between her parents in bed that sheltered her when the stress was excessive, she built a mental wall and withdrew from the world and the people she wanted to block out.

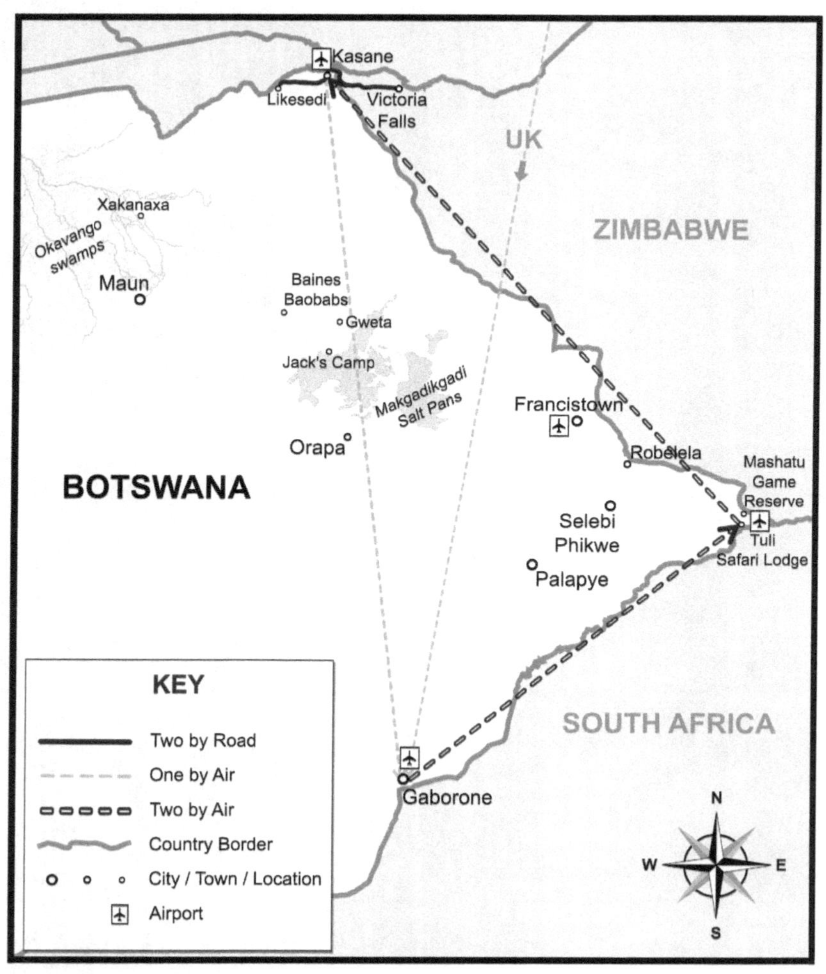

Melissa's Planned Routes by Air and Road for her Tour of Botswana

1

• • • • •

IN THE NORTHEAST OF BOTSWANA, WHERE THE COUNTRY meets Zambia, Zimbabwe and Namibia, the Chobe National Park sprawls westwards along the southern bank of the Chobe River.

It is a place of beauty and diversity, where the river runs through the savanna, and the forest is home to elephants, lions, hippos, crocodiles, and Sam Daniels.

Silent Sam had left his bed at 4:30, as he did every morning. In summer, he saw the first glimmerings of light staining the horizon as if the black sky were blotting paper, sucking up the coloured ink of the coming day. In winter, he saw impenetrable darkness speckled with fading stars, except for a few days after a full moon, when the last moonlight drained from the star-filled sky to the west as the rose tint developed to the east.

Sam liked to watch the sky from his veranda as the sounds of the nocturnal creatures died away and before the day creatures trilled the morning's welcome. He knew both well, for he studied them all. He was the zoologist at Likesedi Lodge in the Chobe National Park.

Likesedi, built on the southern side of the Chobe River, was silent at that hour. Nothing moved, even the bats were still. The sun began to light the thatched roofs of the guests' wooden chalets lining the water, with trees spreading behind them. Further back, the main lodge building with lounge, offices and dining room remained in the shadow cast by the trees. Beyond that, Sam's cottage and the manager's cottage beside it were on the far side of the roadway from

Kasane. The road ended at the workshop and garage, set discreetly out of sight, with the staff accommodation beside it.

Alone on his veranda, Sam enjoyed his moments of freedom from the stress of life as a ranger. He sipped from a cup of his private blend of Kenyan coffee drawn from his cottage coffee machine, a stratagem developed to help him avoid joining the rangers in the lounge in the morning. He believed those minutes of solitary reflection kept him from returning to the depressing world he'd left four years earlier.

The lodge offered bespoke safaris with Sam as guide. The activities provided for the guests and the guests' safety were his responsibility. The rangers worked for him, but that required little effort. The observation and question-answering never bored him, as each day brought something new.

Sam had found that being a bespoke safari guide had benefits. Although free food and accommodation were part of their package, rangers had low incomes. Without the extra tips and gratuities, their off time, after two or three weeks of work seven days a week, would have cost them their salaries. Although Sam had a slightly higher wage due to his qualifications and experience, he relied on the envelopes handed to him as each guest left. Often containing over a thousand dollars, those extra payments had enabled him to buy a good camera, sound equipment, and his Land Rover to use for his off time research.

This morning, carrying a small rucksack, Sam walked the short distance to the workshop car park and drove away in a pickup with Fred, one of the staff. It wasn't his usual ranger routine which involved heading to the lounge and arriving just late enough to miss the rangers' communal coffee time, but punctual enough to meet the tourists for their three-hour dawn drive in an open safari vehicle.

Today's destination was Kasane regional airport, an hour and a half east of Likesedi, for an early morning flight to Gaborone, over one thousand kilometres to the south.

They reached the airport. Fred shook Sam's hand and drove away. Sam felt good until he checked in, and the booking clerk said, 'There's a delay in departure, sir. A technical problem. We'll announce the new departure time as soon as we know. Please don't leave the airport. If you wish, you may go to the departure lounge.'

He knew that time was short, with only two and a half hours at Gaborone before the London flight arrived with his client. He fished his airport security pass from his wallet and went to see what he could learn from the head of security, Baruti Magosi. But Baruti had nothing more to tell him, so Sam returned to the terminal with his worry building. At this early hour, the coffee shop had only stale coffee and yesterday's pastries to offer. Frustrated, he sighed and went to the departure lounge, the only passenger to do so.

He knew the underlying cause of his stress. He didn't like going to cities with their inevitable crowds; they made him tense. The departure lounge, a haven of peace, calmed Sam's worry – for a while. He forced himself to think about his job and client, not the delay. A pretty, young flight attendant came in and looked at him curiously. She seemed about to offer help, but he looked away.

Since his twenty-second birthday, young women had tried to breach his barrier. Sam attracted attention: he was blonde, blue-eyed, tall and muscular, with a suntan – even in England where he spent hours outdoors at Whipsnade Wild Animal Park in all weathers. Sam sidestepped the women and focused on doing what interested him. By the age of twenty-four, with degrees in zoology and entomology, he had managed to overcome some but by no means all of his aversion to social interaction. However, his barrier wall of silence had holes in it because he loved talking about his favourite subject – wildlife. But only when he felt safe.

People liked him, but he encouraged very few to be friends. He might never have a high opinion of himself, but determined that others should not have a low opinion of him, he stuck to his own rules and his nickname: 'Silent'. He liked it, for he didn't need to explain why he talked so little.

Sitting in the lounge, he remembered deciding to go to Africa, where people were few and animals abounded. After writing to every lodge needing rangers in the Serengeti, he'd been surprised at their positive response. He didn't know whether it was his qualifications and desire to study the animals and insects or the reference and recommendation from Whipsnade, where he'd worked during every holiday after his fifteenth birthday because the alternative of a care home was anathema.

He'd selected a lodge at random, signed a year-long contract, and told the others he would contact them a year later.

The lodge owners paid for his flight, although they deducted it from his salary, and Sam boarded a plane, carrying only his suitcase, ten English pounds, and a folder of technical documents – everything he owned in the world.

To Sam's relief, they announced his flight to Gaborone, and the passengers boarded after an hour's delay. For thirty minutes, he sat fidgeting, stress building again, until the engines started, and for another ten while the pilot checked they worked correctly. He only relaxed when the plane finally took off; he would still have forty minutes after arrival to get to the gate to meet his guest when ten was actually enough. He asked himself why he subjected himself to such pressure.

Sam knew the answer. Outside of cities, he loved the life he led. Being a game ranger – away from crowds, concrete pavements, and constant hurry – was heaven. Being one of the few rangers with the specialist knowledge required to conduct personal safaris, limited to a single person or an adult family, allowed Sam the opportunity to talk in detail about the unspoilt lands he loved, for he hardly talked about anything else.

He wondered about his latest client, a twenty-seven-year-old author. Contrary to Carl's insinuation, he hoped she would be tolerable company, for the itinerary included the Tuli area in the east, on the border with Zimbabwe and South Africa, where he would have no other rangers to assist and give him some space.

Carl was the lodge manager, an ex-ranger. Tall, dark, and once built like a tank, he had lost weight in the last year, and his hair had grey streaks. Sam and the other rangers had noticed, but they said nothing. Respect for privacy stopped them from asking. Carl had said a week ago, 'Silent, I have a tough one for you this time.'

'They all are, boss. Some are tougher than others. What's the problem with this one?'

'It's a woman, Melissa … Grouwer. Groover? You'll have to find out. She's twenty-seven, an author who wants to learn about Botswana, so she's looking for unique experiences.'

He paused. Sam said nothing and waited.

'She asked for four days in the Tuli area and ten here. You fly to Gaborone, meet her, fly to Tuli and Limpopo Valley for four days, and then fly to Kasane via Francistown. You must show her Victoria Falls after her safari.'

'Well, that's unusual, but I don't see a problem.'

'I spoke to the travel agent. He said she's a strange character who doesn't smile or talk much.'

'That's better than the guests who never stop chattering.'

'Okay, I guess you can enjoy not talking to each other.'

Sam didn't react to Carl's remark; he was used to them, but thought, *He may be right.*

Carl continued, 'I'll type out the schedule. Fred will drive you to the airport at Kasane on Wednesday morning; the flight to Gabs leaves at 7 am. Do you want me to send your Landy and photographic gear to Tuli, or shall I try to hire a safari vehicle?'

'Send it with Benjy; he needs a holiday and has family in Tuli.'

Although Melissa had a seat in business class that lay flat, she couldn't sleep; the continuous hiss and rumble, only mildly noticeable to others, was enough to keep her awake and thinking about her missing earplugs. She could have read, but that meant leaving her light on. Since a passenger on her first flight objected rudely, Melissa had retreated into a semi-awake dream to find refuge from a blaring world. As on the previous flights she had taken, she tried to remember what had driven her to board the planes in the first place.

Two years ago, she'd returned home from the library. She slid her key into the lock of the heavy wooden door. It stood with other seemingly identical doors, each under a stone portico adorning the row of evenly spaced London townhouses – three-storey Georgian houses with stone facades, once a gleaming pale cream and now fifty shades of grey – stolid, eternal, grudgingly lending, but not giving, status to the occupants. The entrances differed; the gargoyles that spat rainwater onto the flowerbed on either side, carved by diverse stonemasons, had unique faces. A curious observer could tell the stonemason's mood when he sculpted the gargoyle – happy, sad, angry or sleepy.

The doors were identical except for her entrance. Spotting the unique door was like a puzzle in a magazine – Find the odd one out.

It was the feeling that gave a clue. It was the only door that said,

You are not welcome here.

The door, it's dark paint peeling in places, had no polished brass door-knocker to make a cheerfully resounding *rat-a-tat-tat*, the signal of a friendly visitor.

It didn't have a knocker at all.

Melissa turned the key slowly, gently, as if the act of doing so might result in an explosion that would destroy the door and her in a deafening blast. She pushed it open hesitantly, as if expecting a monster lurking in the hall to leap forward and devour her. She couldn't help her cautious behaviour; the habit had built over fifteen years.

There was no monster.

Melissa stepped through the doorway, her shoes silent on the deep carpet, and closed the door behind her.

Slowly.

She held the handle down until it closed, then released it to lock the door.

Gently.

The padded soundproofing, a quilted green baize material, now years old, still did an excellent job. The cacophony outside – from cars, radios, footsteps, the tinkling of an ice cream van, a howling baby, a screaming ambulance, and an ever-present babble of voices – suddenly dropped to a low murmur.

Melissa sighed in relief and quietly walked up the thickly carpeted stairs to her room on the first floor. In front of the white door, she paused and breathed deeply. In a series of flowing movements, she opened the door, crossed to the triple-glazed open window, closed it, pulled the heavy drape across it, and returned to close the door and switch on the light.

Surreptitiously.

With an audible sigh of relief.

Secure in her cocoon, she sat at the dresser. She carefully extracted the two earplugs she'd inserted that morning and had worn every day since her fifth birthday.

Hearing a timid knock on her door, Melissa turned and said, 'Come in, Nana.' She had recognised the knock of Mrs Drew, the housekeeper and her nanny for fifteen years, whom Melissa considered a clone for Miss Marple, Agatha Christie's detective granny. Mrs Drew had the same grey hair, permanent curls, round face, and pale pink lips, and always knew what was 'going on' even when, as usual, nothing was. Mrs Drew entered, saw Melissa at the dresser and the earplugs lying on its surface, and said, 'Melissa, you told me the doctor said you can leave them out now. It's been two weeks; why are you still wearing them?'

'I've tried, but it feels like I've two gaping holes in my head and that something will creep in and start eating me inside.'

Mrs Drew frowned. 'You must try, Melissa. You can't continue wearing them when they aren't necessary. Is there another reason?'

Melissa looked down and hunched her shoulders. Her nanny knew the gesture. She waited, knowing an answer would come eventually.

'If I take them out, strange people talk to me, and I don't know what to say.'

'Wait there, Melissa; I'll fetch something from my room.'

'I'm not going anywhere, Nana.'

'Not swimming?' Mrs Drew had seen Melissa swim, which she did effortlessly for three kilometres or more. It was the only exercise she liked as it was silent and solitary.

'No, not tonight.'

Mrs Drew left her room closing the door softly, habits are hard to discard, then returned with two cellphone earbuds and connecting wires.

'They came with my phone, and I've never used them. Hang them in your ears. People won't think you're deaf, but they won't talk to you either.'

'Okay, Nana. I'll try.'

2

. . . . .

MELISSA WAS IN THE ETHIOPIAN AIRLINES BOEING, FLIGHT ET 823. When the cabin attendant tapped her shoulder, she left her thoughts with a start.

'Miss Grouwer, we shall serve breakfast shortly. Would you like orange juice or coffee now?'

'Coffee, please.'

The coffee came. Melissa tasted it and quickly pressed the button for service.

She found the coffee appalling and undrinkable, but she'd never say anything that might make a scene or draw attention. Instead, when the attendant returned, she said mildly, 'I'm sorry, I've changed my mind; I'd prefer the orange juice.'

'No problem.' The attendant took the coffee and replaced it with the juice. Melissa drank half the glass, laid back again and closed her eyes.

Her first-ever flight was to Kenya. She had been terrified, and the memory of her parents' deaths in a private jet over Sudan had haunted her the entire flight. She had thought about what led to her ever getting on a plane.

She had been researching at the library, wearing her new earbuds from Mrs Drew. She took them out for a moment to speak to the pleasant elder librarian, Mrs Tancred, who reminded Melissa of her housekeeper. Mrs Tancred had asked her, 'You're authoring a book, Miss Grouwer? What are you writing about?'

'Animals, and animal behaviour. I spend hours at Whipsnade Zoo watching them and come here for technical data and background.'

'Have you considered viewing animals in their natural habitat – in Africa?'

'That's a long way to go.'

'Well, I'll tell you what I tell all the budding authors who have come here over the years: it will help if you visit the places you de-scribe in your book. You can read what others say about those places, but you'll never put true feelings onto paper unless you expe-rience them yourself.'

Melissa remembered that first visit; she'd spent a month in Kenya following the migration of the wildebeest and zebra. She'd returned with notebooks filled with observations. She had tried to author a story, scrapped it several times, and consulted Mrs Tancred for ad-vice. Desperate, she returned to Africa after the librarian read what she'd written and said, 'You must return, Melissa. This story is tech-nically good, but it's missing excitement and feeling.'

Melissa returned three times, and the terror as the plane took off was still the same, but it disappeared once airborne. Her writing didn't seem to improve much. She told Mrs Tancred it wasn't going to work. Mrs Tancred encouraged her to keep trying. It was during the fourth visit, when she'd decided it would be the last, that the in-spiration had come.

She met a tracker from the Hadza ethnic group at the lodge near the Ngorongoro crater, and he took her to meet his people. When she re-turned to London, she wrote about the two weeks she had spent with descendants of Stone Age nomads who still lived a hunter-scavenger life.

Unsure what to make of her efforts, she had taken her script to Mrs Tancred to read. 'Melissa, this is wonderful,' the librarian had enthused. 'It's because you participated; you felt what these people felt; you must do it again and write some more.'

So, she could do it; she just needed to practise. She decided to travel again but to change her destination. *Somewhere new might help.*

While the cabin crew served breakfast, Melissa concluded, *I'll have to give up if I don't manage to complete an actual story this time. Perhaps scrapping the earbuds will change something.*

She sipped her breakfast coffee. *The coffee is still undrinkable.*

Destination: Sir Seretse Khama International Airport, Gaborone, Botswana.

'This is your captain speaking. Due to our flight delay, we must wait a few minutes at Gaborone to allow the London flight to land. We apologise for the delay due to factors beyond our control, and thank you for flying with us.'

The stress returned like a hammer blow. Sam grimaced. His guest would be landing before him.

Sam almost ran from domestic to international arrivals, where he joined the greeters at a barrier rail, his rucksack with his clothes for four days and his other gear at his feet. With his small board ready, he asked one of the men he recognised as a tour guide, 'Have any pax come out yet?' Sam relaxed after the negative reply. As the first passenger from the London flight walked out from the baggage hall, he raised his board with 'Melissa Grouwer' written on it.

As he always did, he tried to guess which passenger she was. The first few were all business class passengers; most he quickly identified as business travellers because they carried briefcases.

One woman was wearing a long, loose, grey dress, wheeling a small suitcase and holding a document folder. Expressionless, without a glance at the greeters and their waving boards, she turned directly to the concourse coffee shop. Sam decided she was the right age but, as he'd subconsciously expected a person wearing heavy spectacles, concluded she was waiting for someone.

He discarded all the couples, with or without children. Then a woman came out that fitted the bill, so he waved the placard, but seconds later, two small children rushed up to her, followed by, he assumed, her husband.

Forty minutes later, the stream of passengers had dwindled away. Sam's worry and stress peaked, but he was still hopeful his client had not missed her flight and was reporting a baggage problem; he waited, the sole remaining greeter, shifting his weight from one foot to the other, until he heard an announcement that the airline had closed his connecting flight to Limpopo Valley. Then he went to the airline desk.

The airline from London confirmed a Melissa Grouwer had been on the flight. He went to the local airline counter, where they confirmed she was a no-show, so he cancelled their tickets. Now worried that he'd lost his client, the pain in his neck that signalled stress twinged sharply. He swore under his breath. If anything had happened to her....

Returning to the international customs exit, he passed the coffee shop. It was a service counter surrounded by couches, small tables and chairs on two sides. The woman wearing the grey dress still sat on a sofa, reading a book. She looked calm in contrast to how he felt. He thought, *It's not bloody possible. Or is it?*

Sam approached her and asked, 'Excuse me, are you Melissa Grouwer?'

After a short, yet to Sam, highly irritating pause, she looked up, her face devoid of makeup and expression.

'Yes. But it's *Grover*, not Grower.'

Sam felt his tension peak, quivering like a volcano coming to a boil. 'I was standing with the greeters when you came out, with your name on a board. Why didn't you come to me?'

'I wanted a coffee and expected you to find me.'

Was it his hunger, fatigue, pain, or the lack of the word 'sorry' in her reply? Or how she rudely corrected his pronunciation of her name? To Sam's stressed mind, her expressionless face was a direct assault on his barrier wall. He felt himself lose control. Not since infancy had he lost his temper. His solution to anger was always to walk away. But this was his job. He couldn't walk away. Sam wanted to yell, but he couldn't do that either. He exploded. In a tight, furious voice, he spoke firmly.

'I've no desire to share two weeks of my life with the rudest, most inconsiderate, and offensive b-b-b ...'

Sam had been about to say 'bitch' but couldn't; it came out as, '... b-b-bloody woman I've ever met. Our flight to Limpopo Valley has gone. You can sleep here or try to find a hotel and change your return to London for tomorrow. Goodbye.'

Sam picked up his bag and started to leave the airport building to find a taxi. He hadn't gone far before he began to feel disgusted at his behaviour. The debilitating neck pain that signalled rising stress had vanished, relieved by his outburst, although his burning anger, like over-hot chilli in his stomach, remained as he scolded himself, *I should never have said bloody woman.*

He stopped on the pavement where the taxis queued, but there were none in sight. After a three-minute wait, he decided to call for one. He turned to read the taxi phone number from a publicity panel on the wall behind him and saw Melissa, trolley-bag behind her, standing beside it watching him.

Good manners came to the fore, although his tone was stiff, frosty and formal. 'Miss *Grover*, I apologise for using the words *bloody woman*. That was uncalled for. Do you need help?'

She replied flatly in a monotone, 'Yes, but first, I want to say I'm sorry. People usually don't speak to me, so it's the first time someone's said that to my face. I really am sorry.'

'Thanks for saying that,' he replied, still formal. 'Now, what's the problem?'

'I don't have a phone.'

Sam had to think about this. A woman from England, who had paid for an expensive two-week holiday in Africa, didn't bring a phone.

'You mean you don't have roaming? Why didn't you arrange it before you left London?'

'No, I can't. I don't own a phone.' She gestured briefly with open hands as if to say, 'Look, nothing here.'

It was unheard of to someone who had picked up hundreds of tourists. 'Why not?'

'I don't call anybody.'

Her statement floored Sam, and he thought, *I can't leave her alone; she has no idea what to do. She must have significant social problems and didn't intend her reply to be rude.*

'Okay, Miss Grouwer,' he said gently. 'Let me call a taxi, and you can come with me.'

Melissa's reply was so unexpected it rekindled his anger. 'Call two taxis. You walked out on me, or have you forgotten?'

Furious, Sam snapped back, 'Only because of your careless attitude and rudeness.'

Melissa reacted with a voice that tried, unsuccessfully, to hide her pain at his words. 'Okay, that was my fault, but I wanted a coffee badly. The airline stuff is appalling. You should show some sympathy for your client's needs.'

'You're no longer my client.'

Her reply was louder than she intended.

'I damned well was then.'

Sam saw that she was shaking and there were tears in her eyes. Suddenly, he felt he'd behaved cruelly and had to do something. As a child, when in tears and trembling, he remembered he had felt better after someone hugged him. He stepped forward, wrapped his arms around her, and said, 'I'm sorry, that was cruel. Please forgive me.'

Melissa was quivering, tense, unmoving. Sam didn't move, waiting for her to react. She remained a rigid vibrating bar, but a childhood memory crawled and wriggled its way to the surface of her consciousness – her father hugging her. Then she heard Sam's heartbeat – thumpity-thump, thumpity-thump, thumpity-thump – solid and reassuring.

Sam felt her shaking stop, so he said quietly, 'Can we start over?'

Melissa didn't answer. She was still trying to analyse her feelings. It was the first time since she had left school that anyone had hugged her.

Eventually, her hands moved up and gripped Sam's waist. Unexpectedly, she felt warm and safe.

Sam had to ask again. The mumbled 'yes' from her lips against his chest was encouraging.

3

·····

SAM KEPT HOLDING HER. MELISSA WAS NOT SKINNY UNDER her baggy dress. She might not have any excess fat, but she was well-built and muscular. He had to reassess his first opinion of her as rude and arrogant. 'Are you Melissa Grouwer?' He pronounced it correctly.

He couldn't see her face. She was still clinging to him and didn't look up. 'Yes, are you my guide?'

'I am. Do you know our flight to Limpopo Valley has left without us?'

'No, I didn't notice. I lost myself in my book.'

'Why were you reading and not looking for me?'

'I needed coffee, smelt the coffee, saw the coffee shop, and went straight for it. I'm sorry. I was going to look for you, but the coffee was too hot to carry in those paper cups. I decided to wait a bit for it to cool, but then I began reading ... You can let me go now.'

He thought her body language showed relief as she said, 'Thank you. One taxi is fine.' But Melissa wasn't relieved: she felt something more like regret.

Sam told the taxi driver to take them to the Gaborone Inn.

'It's full, boss. All the hotels are full; there's a big conference at the casino.'

'That's okay. I'll sort something out.'

He turned to Melissa.

'Miss Grouwer, are you hungry?'

She nodded.

'Then we'll visit the restaurant. I haven't eaten anything since yesterday, and I'll ask the receptionist to find us rooms in Gabs. If they can't find two, we might need to share one. Is that okay?'

Sam sensed panic in Melissa's voice. 'Only one room?'

'I'll try to find two, but I can't guarantee anything. Does one room bother you?'

'Yes, I've never slept in a room with another person. I can't sleep.'

'Understood, but I can guarantee you would be safe with me. I don't eat clients,' Sam grinned, 'unless they snore.'

His reward was a twitch of her lips.

'I don't snore.'

'How would you know?'

'Because I investigated it. I left my tape recorder on all night and played it back the next day.'

Sam laughed. He found this hilarious. Melissa's smile widened slightly. *He's definitely not as horrible as he seemed at first.*

She asked, 'What's your name?'

'Oh hell. I did lose my cool. It's Sam Daniels, but the rangers call me "Silent".'

'Why?'

'Because I don't talk much. Only things that matter.'

The Gaborone Inn receptionist confirmed they had no available rooms but suggested that while they had lunch, she would call other hotels and try to find something.

Sam lapsed into ranger-guide mode. He led Melissa to the hotel restaurant and told her that Botswana-raised beef was the best in the world. He was pleased when she ordered a sizeable rare steak. *Nothing wrong with her appetite.*

They ate in silence until Sam said, 'Miss Grouwer...'

'Melissa, please.'

'Miss – Melissa, I know I don't talk much, but please feel free to ask me any questions.'

'I don't have any right now, but I can answer your questions.'

'Then we might have a problem,' he smiled. 'Except when I'm a guide talking about the things I see, I only answer questions.'

'We'll be fine.'

He couldn't read her expression. *Did she want a different guide?*

The receptionist's news was discouraging.

'We've called all fifteen hotels, sir, with no success, not even one room. Here's a list of B&B places. You can try them, but I'm not hopeful.'

Sam decided to ask: 'Miss – Melissa, please tell me, do you want to go on with your safari or take the flight tomorrow to London?'

'I want to go on.'

'Okay, and would you prefer another guide? I can arrange a swap when we arrive in Tuli.'

Melissa had to think about the question. She felt something in her gut as she decided.

At least I know something about him; a different guide might be worse.

'No. I know you say what you think.'

'Okay, I'll call our agent. I'll switch on the speaker so you can hear. Let's sit on those couches.'

'Peter, it's Sam.'

'Sam! I thought you would be in Tuli by now.'

'Unfortunately, I'm not; there was a mix-up at the airport. I cancelled today's tickets. Can you call the lodge, tell them of the delay, and rebook the flight for tomorrow?'

'Sure. Anything else?'

'Yes, I've tried every hotel in Gabs for a one-night stay. Do you have beds for my client and me for tonight?'

'I can put Sophy into her brother's room, so I have one room with two beds and a couch in the lounge.'

Sam looked at Melissa and raised an eyebrow.

Melissa nodded.

'Okay, Peter. What time should we arrive at your place?'

'Say, 6 pm?'

'Right, see you then.' He hung up.

'Okay, that's arranged. Now, um, please come and sit next to me. I must discover something.'

Intrigued, she moved across to his couch. 'What is it?'

'When I held you, I could smell you.'

Her reaction was sharp, 'Well, after eighteen hours without a bath, what would you expect?'

'I don't mean like that; that would be a natural smell. I think it's your hair.'

Still tense, she replied, 'What's wrong with my hair?'

'Nothing. You smell fine but will smell like a rubbish dump to wild animals. If you want to walk with me in the bush, you must use cosmetics, soaps, shampoos and deodorants that don't smell of anything. So let me smell you to find out which ones need to be changed.'

Sam's reward was an even bigger smile when she said, 'You're a very peculiar person, Sam Daniels. What will smelling me tell you? Weren't you close enough when you grabbed me at the airport?'

'Only your hair, then. And I didn't grab you.'

'You did. I distinctly remember you did.'

Sam had a reply. 'It was a hug to calm you down.'

It didn't convince Melissa. 'Okay, but it started as a grab.'

'Let's just agree to differ. Lean towards me.'

Sam sniffed loudly around her head and arms *like*, she imagined, *a puppy dog sniffing me.*

'Melissa, you're wearing a scented deodorant, have used an aromatic or perfumed shampoo or conditioner, and you've sprayed perfume on your neck. Your face cream has a smell. I think it's sunblock.'

'How can you smell all that?'

'Practice. An animal could tell you which factory made the perfume and on what date. But tell me, do you have any cosmetics that don't include perfume?'

'No, I don't. And seriously, how can you smell all that?'

Sam explained, 'Watch a dog; you'll see it opening and closing its mouth, pumping air through its nostrils. Half of our ability to smell comes from the buds on our tongues.

'Now, you must be clean of any artificial smells. We can go to a pharmacy that sells cosmetics, see what's available, and you can buy enough for your stay. Do you have sun lotions?'

'The one you smelt. But won't I smell horrible?'

'No, if you shower twice a day, you won't. You'll smell like a beautiful woman should.'

'Okay, I'm ready. What about our bags?' Melissa had to think about Sam's words; she'd never received such a compliment from a man. *He said a beautiful woman; he can't mean me.*

'We'll leave our bags with the concierge and come for them when we go to Peter's.'

'…Sam?'

'Yes?'

'That's more conversation than I've had in ages.'

'It was all question and answer, Melissa. That works for us. Although you nearly started us going again when you said I grabbed you.'

'Well, you did.'

'Don't start.'

Melissa thought Peter's house looked lovely. It was in a suburb some way from the centre of Gaborone, surrounded by a small, lush garden and an outer wall. Peter came to answer Sam's doorbell ring, 'Hello, Silent.'

Sam shook the proffered hand, 'Peter, this is Melissa *Grover*, our client.'

'Melissa, Peter Reynolds, agent extraordinaire.' Melissa shook hands and wondered, *Why are all the men here so handsome? Is it the suntans? Peter could be a film star. He's tall and rugged and smiles with his eyes.*

'Come in, come in. Sally's feeding the kids. She'll join us in a few minutes.'

Sam asked, 'Peter, did two packages come?'

'Yes, they're behind the couch.'

Peter led them into his lounge. 'Please, sit anywhere. I know it's a beer for you, Silent. Melissa, what would you like? I have fruit juice and Appletiser if you want something non-alcoholic.'

'What's Appletiser?'

'Sparkling apple juice. It's like a sweeter champagne and non-alcoholic. Would you like to try it?'

'Yes, it sounds interesting.'

When Peter went out to fetch the drinks, Melissa whispered, 'Was he a game ranger?'

'You can ask him, Melissa; he won't mind.'

'Do you only drink beer?'

'A fellow worker at Whipsnade gave me one when I was eighteen and said I could have it if I promised to drink nothing else until I was over thirty. I promised, so I'm sticking to it.'

Melissa didn't miss the titbit of information. *He's under thirty.*

Peter fetched the drinks and a beer for himself and asked, 'What was the mix-up at the airport, Silent?'

'We need to change our instructions to the clients. I was waiting for Melissa at arrivals, and she was waiting for me at local departures.'

Melissa heard what Sam said. She felt guilty that Sam took the blame when it was her fault, so she forced herself to explain.

'Peter, Sam's being kind. It was my fault. I arrived, didn't see him, sat at a coffee shop and lost myself reading my book until he spotted me.'

Melissa couldn't analyse Sam's reaction as he thought, *She has guts, and she's honest.*

Peter smiled, 'No harm done; the keys to your Landy are with the Limpopo airport staff. The ranger who drove it from Likesedi with all your expensive gear has flown back; he left the gear and the guns with Hennie at the lodge. I've confirmed your bookings for 10 am tomorrow; a taxi will arrive at 8 am.'

Melissa took a sip of her drink and thought it delicious.

'This is super. Were you a game ranger once?' she asked Peter.

'Yes, that's how I met Sally. She came to re-organise the catering when our lodge expanded, and I applied for a town job before the kids needed schooling. Then the directors gave me this one much sooner than I expected.'

Sally came in, and a little boy and a girl rushed in and jumped onto Sam's lap.

'Uncle Sam, did you bring my elephant?'

'And my giraffe?'

'I gave them to Auntie Melissa, Jimmy, but she might have lost them.'

The children turned to Melissa, who remembered what Peter had said.

She looked at the children for a long moment, the two faces looking hopefully at her. After twenty-three years of no interaction with children, she had no idea what to say or do. Then her earliest memories returned, those formed before she had earplugs, and a dam inside her broke. 'I put them down somewhere; we must look for them.'

Melissa slid off the couch onto her knees, then fell forward onto her forearms, and felt she was a child again as the two children followed suit. 'Sophy, you go that way, Jimmy, that way; they must be somewhere.'

A minute later, after the three had crawled around the room, Sophy found the parcels, and squeals of happiness filled the room. Melissa had a wide grin. It pleased Sam when he saw it. *Lovely. She seems okay with small children. Touchy with adults. I must learn her story.*

After the drinks and a light supper, Sally showed them the room.

'I've put towels on the beds and bottles of water on the tables. Have a good night's sleep. I know you must be exhausted, Sam; if you prefer the couch, go to the lounge. Did you sleep on the flight, Melissa?'

'Not much; I keep waking up.'

'Well, good night. I'll bathe the kids in our bathroom tomorrow morning, so use the family one as you wish and come down for some breakfast at 7:30 am.'

As Sally went out the door, Sam asked, 'Will you go first, Melissa? The bathroom's at the end of the corridor.'

'No, you go; I must find my nightie and my clothes for tomorrow.'

Sam returned, 'The bathroom's clear, Melissa. I'll go downstairs.'

Melissa felt it was her fault they were there, so she said, 'Sam, I know you're tired. I've had eleven hours lying in an aeroplane, so you sleep here. The couch will be fine for me.'

Melissa went off to the bathroom, and when she returned, Sam was asleep. She stood watching him for a few minutes. *I must learn to sleep in the same room with someone. Is this my chance to try?* She slid quietly into the other bed, turned out the light and whispered, 'Good night, Sam.' He didn't hear her.

She couldn't sleep. She could hear Sam's breathing, but after a while, the memory of Sophy and Jimmy popped up, and she remembered they were now like Sam and her: in the same room together. *I'm Sophy, and he's Jimmy.* Sam's breathing seemed to fade, and she slept.

4

· · · · ·

SAM WOKE AT 4:30 AM, A RANGER'S BODY-PROGRAMMED TIME, but he didn't move in the darkness. The desire for his morning coffee began to build. He tried to figure out if he could reach the kitchen without waking Melissa on the lounge couch at the bottom of the stairs. After deciding it was impossible, Sam closed his eyes and tried to sleep, but his senses had awakened, and a minute later, Sam heard Melissa's breathing. He tapped his phone, saw Melissa in the faint light, and wondered when she'd come to the bed. Sam supposed the couch had been uncomfortable. After another minute, he decided to slide out quietly and go downstairs to the kitchen.

Melissa heard him the moment he tapped the phone. She woke as she always did, cautiously. She didn't move, still assessing her environment for painful sounds, though her hearing sensitivity had dropped and she no longer needed earplugs.

She heard the rustle of sheets as Sam left the bed, then the pad-pad-pad of bare feet on the tiled floor. She listened for the slight screech and the click as he pressed the door handle and felt the movement of the air as he opened the door. She didn't hear the lock again and knew he'd left the door ajar.

She heard his bare feet walk down the stairs, the creak of the handrail as he reached the bottom, and the dwindling noise as he went to the kitchen. She continued to listen and smiled.

She heard the light switch click as he turned on the kitchen light. She perceived the kettle singing and could tell the moment it reached the boil, the click as the auto switch triggered. The clump of a mug, placed carefully on the countertop, and the glugging sounds while Sam poured water through a coffee filter, then the tinkling as he stirred in a half spoonful of sugar. She smiled again when she heard him sigh as Sam drank his first mouthful.

Then, the aroma of freshly brewed coffee reached the bedroom. It was too much for Melissa; she followed Sam but moved in total silence.

Sam, standing in the kitchen, staring out the window at the first glimmer of dawn, his coffee mug in his hand and peace on his face, suddenly had that feeling. The one that warns, *There's someone or something behind you.*

He turned, tensed to react, to see Melissa watching him; she had a half smile, and her eyes gleamed.

Sam's jaw dropped. He hadn't heard her arrive and seeing her in her ethereal nightie seemed magical. Then she raised a finger to her lips and whispered, 'Sam, if you don't give me a mug of coffee, I'll hate you for the rest of my life.'

Sam's mouth snapped shut. He moved to the counter and handed Melissa a mug half a minute later. She moved to look out the window, and Sam realised she glided silently. He joined her, and they watched the glowing horizon side by side.

She whispered, 'My first sunrise in Botswana. The colours are lovely, and it's quiet.'

He whispered too, 'It's better in the bush, and the city will begin to wake now; the silence will shatter.'

Five minutes later, Melissa whispered, 'Sam, I need another mug.'

He refilled both. They didn't speak for half an hour until the first sliver of the sun rose above the horizon, and the crescendo of the city began to grow. Sam struggled to understand why a woman who at first wouldn't sleep in the same bedroom as him was now beside him wearing a nightgown. In his confusion, his only unhelpful con-clusion was: *she's unusual and unpredictable.*

He didn't know she had never had someone to tell her the things most young girls learnt, like hiding from boys and men when wear-ing a nightgown.

'Sam, I'll use the bathroom first. I must wash my hair to remove the smells. I can dry it in the bedroom while you shower.'

'Okay, Melissa. Do you have a nickname? Don't tell me if you don't want to.'

Sam saw Melissa clasp her hands together and then look down at them. Melissa was aware of the gesture but couldn't avoid it. 'I must, Sam; answering questions is all I've done for years. Kids can be cruel, Sam, and they often use hurt to establish hierarchy. I used my aunt's perfume once, and the kids called me *Smelly Melly*. It stuck, but I lost it when I went to high school.'

'Well, I would never use that.'

Melissa remembered him saying 'b-b-bloody woman.'

'You used *whatsit!*'

Sam knew to what that referred. 'Not as a nickname.'

'That was just as bad.'

'Far worse, Melissa, far worse. I'm sorry I did, but let's avoid an-other fight, although I would like one.'

'Why?'

'Well, I liked the way the last one ended.'

Melissa grinned at him. She had a feeling she hadn't experienced before. 'I win, Sam.'

A puzzled Sam asked, 'Win what?'

'You grabbed. I'm going to shower.'

Sam sat beside Melissa during the hour-long flight. She was next to the window. He wanted to ask her about her childhood but thought, *It's not the right time or place; it'll keep.*

'Melissa, the lodge we're going to is on the bank of the Limpopo River in an area known as the Tuli Block. Originally, Tuli was a British possession, ceded by the Botswana King a century ago. As has often happened in history, the people in London had nothing but an early map and happily drew lines to decide what they did or didn't want. Tuli was a mistake. Cecil Rhodes discovered he couldn't build a railway through it to Rhodesia, and the farmers found they couldn't grow much.'

'Why not?'

'It's nothing like the rest of Botswana. The land is rocky, grazing is sparse, and the rivers are dry for months each year; they must pump water from wells. But the area is an important ecosystem of its own, with animals migrating to where they can find water. It is now eight thousand square kilometres of private game reserves. The scenery is fascinating, the rocks are ancient, and there are dinosaur fossils on the surface near the Limpopo in Zimbabwe. I'm sure I can find things that will interest you.'

'I'm looking forward to that, Sam. You saw me in my nightie this morning but didn't tell me your impression.'

She needs reassurance. 'You don't wear makeup, Melissa, your nightie is lovely, and I was hungry. With your ruffled hair, you looked good enough to eat.'

He earned the laugh and the smile he hoped for as she said, 'So you do eat clients.'

'Only when I'm hungry!'

Sam fetched his Landy keys from the Limpopo Valley airport office after landing. 'Sam, this Land Rover is beautifully fitted out, better than any I saw in Tanzania.'

'Rangers' rules. All the rangers must own their gear, binoculars, rifles, cameras, and even guidebooks. I needed it for my research and spent everything I earned fitting it out.'

'Why are you doing research? I thought you were a ranger and tourist guide.'

'I am, but I'm also a zoologist and have registered for a doctorate by research. I organised things so I could do both. It helped me earn the exclusive guide label, and the lodge doesn't need to supply me with a safari vehicle. But they pay the running costs.'

As they drove along the road, Melissa thought it odd that she should feel guilty about never working.

The road wound between bands of giant nyala and fever trees along the Limpopo River bank until Sam stopped close to a huge rock, a twelve metre vertical wall beside the road.

'We'll return here tomorrow night, but I want you to look at the base of the rock in daylight.'

They walked towards it, and Melissa exclaimed, 'It stinks here; it's horrible. I don't want to go closer. What is it?'

'Don't speak. Keep your mouth shut. Look carefully. The black stuff is baboon crap mixed with baboon pee. Sorry, I should have said faeces.'

Melissa looked, then turned away and returned to the Land Rover. 'Crap is okay. There's tons of it.'

'Look up at the rock. It looks like a smooth vertical face, but there are cracks and protrusions that the baboons can cling onto at night to sleep, safe from leopards.'

Melissa had an unusual question, 'Do the highest baboons pee on those below?'

It surprised Sam. *I expect authors want to know details, but no other tourists have asked that question, even if they thought of it.*

'No, they pee on the rock, and the others avoid the rivulets; those are the yellow streaks. The bottom baboons, primarily females and young ones, crap where they are; higher up, they move to the three long drop toilets, the ledges above the big crap piles.'

'That's fascinating; they must have been doing this for hundreds of years.'

'Maybe thousands. It's an ingrained behaviour in this troop of baboons. We'll return at sunset tomorrow when I have my lighting. Let's continue and have lunch.'

'Sam, if you have a sense of smell good enough to smell my cosmetics, how can you stand the baboon poo?'

'I keep my mouth shut near baboon poo like I told you to.'

They drove into the lodge grounds where Melissa remarked on the accommodation, 'Those are tents on top of long stilts.'

'Yes, every few years, the Limpopo floods. In the worst years, the damage was enormous, with all the buildings flooded. Several years ago, the insurance companies refused to renew the insurance unless the owners raised everything above the highest water level. The lounge is stone on a high plinth; the accommodation was easier to perch on stilts.'

'That's a massive amount of water.'

'It's a massive river.'

After they greeted Hennie, the lodge manager, Sam asked, 'Melissa, do you want to go to your room first? I'll meet you back here.'

'Okay, Sam, I want to wash off the dust.'

As she walked away with one of the staff carrying her bag, Sam turned to the manager, 'Hennie, what game lives on the grounds?'

'The leopard still hides in the rocks behind the boma. The bushbuck, four of them, come regularly. Half a dozen squirrels, a warthog with two babies, vervet monkeys, and the mongoose family.'

'Any pups?'

'A litter of three; I saw them a week ago.'

'Have you given them an egg?'

'No, I didn't forget you wanted to be here to film them.'

'Thanks, Hennie. Where's our table?'

'Under the nyala tree by the river bench.'

'That's perfect.'

Melissa returned and Sam took her by the hand. 'We'll walk to the river and our lunch; the ground is uneven and has rabbit holes, so hold my hand.'

When Melissa saw the table beside the river, she exclaimed, 'This setting is straight from a romantic movie. Are you trying to seduce me?'

'That I do at night: candles, champagne, soft music and heart-shaped balloons hanging in the tree.'

'I'll bet that's true, and the music would be "Younger than Springtime", but why are we here and not in the dining area?'

Sam opened her Appletiser, filled her glass, and then flipped off the top of his beer, deftly catching the top as it popped skyward.

'So we can talk quietly without interruption. I need to learn what I must do to make your trip unique.'

'You have already, Sam.' *Does he sense that I don't like noise?*

Sam thought, *Now's the moment to ask.* 'Melissa, what have you written about? I don't want to repeat anything you already know.'

For at least a minute, Sam watched her face. *There's something she doesn't want to tell me.*

'I don't know if I can tell you.' Melissa looked down at her lap.

'How can I learn if you don't tell me?'

Without looking up, she said, 'Do you want to help a rude, inconsiderate, and offensive *whatsit*?'

Sam blanched when he *felt* his reaction, *Oh shit! That must have hurt.* 'Melissa, please forgive me; that came from frustration and fatigue. If I could take it back, I would. You're nothing like that. I do very much want to help you.'

Melissa didn't need to answer as a waiter came, laid a plate with roast chicken before them, and offered a dish of assorted vegetables. 'What would you like, madam?'

'A bit of everything, please.' *Does the waiter think we are married?*

Sam had the same, then Melissa asked, 'Sam, why did he call me madam?'

'Because it's a term of respect for women. Miss and missus are considered familiar by the people here.'

Melissa looked down at her plate and, in a small voice, said, 'I haven't written anything yet. Only a short story.'

Sam had almost expected it. *I must congratulate her.* 'That's great, Melissa.'

Shocked by his reply, she looked up and asked, 'Why?'

'Why what?'

'Why's it great that I've written nothing?'

'Because I'm relieved. The idea of having to read and comment on what you've written has terrified me. I'm a bad reader.'

Melissa forgot herself, for Sam's statement interested her. 'I don't think I would have done that to you. But why a bad reader?'

'I'll explain later, but now tell me what you want to write, and then we can think about how I can help.'

'I decided to write about travels and animals in Africa. I've made books of notes. I spent months on four trips following the Serengeti migration, but everything I saw, except one experience, is already in dozens of books. That's why I came here, for something new.'

'Let's eat while I think about it....'

After finishing her ice cream dessert and the waiter had filled their cups with coffee, she sat back, sighed, and asked, 'Have you found an answer, Sam?'

'Perhaps. Correct me if I'm wrong: you've seen and studied many animals but haven't seen unusual behaviours. If I can show you some, will it be worthwhile?'

'Yes, definitely, Sam. What do you have in mind?'

'I can't promise I'll find them, but we can start with one. I'll find you unique experiences. You can write about them like a chapter in a book, then read them to me, and we'll correct anything we think wrong before writing about the next experience.'

Melissa suddenly felt lightheaded, as if an enormous weight had disappeared, and she smiled. 'Can you do that, Sam, find experiences? The rangers never found any for me in the Serengeti.'

'Yes, I've two already.' *For that smile, anything.* 'The standard game drives provide what most tourists want: a sight of animals at a safe distance, with minimal information to remember. I'm sure you'll learn what you need if I show you the underlying details.'

'And the safe distance?'

'Stick close to me, and you'll be safe, although you'll be closer than you've been before. And don't wander away without asking me first.'

'When do we start?'

'When we finish our coffee.'

The smile grew wider. 'Okay.'

5

· · · · ·

THEY COLLECTED SAM'S CAMERA CASE, A TRIPOD AND A FOLD-ing sun reflector from his room, and then Sam said, 'Now, we need an egg from the kitchen and two folding chairs.'

'What's the egg for?'

'The experience. We'll use the reflector for cooking an egg on a rock in the sunshine.'

Sam could see she was disappointed, 'That's a school experience. Why do we need a professional's camera and equipment to film that?'

'We don't, but in this experience, a mongoose will cook the egg.'

Melissa exclaimed, 'Now I *know* you're pulling my leg!'

'Wait and see.'

Sam led the way across the open ground towards the mongoose burrow halfway to the river, but before they reached it, Melissa asked, 'Sam, what's that funny-looking bird with the long legs? It has a hat.'

'Where?'

'It's grey. Over there.' Melissa pointed.

Sam saw it, laid the equipment and the chairs on the ground, except for the camera hanging around his neck, and said, 'That's a crowned plover. They are quite common, but we don't see them because they choose nesting grounds with the same colouring as their plumage. They are interesting birds. I'm sure that one has eggs close by.'

'I can't see a nest.'

'There isn't one; the bird picks a spot in open ground and lays a clutch of two or three eggs on the bare ground.'

'But that must be dangerous; anything walking by could step on them.'

'That's true, but the chance of it happening in a large area is small, and the bird will try to lure away a predator.'

'How, Sam?'

'Melissa, walk towards its eggs – I guess where its shadow falls – and tell me what you think the bird is doing. I'll walk behind and film you.'

Melissa sauntered forward. 'The bird is becoming agitated, Sam.'

'Go on.'

'It's injured, Sam. One wing touches the ground.'

'Keep walking. If it tries to escape, follow it.'

The plover tried to jump into the air, flapped the uninjured wing, and landed badly, with a flutter of feathers three metres further away.

'Sam, it also has a bad leg; it's limping.'

'Then it's in a bad way; just follow it.'

Melissa didn't see Sam behind her. He bent down, grabbed a clump of grass, and bent it over.

'Wow, Sam. That time, it went further, but it tumbled on its head. Aren't we being cruel?'

'It'll give up once it gets further, Mel.'

After Melissa had followed it for thirty metres, what looked to her like a seriously injured and panic-stricken bird miraculously recovered, took off and flew away.

'Sam, how did it manage that?'

'The whole sequence is known as paratrepsis or distraction display. It's anti-predator behaviour; many bird species do it, and some animals. That bird wanted to convince you that it would be easy to catch and eat, and you're now thirty metres away from its eggs.'

'But I can return.'

'Try, Melissa.'

She walked about the same distance back, and began searching the ground for the eggs. Sam allowed two minutes.

'Well, Melissa. Can't you find them?'

'No, Sam, they must be hard to see.'

'Look straight ahead...

'Now turn sixty degrees to the left. Do you see a bent clump of grass about five metres away?'

'Yes.'

'A ranger's lesson, Melissa; you can never return to where you were unless there's a marker. I bent that grass. It's where the bird was when you saw it. Go and look around there.'

Melissa looked carefully at the ground, and a minute later, the three speckled eggs jumped into focus. Excited, she exclaimed, 'I've found them, Sam.'

'Don't touch them; we'll return to pick up the chairs.'

Melissa looked back as Sam bent down to collect the chairs and camera gear.

'Sam, the bird is back where we first saw it.'

'Good, then we didn't upset it.'

As they arrived at the mongoose burrow, Sam said, 'Look for the bird again.'

'It's gone away, Sam.'

'It hasn't. It's sitting on the eggs and has flattened itself down until it's almost invisible.'

'That experience might make a story, Sam, or part of one, but you must explain why I couldn't walk back to the same place.'

'Later, I will, but let's cook the egg.'

Sam positioned the chairs three metres from the mongoose burrow, then set the camera on the tripod, the reflector to reduce shadow, and said, 'Now sit there, Melissa, and don't talk above a whisper.' Holding the camera's radio remote, he sat in the other chair.

'What's in the burrow, Sam?'

'The mongoose.'

'But where's the egg?'

'Here.'

He took it from a pocket and gave it to her, 'Now, place the egg halfway between the burrow and that rock in front of it. Return, then *don't move.*' He set the camera running. *I reckon that will give an exemplary sequence of Melissa placing the egg.*

Nothing happened for four minutes, and then the mother mongoose's head and twitching nose appeared momentarily before disappearing again. Fifteen seconds later, three pups shot out of the burrow and attacked the egg. It began to roll around the area in front of the den as they tried to bite it. The mother came out and sat watching.

Melissa whispered, 'Sam, what are they doing?'

Sam whispered a reply, 'The pups are learning that the egg is too big for them to bite into, and the mother is waiting until they give up. Just watch.'

Half a minute later, one of the pups appeared to have a grip on the egg, but a second later, it shot from its grasp and finally rolled to a stop a metre before Melissa. She reacted by leaning forward and stretching her hand ahead to roll the egg back. She didn't move far before Sam smacked her forearm away.

Melissa remembered to whisper. 'Owww! Sam, why did you smack me?'

'We gave the egg to them, so the mother thinks it's hers, and she will bite if you touch it. They are lightning fast, and her bite can pierce the head of a large cobra. You could lose a finger or part of one. I didn't have time to warn you, but I did say, *Don't move*.'

The mother mongoose rolled the egg back to the pups, but a minute later, two of the pups had lost interest and Melissa saw the mother come and move the egg to a position in front of the rock. The mother chattered for several seconds, turned her back to the stone with the egg between her front paws, and suddenly hurled the egg backwards between her legs so it crashed into the rock and broke open. The pups leapt on it in delight.

'Sam, that's fantastic. Thank you, thank you, thank you. I'm sorry I moved. Thanks for saving my finger.'

'You could try the chapter title "The Mongoose Cook". You can write and then read the chapter to me when ready. If you see any bruising where I slapped you, say so. I have arnica ointment.'

'You want me to read to you?'

'When I read, I'm a fact checker. I have difficulty imagining the picture the author creates. I need practice. You know what feeling you want the story to tell, and I'll hear that.'

'Okay, I'll read it. What will you do with the film?'

'We'll look at it now on the TV in the lounge, and if it's any good, Hennie will tell the guests at dinner in the boma, and we can show it to them. At Likesedi, I can edit it, and then we can decide what to do with it. You can use it for marketing your book if you like.'

In the lounge fifteen minutes later:

'Sam, you filmed me.'

'Of course – you're the author; it's all part of the plan.' He looked away.

Is he blushing?

'What plan?'

'You'll see.'

Hennie came to see the film and said they had to show it that night. He agreed to do the presentation if Sam answered questions.

Melissa asked, 'Now, Sam. Tell me about why it was so difficult for me to walk back to find the plover.'

'You walked from where you saw the bird towards it and then turned to follow it. It wasn't a straight line, although you might have believed it to be so. The plover changed direction slightly with each jump. When you turned to go back, you saw a completely new image without previous references. There was no way you could return to the starting point.

'Now, if you had gone to where you first saw the plover and then walked to where it was standing, you would see in front of you an image that you had already seen, and you would have been closer; it's the difference between taking a known route or a road that you've never taken before. Following a path you know, you can remember the next corner.

'Have you heard of people in a forest cutting marks on trees so they could find their way home?'

'Yes, but I didn't think it necessary for short distances.'

'It's the same, Melissa: leave markers if you need to return to a place. I bent that grass over.'

After dinner, Hennie introduced Melissa, who had, after the screening of the video, become the centre of attention. Hennie gave Sam a guest list with email addresses; all of them wanted notifications when Melissa published her book, and Hennie added, 'Sam, one of the guards saw *Ingwe*; I think our leopard's back for a few days.'

Sam walked Melissa back to her tent on stilts. She turned to him at the bottom of the steps and said, 'Sam, you're incredible. All that in one day.'

Stepping onto the first step, Melissa began to lean forward. *I want to kiss him, but I can't. I don't know how.*

'Good night, Sam. Your plan is working.'

Sam returned to his room happy and fell asleep instantly, but Melissa tossed and turned for an hour.

6

· · · · ·

MELISSA WOKE EARLY THE FOLLOWING DAY, SHOWERED quickly, opened her notepad, and began to write. She started with the title, 'The Mongoose Cook', paused, and opened a new document. The title she wrote was 'Preface'.

The first paragraphs she wrote were sparse, almost a series of notes, in which she described her past, how her parents had died and how her aunt had barely taken their place. She told how she'd become withdrawn, barely speaking. She explained she'd lost herself in books, eventually deciding to study English at university, continuing to a master's degree, and then her desire to write.

She described how she'd read several books about Africa, had one day decided to visit the continent, and had spent months following the migration in the Serengeti in Tanzania and Kenya.

The last of these short paragraphs described her desperation when she found nothing worth writing about and her decision to try Botswana.

The paragraphs became more detailed after she stepped off the plane in Gaborone; they described Sam, what he said, and how it affected her. She recorded how they had sought a room and stayed with Peter, his wife, and children, sharing a room, and everything she remembered about her arrival at the lodge, including the last lines:

'When do we start?'

'When we finish our coffee.'

Melissa read what she'd written, making some minor corrections. Everything that needed remembering was there, so she closed and saved the file. She was about to return to 'The Mongoose Cook' when Sam arrived.

'Melissa, I was expecting you for breakfast. You can't work on an empty stomach; come.'

'I was about to start writing about the mongoose, Sam.'

Sam felt she was trying to withdraw. 'Melissa, authors have a public they must nurture. If you write, you can't escape it. Five children are waiting for you at breakfast, and they have an egg. They want you to show them how the mongoose breaks it. Please don't disappoint them; I've promised.'

'Children, Sam?'

'Yes. Although Hennie will be there to keep them from pushing the egg around.'

Melissa thought, *He's reminding me. I suppose I must, if not for them, for Sam.* 'Okay, Sam. Let me wash my hands.'

Melissa ate well and after breakfast, followed by five children, she left to visit the mongoose. Sam promised to see her later, for he had something to do.

He unpacked his artificial moons from his equipment case. Large diameter LED floodlights that gave a wide beam of moonlight strength, but finding sufficient battery power proved difficult. With the help of the workshop crew, he cobbled together a collection of batteries and put them on charge.

Then he unpacked his sound equipment from a foam-filled box:

his recorder and parabolic microphones. He connected the cables and checked them.

At 11 am, he went to see Melissa, carrying two cups of coffee.

'Hello, Mel. How's the writing progressing?'

She looked up from her notepad, 'Are you going to call me Mel, now? No one has ever called me that.'

'Do you mind? It just seems easier, and I like it.'

'It feels more intimate.' *Does Sam like me? No one has except my parents, aunt, and Mrs Drew.*

'Well, we did sleep in the same room. It might make the next time easier.'

Melissa smiled, 'Do you want there to be a next time, Sam?'

'A guy can hope, can't he?'

'Okay, Sam. Just between you and me.' Melissa felt something new. *He wants to be with me. I never expected that.*

'I'll finish in an hour or so. Come and fetch me for lunch.'

'Okay, I came to say we won't go to Baboon Rock tonight; we'll go tomorrow. The batteries need time to charge.'

'So, no more experiences today?'

'Well, I can think of one. I'll fetch you for the buffet lunch in the garden.'

Sam went to the kitchen, gave instructions for an after-lunch coffee, and fetched his camera, tripod and the motorised platform that he screwed onto the tripod with the camera on top. His wireless remote had buttons for zoom, right and left, up and down. He removed the view screen from the camera and switched on the Bluetooth connection. He set it up beside the table on the stone terrace in front of the lodge lounge.

Sitting at the end of the table, facing the lounge, and looking at the little screen, Sam checked the camera would give the views he wanted from himself to the lodge corner and from the roof edge down to the table. He had to move the tripod three times before he was satisfied, and as he finished, the staff member he'd asked for arrived to watch and make sure the vervet monkeys didn't come to investigate and damage the equipment.

Then he went to fetch Melissa.

'Mel, have you finished?'

'Yes, I'll probably revise it several times, but I can read it to you.'

'Well, come to lunch. You can read it to me this afternoon.'

Sam was pleased during the buffet lunch. Melissa seemed relaxed and talked to the guests, answering their questions openly, and Sam sensed her pride when she said that she'd written the first draft of 'The Mongoose Cook'.

When they finished eating, Sam said, 'Mel, come to the lounge. I arranged our coffee there.'

When they arrived, Melissa asked, 'Why are the camera and microphones here?'

'You'll see in a few minutes. Sit there, with your back to the lounge, opposite me.'

Sam started the camera before she sat, and a waiter brought three tin cups, two for Sam and one for her.

Melissa lifted the cup, sipped it, and said, 'This isn't coffee; it's chocolate, lukewarm and very sweet.'

'I know. Leave it on the table and slowly turn to look over your right shoulder at the roof's eave.'

She did. 'There's a monkey up there. It's cute and looking at me.'

'Yes, he's our guest. He can smell the chocolate. Come and sit next to me. Your coffee's here. Go to your left, and then watch the monkey.'

The camera tracked her until she sat, then back to a close-up of the monkey. It zoomed out until the monkey, mug, and table were in view.

The monkey finally decided, dropped from the eaves, scampered across to the table and reached the mug of chocolate after two leaps to the stool and table top. It grabbed the cup with both front paws and, standing on its back legs, stuck its muzzle into the mug to drink the chocolate while keeping its cheeky eyes on Melissa and Sam who were less than three metres away.

'He's lovely, Sam. Just like a naughty child.'

'Now go and shoo him away.'

Melissa stood, and the monkey, eyes fixed on her, continued to slurp as she approached until she spoke, 'Go on, scram, you thief. Leave my drink alone.'

The vervet pulled its head from the mug. As Melissa continued to approach, it dropped the cup and scampered back to the lodge and up to the eaves. Melissa bent down, her back to Sam, to pick up the cup.

The camera, and Sam, had a direct view of her butt in tight pants. Sam forgot the monkey.

Melissa stood up. 'I now understand why the mugs are metal and chipped. What kind of monkey was that?'

'A vervet, common in riverine forest. Very clever little buggers, they are born thieves.'

'Why born thieves?'

'They seem to enjoy stealing from under your nose. Even if they have more than enough food, they'll steal yours but often not eat it.

That monkey decided to steal the chocolate the moment you sipped it.'

'I'll call the chapter "A Guest for Coffee".'

'That's a good one.'

'I'll write it tomorrow. But now, do you want to listen to what I've written?'

'Okay. Two hours, then we must take a short walk: exercise with something to see.'

Melissa read her story. Even if it had been terrible, Sam would have said it was wonderful, but he didn't need to lie. It was, to his ears, superb.

'So, Sam. What do you think?'

'It's excellent. Although I'm far from a literary critic, I can make some suggestions. How about something about what mongooses eat? Then, how long does the mongoose care for her babies, and how much must she teach them? You can find all that on the web. Please don't copy or put everything in; you want to add something relevant to the story.

'There are also one or two places where I wasn't sure if it was you, the mongoose, or someone else telling the story. You should reread it and see if you can find those places.'

'Can't you point them out?'

'I can try, but you would have to read it to me again. Let's go for that walk, then we'll have dinner. After dinner, you can read it to me again.'

Sam carried two small folding chairs and led the way out of the lodge. Melissa saw he had a pistol in a holster at his belt. 'Why the pistol, Sam? You've never carried it before.'

'There are times when I carry it. We're going into a rocky valley, and if your back is to the wall, you don't have much choice except to stand and face an animal. The pistol doesn't have bullets, only blanks, so I can face a cat or hyena on equal terms. He can growl, and I can growl back with a bang.'

'But you could have bullets and fire into the air.'

'I make my cartridges, and I make my growl terrifying. It fires an exploding firework, and all wild animals are terrified of fire. I'm a dragon.'

Melissa saw an image in her mind from early childhood. It somehow released her from only answering questions. 'Wow, now I'm beginning to understand you, Sam.'

'Understand what?'

'You said that in my nightie, I was good enough to eat, and in all the stories my mother read me that had dragons, they all wanted to eat the virgin princess – you're a dragon in disguise. Is that why you smelt me two days ago? Deciding if I was tasty?'

Before Sam could reply, Melissa added, 'That explains why I had to buy creams with no scent; you don't like sauce on your food.'

His reply confused her for several seconds.

'I'm sure you're exceedingly good to eat, although I shall take off your nightie first; I don't like strings between my teeth. And you're right. No sauce.'

Disconcerted at the mental image of Sam removing her nightie, Melissa blushed.

Sam continued as if he hadn't noticed. 'Now, do you see the rocky outcrops and the Baobab tree ahead of us?'

'Yes.'

'We're going to climb the outcrop on the right of the Baobab. About two-thirds of the way up, there's a flat piece of rock where we can sit. We'll be in the shade from the setting sun. On the other outcrop, a leopard uses a cave when it's in the area. If it's there, it will come out just before sunset.

'All we need to do is sit quietly and watch.'

Minutes later, they were sitting in the chairs. Sam pointed out the cave entrance.

'How long will we wait?'

'Until it's dark. Now's when I practise listening. Shut your eyes and concentrate on what you hear. Turn your head six or eight steps from right to left. For each, listen for three minutes. First, concentrate on anything close, then farther away, and then far. Tell yourself you don't want to hear anything outside the area you're concentrating on. It takes practise, but it's wonderful once you can.'

Melissa smiled. Sam didn't see her eyes twinkling in secret amusement, 'How do I tell I'm doing it right?'

Her voice alerted Sam, *She sounds like she's teasing me!*

'When the sounds you hear from one place differ from those you hear from another. Build a picture in front of you of where the sounds come from. You can see darkness filled with creatures when you know what makes the sounds and refuse to hear anything that comes from all around.'

Silence fell, and an hour later, Melissa gave a start when Sam poked her, but she didn't move when she saw the leopard come slowly from the cave.

It's beautiful and much bigger than I expected.

The leopard looked at them from across the small valley for what seemed like ages. Then it lay down under the fading sunlight on the warm rock. Melissa knew that although it was lying down, it was watching them.

As the growing shade from their outcrop crept across the leopard's shelf, it stood and stretched, and Melissa remembered, *like a big pussy cat*. It stepped off the ledge and, leaping gracefully from rock to rock, reached the valley floor, only eight metres in front of them, where it stopped and fixed them with a long stare before casually walking away. Melissa felt a frisson of fear rippling down her spine.

'We can go now,' said Sam.

'Sam, what would you call the chapter if I write about it?'

'Thirty Minutes with *Ingwe*.'

'What's *ingwe*?'

'The name for a leopard in Zulu. What will you write about?'

'It's difficult. I must write down what we saw and what happened, but there's the beginning of a story there, maybe not about the leopard.'

'Then what?'

'Just before you poked me, I heard the sounds change.'

'They did; you're the first-ever visitor to tell me you can hear it too. Keep practising, and you'll belong and feel happy here. Now let's go for dinner in the boma, and then you can read to me again.'

'In my room?'

'You choose. There, or in the lounge.'

Melissa came to dinner carrying her notebook, so Sam knew she'd decided on the lounge, but after a splendid meal and a staff traditional dance performance, they entered the lounge to find six adults and four children watching the TV.

'Sam, I can't read to you with people listening. I don't understand why I'm reluctant to take you to my room. It's not you. I'm the problem. Peter's room wasn't yours or mine. I've never taken anyone to my room in London. What have you planned for tomorrow?'

'Breakfast, work, a ride to the Shashi River for a picnic lunch, more work, then a visit to Baboon Rock at sundown, and dinner. Remember, the day after tomorrow, we fly north.'

'How about I write the monkey story tomorrow morning? Then we'll go for your picnic lunch. I'll take my notebook, and I can read the stories to you. We can then return in time for Baboon Rock.'

'Whatever you want, Mel, this is your trip. The Landy has a USB connection for a notebook.'

'Can you film those baboons installing themselves, Sam?'

'No, I need a special low-light lens; they look more like telescopes.'

'Why don't you have one?'

'First, they're a luxury I can't afford, and second, they have limited use, and there are better things to spend my money on.'

Melissa decided to find out more later.

'Why are we flying?'

'The agents agreed on flying to fit north and south into your schedule. Because the distance is seven hundred kilometres in a straight line, more like a thousand by road, and most of it gravel road, the agents would never suggest anything else to an exclusive guest.'

'Is there anything to see on the way?'

'Only occasional animals, but there's endless wild Botswana and some spectacular places. It's the kind of trip worth doing once in a lifetime if you don't have arthritis, and animals are not the only thing that interests you. Some, including myself, adore those places and return often.'

'Okay, let's do the reading at Shashi. Take me to my tent.'

'Have you been watching silent movies?'

'Why?'

'I remember it as "Take me to your tent". Then the sheikh lifts her onto his horse and rides off.'

'Well, if so, she was dressed in revealing gossamer drapes, and I don't fancy riding away.'

Sam grinned. Melissa was sure it was devilish, 'You have a nightie.'

'Before you start a fight: good night, Sam.'

'Good night, Mel.'

Melissa couldn't sleep. She rose twice to drink some water. The question she had to resolve was: fly or drive? When she finally cracked it, she slept well.

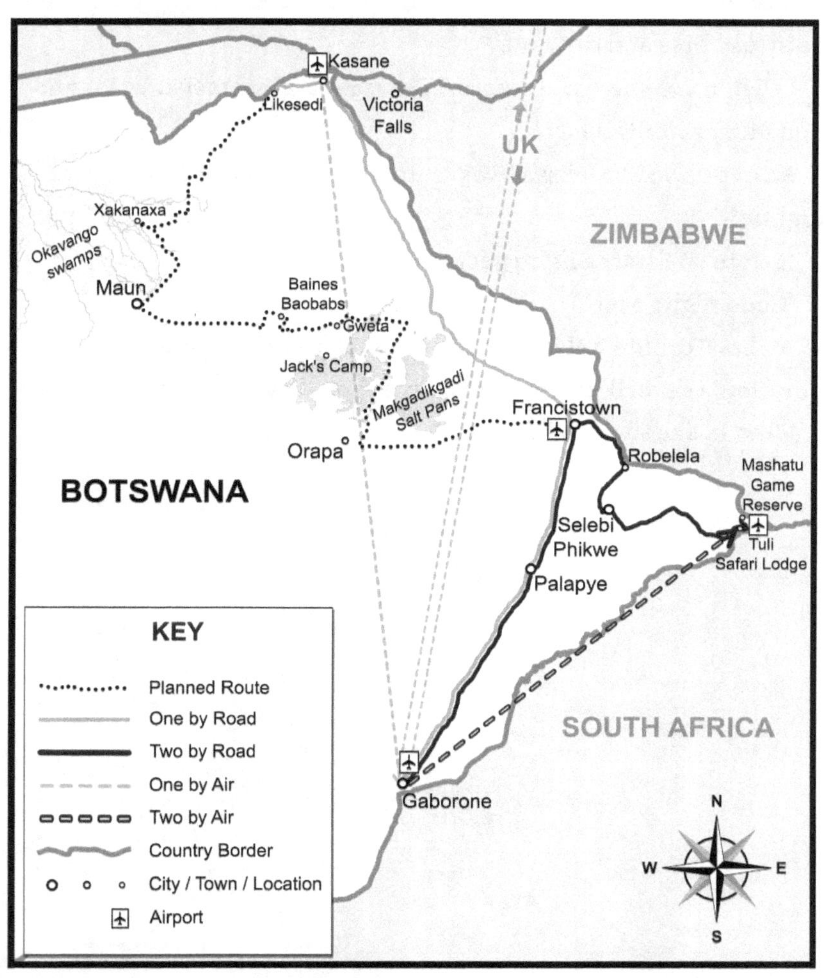

Sam's Modified Planned Routes for the Remainder of Melissa's Tour of Botswana

7

·····

SAM FETCHED MELISSA FOR BREAKFAST, THEN TOOK HER BACK
to her tent and said, 'I'll be waiting at the parking at 11:30 am. I'll organise the picnic.'

He didn't: he asked Hennie to do it.

Sam sat down in the lounge with a road map and devised an itinerary from the lodge to Likesedi. It would take fifteen days.

He washed out his Landy's water tank and checked he could borrow an extra sleeping bag. Then he called Peter.

'Hi, Silent. How's it going.'

'It's going fine, Peter, I'm calling because Melissa asked for information.'

'What does she want to know?'

'She likes Botswana and wants to know if we could drive to Likesedi.
If she decides to go by road, she'll extend her stay. I've worked out an
itinerary for fifteen days, starting tomorrow. I can take care of it, but I'll
need one night at Mashatu or nearby tomorrow night. I can update you
with my position during the trip, so you'll know when we'll arrive.
Lastly, will there still be room at Likesedi, and for how long? If we do go,
you must cancel the flights to Kasane.'

'Okay, Sam, I'll call back within an hour on the accommodation. I
need your confirmation before 4 pm to cancel the flights and confirm
the first night.'

'Okay, I'll charge my satphone. If I don't answer my cellphone, call
that.'

Sam checked out his winch, jacks, and sand tracks in the garage and serviced the engine.

Peter called back. 'Mashatu has one room in the tented camp, but nothing for you as the pilots' and rangers' rooms are full. You'll need to share as you did here. At Likesedi, Carl confirms they should have a room for two or three days, but he has bookings afterwards.'

'Thanks, Peter.'

At 11:30, Sam was waiting when Melissa arrived with her notepad in a bag.

She surprised him once again. 'Sam, let's go into the lounge; I've something to say.'

In the lounge, Sam asked, 'Okay, Mel. What's it about?'

Melissa took a deep breath, 'Sam, I've spent three years trying to write and achieved one short story; it's been my only ambition or objective since I graduated. It may be my fault, but I've never had a social life; all I've done is study, and I believed that authoring a book would prove that I haven't wasted my life. Until I met you in Gaborone, I was terrified that I had wasted my life.

'In three days, you've changed my life entirely. You've taught me I can overcome whatever has dogged me for years. I've no right to ask you, but I must do everything possible to keep the momentum going. I'm ready to extend my stay for as long as it takes, and I would like you to take me north in your Landy.'

Sam smiled. Melissa felt it was affectionate, 'Mel, are you prepared to miss two or three days of showers, using only a cloth and chilly water? Can you stand naked in a camp shower, with only a can with a dozen punched holes above your head, while I pour icy water into the can with a bucket? Are you ready to share a tent and sleeping bags with me? Share a bedroom with me? Share a bed with me?

'Are you ready to squat over a small hole I dig for you in the open while I watch for predators? And drop your pants and pee in the open while I keep a lookout?

'I'll protect you, but will you have hysterics when you meet a furry spider the size of your hand, a scorpion even bigger, or a snake big enough to swallow you whole?'

Melissa paused, then raised her chin and replied, 'None of that frightens me, Sam, nowhere near as much as returning to where I was, but if you don't want to take me, I'll accept it, and if you can't organise it, then please suggest something else.'

Sam picked up his mobile, tapped in a number, and passed the phone to Melissa. 'That's Peter, our agent. Tell him.'

The phone rang for fifteen seconds.

'Yes, Silent, I'm listening.'

'It's not Sam; it's Melissa.'

'Oh! Hi Melissa. How can I help?'

'Sam says I must tell you I want him to drive me north.'

'That's okay, Melissa. Has he told you that when you arrive at Likesedi, there may not be more than a day or two of accommodation?'

'No, but that won't be a problem.'

'Okay, Melissa. Have fun. Bye.'

Melissa closed the call, turned and looked at Sam for five seconds. He could see the daggers in her eyes.

'Sam Daniels, you're a scheming, devious, sly, underhanded *what-shim*. You had it all organised before you asked those questions. I don't know whether to hit, hate, or kiss you.'

'I had to be sure. It won't be easy for you. There are no taxis where we go, so once in, you stay in. Am I supposed to guess what a *what-shim* is?'

'The male equivalent of a *whatsit*.'

'Then you should have used *whatsher* the first time.'

She grinned. 'I wasn't thinking grammatically.'

Relieved, Sam said, 'Well, now we're even, and if it helps you to decide, I'd prefer a kiss. Let's go to the Shashi and read.'

Although not far, it took them over an hour. The journey needed a slow four-wheel drive in the sand. When Sam stopped at the Shashi and the Limpopo confluence, Melissa exclaimed, 'But the Shashi is much wider than the Limpopo.'

'Two million years ago, this was the Zambezi; the Limpopo was only a tributary. Today, the Shashi only flows for a few days of the year, but the Limpopo backfills the confluence, and what you're looking at becomes a vast lake.'

'Sam, it's empty and peaceful. We saw only a few animals on the way here.'

'Oh, they're there, but although it may not look like it, there's more to eat at the lodge than around here. There's a nice shady parking spot under the nyala trees at the point. I'll park there, take some drinks from the cooler, and we can eat or read in whatever order you prefer.'

'I'm hungry. Let's eat first.'

Sam set up a folding table and two camp chairs before placing the salad, plates and cutlery on the table. After they ate, Melissa said, 'Sam, I've read the story and corrected what you pointed out. I've also added facts about the Mongoose family, though not too much. Let me read it.'

Sam closed his eyes as she read. When she finished, Sam said, 'Mel, everything you wrote is accurate, and it's a great little story, but I think something's missing. When I drafted my first thesis, the professor rejected it and gave me a booklet about how to draft a thesis, and I learnt about points of view. You must know this from your studies. You've written this in first person, telling your account, but the story is not about you: it's the mongoose's.'

Melissa considered what Sam said, frowned, and asked, 'What can I do?'

'You can't talk to the mongoose; it can't talk back and tell you what it thinks. Animals are a difficult subject to write about. Have you read *Jonathan Livingston Seagull*?'

'Yes, that's third person but omniscient. It was a lovely story. I don't think I could write that.'

'I'm sure you could, but it will become confusing if you have stories about different animals. What about including me in the story? Just call me "My guide Sam". Then you can write, "I asked Sam if she was smiling?" If you were drafting a thesis, it would be formal and dry facts. I had to use what the booklet said was third person detached. It would help if you made this story interesting but easy to understand. People don't keep reading if it's full of facts and difficult to follow. You can also say Sam was terrified, horrified, shocked, surprised, disgusted and words like that. We can also argue, and you can lose your temper.'

'You mean like we do every day?'

'Yes, just think: we're living this story, but you're writing excerpts from it. Won't they sound more real and interesting if they include what we say and think during that episode?'

'Let me think, Sam.'

Sam opened another beer and sat back, watching Melissa and her frowning face. *I think she's running a variation of the story through her mind.*

...

Melissa suddenly began to type. She typed for five minutes without a pause, then said, 'Sam, the first four paragraphs.'

Then she read them.

'Mel, read each sentence, stop, play it back in your head, and see if you can improve it. That's what I do.'

She read three paragraphs, making two minor changes, but she stopped and said when she read the fourth. 'That's not right.'

'Then you should make it right.'

Ten minutes later, she said, 'Let me read it to you again, Sam.'

He closed his eyes again, and she read.

Her voice and the words are like beautiful music.

'What do you think, Sam?'

'Mark it as perfect. If the rest follows like that first bit, it will swat *Jonathan Livingston* out of the sky.'

'I'll write the rest, and you can have a snooze, but before I do, stand up.'

'Why?'

Sam looked at her, saw her smile, and suddenly felt afraid; her eyes shone. 'Because if I sit on your knee to kiss you, the chair will collapse.'

Sam stood, and Melissa wrapped her arms around him, looked up, and said, 'This is another first for me. Kiss me, Sam.'

He gave her a gentle kiss.

'Sam, I've seen kisses, although this is my first. You can do better than that.'

'I'm afraid to.'

'Try.'

It lasted over a minute...

'Wow! Now have your snooze; I've work to do.'

Sam lay back in his chair, *Is 'wow' is her equivalent of 'holy shit'?*

Ninety minutes later, she woke him, 'Sam – wake up, Sam! I finished the first draft, and I need a pee. What do I do?'

'Remove your trousers. I'll check for a place.' Sam jumped off the low riverbank and checked out the sand. 'There are no snakes or scorpions here, and there's no toilet paper roll on a convenient holder. Remember that. Do you have a tissue?'

'I'll take one from my bag and come down.'

She joined him, wearing her top and panties, and Sam said, 'Right, pull the panties down, squat, and fill the river.'

He turned and climbed the bank.

She followed a minute or two later, 'Thanks, Sam, that was easier than I anticipated.'

'It always is, but always ask me to look and watch out first. There are hidden surprises everywhere.'

'You guys have it easy.'

'Mel, don't think that. I check for bugs and beasties first. They don't like being peed on and can sting your foot, so it swells like a balloon. What did you do with the tissue?'

'Pushed it under the sand.'

'Don't do that again, Mel. Drop it on the ground and use your shoe to kick dirt or sand over it.'

'Why?'

'Centipedes and other things can sting a finger.'

'Okay, I'm learning.' If Sam had seen her grin and eyes before he turned away, he might have realised that something wasn't quite as simple as it seemed.

'I'll make us some coffee while you work through what you've written. We have an hour before we leave.'

They reached the lodge a half hour before sundown, collected the moon lights, a spotlight, the batteries, the camera and sound recorders and returned to Baboon Rock. Everything was in place before dark, and Sam whispered, 'Now, this is the worst part ... waiting.'

He placed the two chairs with their backs against the Landy and added, 'We wait and listen. When I'm sure the baboons are on the rock, I'll use the spotlight and highlight them for you to see, but until then, when they arrive, they'll be shadows in the moonlight. At times like this, I practice listening. We'll hear the guard baboons signalling either warnings or all clear, mothers calling their young as they climb down, a leopard may grunt or snarl, and if one gets too close, the terrible noise of a scrap between baboons and the leopard. Everything is a picture from sounds, so do as I told you and concentrate on separate areas in succession.'

'Is there a reason we sit with our backs to the Landy?'

'Yes, in the open at night, we're prey. With our backs to the Landy, as long as we don't stand up, we're part of it and much too big to attack, so don't stand.

'And while I think of it, if you want to pee at night when we're camping, pee beside the Landy as I do, and don't squat if you can't check out the ground. Remove your panties and spread your legs.

'Right now, if we need to, we pee where we sit. We're inside the boundary of the leopard's larder.'

Melissa shivered.

She sat on Sam's left, close to him, and said, 'Hold my hand, Sam.' They sat for an hour while complete darkness crept over the land. Melissa closed her eyes and listened. The continuous chirrup of the crickets blended into a featureless grey background to her mental picture. She heard the bark of the guard baboons to the left as they came and replies from the right, and then from higher up her image as they climbed the rock to the top.

She heard a different bark; it seemed reassuring, carrying the message, 'All clear'. Then Sam poked her. She opened her eyes. In the pale light from Sam's moonbeams, the rock had fireflies wherever a granite crystal concentrated and reflected a pinpoint of light. Melissa saw the shadows of baboons climbing down the face, only to freeze at a perching spot, where, motionless, they became instantly invisible, only a patch of a darker shade. One or two called; she thought it was a baboon whisper as they gave instructions to their children. Then silence fell again.

Sam switched on his spotlight and swung the beam along the rock face. He didn't stop in one place but kept it moving. Melissa saw the baboons as individuals, mothers with babies at the lowest level, yet too high for a cat to leap. Her mind filled her grey picture with dark shapes, glued to the near-vertical rock face. As the spotlight beam swept higher, she saw the older adults and the prime males, who looked directly at her and Sam, their eyes reflecting the light.

Sam switched off the spot and whispered, 'We'll wait a bit; listen.' Melissa closed her eyes again.

...

A half-hour passed, and then an expanding hole of nothingness grew on one side of Melissa's picture, and she felt a ball of fear at the unknown. Sam gently touched her leg and sighed, 'Sshhh.'

Melissa opened her eyes, and the picture was still the same, but the hole was moving; she felt tension she'd never felt before. An urgent bark came from the top of the rock, followed by another, and Melissa sensed movement. A leopard walked silently between her and the rock, only metres away. It stopped and turned its head to look at them, and Melissa saw its eyes reflecting the moon lights. The shiver returned. She felt primitive fear. *They are terrible eyes; they could frighten anyone. It's deciding if it should eat me.*

Before the leopard turned away, Melissa *felt* a whisper; she knew she hadn't heard it. *'You're too much to eat.'*

Sam gave the leopard time to distance itself, then said, 'That's enough for tonight. Let's go.'

She didn't speak until they reached her tented room, where Sam said, 'We have a long day tomorrow. Come to breakfast at 8 am; we'll leave at 9 am. We can talk about tonight then.'

'Good night, Sam. Thanks, I'm glad you held my hand.'

'Why?'

'The leopard told me we were too much to eat.'

Sam didn't know what to think, so he said, 'Good night, Mel.'

8

· · · · ·

MELISSA WAS ON TIME FOR BREAKFAST. AS SHE SAT BESIDE HIM at his table, she asked. 'I'm all packed, Sam. Where are we going today?'

'Mashatu, unless you want to read me the whole Mongoose story first.'

'Okay, come after breakfast, and then you can carry my suitcase down the stairs.'

'Sam, are you ready for this?'

'Go ahead.'

Sam listened again, with his eyes closed, and said not a word until after she ended and said, 'Sam, are you asleep?'

'No, I'm in mongoose-land. That's where your story took me. It carried me away to somewhere magical.'

'So you liked it?'

'I adored it. I think it's perfect. File it under approved by Sam.'

'Okay, now answer my question: where are we going today?'

'I've decided to go the wrong way today. It's not far, but tomorrow, we'll retrace our steps. We'll drive through the Mashatu reserve, stop at the main camp for lunch, and then go to their tented camp for the night. They have a room for us.'

'Why do you want to go that way?'

'Well, I want to show you a unique moth and caterpillar; the life cycle takes a year. In the Mashatu area, it's still hot and dry. We're approaching the second and final moult stage, and the caterpillars should be easy to see unless they've moulted and gone to ground.'

'Again, why?'

'Well, if we can find a mopani tree with a load of caterpillars, we can collect a few. Then we'll dry them and eat them. They love mopani, and mopani is dense in the area, and by now, they should have eaten most of the trees' leaves. You can write a story about the emperor and the caterpillar, although their common name is the mopani worm.'

'Emperor, Sam?'

'The caterpillar metamorphoses into the emperor moth, with a wingspan up to a hundred and twenty millimetres.'

'Wow. I'd love to see the moth. So we'll look for a tree with no leaves?'

'No, there will be some leaves, though very few. I'll show you the leaves. They're distinctive, in pairs like butterfly wings, and they change with seasons from bright green through orange and yellow. If you want to see the moth, I've one in my sample case in Chobe, or you can return in November.'

'I might do that; it's something else to write about.'

Sam drove out of the lodge area, and as they passed Baboon Rock on the way to the airfield, he said, 'Mel, tell me what kind of pictures you managed to form in your mind when you listened last night. Tell it as if you had written it as a story.'

'Where do I start, Sam?'

'Start when we arrived, describe what it looked like as the light faded, and then when you closed your eyes.'

Melissa did, and then closed her eyes and, after a minute, said, 'When I closed my eyes, it was just all black, and then the sound of the crickets and Sam's breathing began to die away, and either side of the rock the black changed to grey, getting lighter until I could hear nothing. It was still black above the rock and in front, but I could see the rock outlined by the grey.

'Then I heard the baboons' calls; they showed as bright flashes, so I could tell that they climbed up onto the rock as the flashes rose. When Sam poked me, I opened my eyes and saw the rock with hundreds of tiny lights where the rock crystals reflected the moon lights. I saw the shadows of the baboons climbing down and perching as they blocked out the glint of the crystals. When I closed my eyes again, I could see them as dark patches on the rock. Then I saw the leopard come.'

'Because I poked you?'

'No, first it was a small black hole to the right, then the hole grew and moved across until it reached the rock. That's when you poked me, and I saw it when I opened my eyes. Was it the same one we saw in the rocks?'

'More than likely. Leopards stick to known ranges.'

'Well, that was when I felt it told me we were too much to eat and went away.'

Sam laughed, 'It did look like it was trying to decide now or later. You did brilliantly. I don't know how you managed that on the first try; it took me months to reach the first step of the grey. That's the background noise. The hole is where the crickets stop chirruping; they stop when something moves in their area.'

Sam glanced at her. Melissa was sitting, her hands clasped in her lap, shoulders hunched, looking at her hands. *That posture tells me something. I think she's unaware of doing it, but it's when she wants to withdraw because she's scared to tell me something. It must be an in-grained habit to avoid criticism.*

Sam braked, stopped the Landy, and turned to her.

'Mel, is there something you're scared to tell me?'

She raised her head and looked at him.

Her eyes are grateful; she needs someone to ask before saying something.

'Yes, Sam.'

'You can tell me anything whenever you wish.'

'I have perfect pitch. I was born with it.'

'What's that mean?'

'If you played ten sounds. Short, sharp ones, like a baboon's bark, but three or four were the same, I can tell you which ones are the same. If two baboons bark and one twice, I can tell you which one barked twice. And even if I'm standing by a running car engine, I can still tell you. My mind breaks up sounds and sees them as separate things.'

'But that's marvellous. Why didn't you want to tell me?'

'It's not, Sam.'

'Not what?' *She's looking at her hands again.*

'Not marvellous. I can hear what someone says even when they think I can't, and often I hear hurtful things.'

Sam had to think about what she said. *I understand that and know that withdrawing from conversations would follow. She needs something else to think about.*

'Mel, I don't tell people unless they ask, but I'll tell you because you told me about your perfect pitch. I'm an orphan.'

It electrified her. She snapped back and turned to Sam. Her face was expressionless, but her eyes were bright. 'Sam, you too?'

I seem to have accidentally hit the proverbial nail on the head. 'Are you an orphan?'

'Yes, Sam, my parents died when I was nine, and an aunt took me in. How old were you?'

Sam felt like he had when he called a female teacher 'sir'. *That explains much. It also confirms I'm an asshole, making assumptions about her without asking.* 'I was five, none of my uncles or aunts wanted me. I went to a care home.'

'That's a shame! So you were like me: you didn't talk much, and the kids called you Silent?'

She remembered that, and I only said it once. 'Yes, we'll discuss this more in the next two weeks. Now, we must drive on, but I want you to believe you have a magnificent gift and should be proud of it.'

His reward was a marvellous smile. 'Thanks, Sam.'

Half an hour later, Sam drove off the road and stopped the motor.

'Mel, this is where we go for a walk.'

She climbed out and came around the Landy to his side, 'Where are we going?'

'To look for the mopani worms, there's dense mopani in this area, so we should be lucky. Let's walk that way; any direction might be okay, but there will be more change in the vegetation as we go down the slope.'

The vegetation changed, but it was predominately mixed acacia thorn at first.

'Mel, be careful of that bush on your right; that's a wait-a-bit thorn.'

'Why wait a bit?'

'The acacias have straight thorns; the subspecies' thorn length varies, but that one has a hooked thorn with an extremely sharp point. It catches your clothes and can be a devil to extract, so you must wait a bit. Its scientific name is *Biancaea decapetala*; we call it by its Afrikaans name, pronounced *vagh uh beekie*. They call it Mauritius thorn elsewhere because although it came from India, it went first to Mauritius.'

'Okay, Sam, I'll watch out. Damn, there's another spider web; where are the spiders?'

'We'll see one in a moment, Mel. They spin the webs between bushes but choose another place when something breaks the web. Look, here's one. It's named the golden orb spider after its web. The golden silk shines in the sunlight.'

'The spider is huge, Sam, and quite beautiful. Is it poisonous?'

'Yes, it can give you a nasty bite, but it's not lethal. The spider webs are so strong they can catch a small bird. Spiderman would use their silk if the films weren't fiction.'

'Can I just push through?'

'Yes, the spider will run off the web and then rebuild it.'

'I'll go round if there's another route.'

Sam smiled and followed her, pleased.

As they approached the dried river, he said, 'Here we are, Mel. Mopani. Look at the leaves.'

'I see why you said they are like butterfly wings; they look alike. Let's search for the worms.'

Forty minutes later, after investigating every clump of mopani, they reached the dry river, and Melissa said, 'I think we're too late for this area. The caterpillars have gone to earth.'

'I hate to admit it, but you're right. We'll turn back and find the Landy. There will be other places somewhere on the way north.'

'We can't go straight back, Sam.'

'Why not?'

'A herd of elephants is coming through. I can hear them.'

About to say, 'Then let's go this way,' Sam had an idea: *It should help her confidence if she leads the way.*

'Then you can do your first guiding job; take us around them. This reserve has some of the biggest elephant herds in Botswana. They can migrate from the Chobe River, where we're going, via the Hwange reserve to the Limpopo. But we won't look at them, only avoid them. Mel, you must learn this gesture.'

Sam raised his right arm above his head, bent the wrist with fingers and thumb together and then waved his arm sinuously. 'I learnt it from a tracker at a lodge in the Ngorongoro.'

'Was his name Chacha?'

'It was. Did you meet Chacha?'

'Yes, he told me some stories; one was about a man who made friends with the elephants by making that gesture.' Melissa waved her arm in a perfect imitation, 'I didn't see him use it.'

Bloody hell. Wonders never end with this woman. 'Well, if we accidentally find ourselves in front of the herd, we'll see if it works here. Never say a word: human voices upset them. And never turn and run: we can only back away slowly.'

Melissa led the way, listening for the sounds of elephants breaking bushes and small trees. Three hundred yards later, with the sounds of breaking brush ahead, Melissa turned away, trying to go around, but then she heard the elephants on all sides. They were in the centre of the herd's path.

Sam stopped her in a clearing, placed a finger on his lips, and raised his arm in the gesture, waving it slowly. Melissa, standing beside him, her heart thumping, did the same.

The herd passed slowly. Two elephants came closer, looked at them, and continued. The others were only dark grey shapes behind the remaining foliage.

Twenty minutes later Melissa whispered, 'They've all passed', and started walking.

Sam didn't reply. He took her arm, and gestured – *That way.*

When the Landy came in sight, Melissa said, 'Sam, that was incredible, but how did you know where to go? I would have lost myself.'

'I could claim I have a GPS in my head, but you must learn something simpler. I kept track of where we had been all the time we walked. I could always find the road easily. But before we started, I noted two points on the opposite slope. Look over there. Can you see two dark green trees in a line, one closer than the other?'

'Yes, they're quite clear.'

'Well, if you're in line with those trees and haven't crossed the road, you can find the Landy by walking away from them. All I had to do was ensure we could always see those trees.'

'And if we had crossed the road, walking towards them?'

'Correct. Do you remember what I said about markers? They are my markers.'

'Were you afraid of the elephants?'

'I didn't sense any reason to be scared, It was interesting, and I'll remember what you've said. It would make a story, "Lost with the Elephants". But where were the elephants going?'

'For water, they must have a waterhole upriver. Okay, let's go for lunch at the lodge. But remind me to tell you more about how not to become lost – you may need it.'

They spent a pleasant lunch break watching the guests. Judging by the lack of suntan, Melissa tried to count the foreign visitors, and Sam was looking to see if he recognised someone. As they sipped their coffees, the lodge manager approached them with another man. 'Hello, Silent. Good to see you again. Have you met our tracker?'

'Yes I have, Gordon. Dumela *N!ki'ka*' Sam used two click sounds in the name; he knew the tracker was from a San tribe.

'Gordon, this is my guest, Melissa Grouwer.'

Melissa put out her hand, 'Pleased to meet you, Gordon.' Then she turned to the tracker, smiled, and said, '¡Hola! *N!ki'ka.*'

It shook Gordon, and Sam gaped, but it delighted the tracker. He replied with a smile and a clap of his hands.

Gordon recovered first. 'Sam, can you take him to the tented camp? They need him there. He'll also make sure you find the camp.'

'Of course, Gordon. We'll leave now.'

It was only six kilometres in a straight line. Still, with no roads, their route had to divert around several deep watercourses and rocky outcrops. The distance they covered was closer to twelve kilometres, all in deep sandy soil in low-range and four-wheel drive. Sam wrestled with the steering and the gearbox. Sitting in the middle, Melissa talked with the tracker on her left. Sam couldn't understand their conversation because the clicks were almost continuous. He could only catch the few words he knew in the San dialect of the Chobe. He missed hearing when *N!ki'ka* asked her for her name, and she told him what the Hadza called her, with its three different clicks. 'Vixen.' Melissa knew that he understood what it meant. 'The fox hears insects underground.' The bat-eared fox has acute hearing.

9

· · · · ·

WHEN THEY DROVE INTO THE TENTED CAMP, IT WAS IN AN UP-
roar. Everyone there was running back and forth. When Sam
stopped, a ranger ran over, 'Silent, I'm glad you're here. The main
camp said you were coming with *N!ki'ka*. The four-year-old son of
one of the guests has disappeared. Can you tell *N!ki'ka* and ask him
to help find Robbie?'

Sam couldn't, but then he remembered Melissa. 'I can't, Koos, but
Melissa can.'

Melissa turned to *N!ki'ka* and explained with a gesture and three
clicking words. *N!ki'ka* replied.

'He says you must show him the boy's tent.'

Koos and the tracker ran off, and Melissa looked around. She spotted a massive anthill, ran to it and began to climb. *N!ki'ka* looked
back, saw her climbing the anthill, and muttered a prayer to his gods
to help her find the boy, but didn't forget to include himself.

Sam found himself alone, joined the ranger distributing searchers
to areas and said, 'Give me a sector to search.'

'Take the area from here to the big nyala tree over there', the
ranger pointed, 'and to the right to the big fever tree. I can't send any
tourists in that sector; the elephants are there.'

Sam set off. He saw Melissa on the anthill and wondered why
she'd gone there. It wasn't high enough to see anything distant, but
he felt she would be safe.

Melissa wasn't looking. She sat down, eyes shut, and listened. A minute later, her picture had greyed out, and a minute after that, she saw a small hole in the fabric of the grey space. It was moving. After another two minutes, Melissa confirmed it moved erratically, but another emptiness far to the other side was not erratic and growing. She ran down the anthill and ran on, headed along as straight a line as possible to where she estimated the first small hole would shortly be.

It was seven hundred metres. Luckily, she didn't put her foot in a rabbit hole, and as she began the last hundred metres, she saw the tracks of a little human foot and those of an animal pack. The small footprint wandered, but the animals tracked straight. She followed the animal spoor – hyena tracks.

Sam was zigzagging from one side of his search area to the other, each time advancing ten metres. At first, he moved rapidly away from the lodge, but as each zig and zag grew longer as he descended further into his wedge-shaped sector, he became worried. The search was going to take a long time. Then he spotted some small footprints; it could only be the boy, so he followed them as they wandered. Sometimes, Sam had to cast around when he lost the trail.

N!ki'ka in the next sector was doing the same. He picked up the same tracks slightly ahead of Sam only moments later.

Melissa came out of the bush into a cleared area and slowed. Forty metres ahead, the little boy stood, right thumb in his mouth, waving the other arm at a small herd of elephant forty metres ahead of him. In the direct line between him and the herd, at about twenty metres, stood the elephant matriarch, a colossal beast. Robbie's left arm was in the air, his hand stroking as if he wanted to touch the elephants.

At the sound of Melissa's running footsteps, the hyenas had moved well to one side. She was an unknown element that needed evaluation. They were about fifty metres away.

Melissa kept walking fast, raised her arm to the elephants in what she believed was the friendship signal, reached the boy, stooped without breaking her stride and took him by the hand. She continued walking, almost dragging the surprised child. She looked to the side at the hyenas that had begun warily closing in on her, decided she didn't need to run, and faced the colossal elephant watching her. If voiced, her thought would have been a shout, *Please help! I must save this child.*

She felt desperate at ten metres, and then the elephant charged.

The relief almost made her legs wobble. *She's charging the hyenas!* The people at the camp heard the shrill trumpet blast as the matriarch passed her.

Sam heard it too and broke into a run. *N!ki'ka* also heard it, recognised it as a predator warning and began to run. The two of them met, and Sam followed the tracker. When they noticed the footprints of a woman and hyenas, they ran as hard as possible.

Melissa didn't stop until she reached the herd, where the matriarch caught up to her. Melissa felt the matriarch sniff her and the boy, drinking in their smell before she pushed them gently into the centre of the herd where they joined the young elephants as the herd started to move off.

Sam and the tracker arrived in the cleared area. Sam looked around wildly. He couldn't see the boy or Melissa. *N!ki'ka* examined the tracks and smiled. Bewildered, Sam stood beside him as he pointed at the footprints, then darted back and forth, learning the story they told.

After two or three minutes, he gestured to Sam and set off after the herd. Sam could only follow. He noted the signs left by the moving elephants and every time *N!ki'ka* pointed at the ground, he saw a footprint, either of a little boy or a woman. Sam could not understand why Melissa should move ahead of the herd. When *N!ki'ka* burst into a run, in a direction away from the tracks, Sam ran too, feeling a mounting panic. *Something is happening to them!*

N!ki'ka knew the terrain intimately. The tracks had told him where the elephants were going and four minutes later, followed closely by Sam, he came to another clearing, stopped and calmly squatted. Sam felt his eyes were laughing when he turned to him. Sam crouched beside him.

He couldn't understand what the tracker was saying, except it had something to do with elephants. Moments later, when the herd came into the open area, *N!ki'ka* pointed towards them. Sam couldn't see anything, but as the adults moved, he caught sight of Melissa, holding one of the boy's hands while he stroked a baby elephant.

Sam felt something completely new that he couldn't understand. Was it awe, pride, or something else?

Melissa glanced up and saw them, then holding the little boy's hand, she walked over to the massive matriarch, seemed to hug her trunk, and stood back as the elephant caressed her hair. Then Melissa turned and walked straight towards them with the child. Sam and *N!ki'ka* stood up, and when Melissa reached them, Sam picked up Robbie and could only say, 'Come on, mister, your mummy's looking for you.' Melissa took Sam's free arm, and *N!ki'ka* walked on the opposite side.

After fifty metres, Melissa stopped and said, 'Put Robbie down, please, Sam.'

He did, and Melissa said, 'Robbie, wave your hand at the elephants; we must say goodbye.' He did, and Melissa did, too. When the matriarch trumpeted a reply, it didn't surprise Sam. His emotions were already overloaded.

'Okay, Sam, let's return to the camp.'

They had walked another hundred metres when the first safari vehicle, driven by Koos, arrived.

At the lodge, Robbie, enveloped by his mother, said several times, '*Ellyfumps*, nice *ellyfumps*', before his father arrived.

Koos asked, 'Where did you find him, Sam?'

'I didn't, Koos. Melissa found him watching a herd of elephants, and then *N!ki'ka* and I found her.'

'Sam, we owe you and Melissa big time.'

'Melissa and *N!ki'ka*, Koos. I followed.'

'I won't forget. I imagine you want a shower. I'll show you to your tent. Relax. What will you drink? I'll send a waiter.'

'Beer and an Appletiser, thanks.'

When Koos left them at their tent, Melissa peeked inside and said,

'Sam, there's only one bed.'

'Peter didn't tell me that. I'll ask Koos for blankets to lay on the floor.'

Melissa thought. *Sam asked if I was ready to share a bed with him during the trip, and this may happen several times. I said yes. I'm sure he won't take advantage, and I'm not going to chicken out on what I said.*

'Just stay on your side, Sam, and we'll share the bed.'

Melissa wasn't the only person who could understand *N!ki'ka*. One of the staff was half San. *N!ki'ka* told him the story, including how Melissa had climbed the anthill and 'sniffed him out' with the help of the gods. Sometimes, things in an ancient language have no direct translation. The signs of the hyena and the elephant charge were clear, and *N!ki'ka* said he'd seen her and the boy in the middle of the herd, stroking the babies, and the San don't lie.

Robbie's father couldn't understand why Robbie kept saying, '*Ellyfump* tickle.'

Soon, the entire lodge knew the story, and Sam asked Melissa, 'How did you find him, Mel?'

'I listened, Sam. I heard the emptiness around Robbie and then the emptiness as the hyenas came, so I ran. When I found him, he was waving an arm at the matriarch only twenty metres in front of him, and the hyenas were forty-plus metres to one side of me. I didn't have a choice, Sam, I had to have the protection of the matriarch.'

'So you grabbed Robbie and went to the matriarch?'

'The matriarch hadn't attacked Robbie. She seemed curious, and I did make the friendship sign. She knew the hyenas were far more dangerous than me. I had almost reached her when she attacked the hyenas. I had to stay with the elephants because I didn't know if the hyenas were still watching. When I saw you, I knew it was okay.'

A light bulb went off in Sam's head. 'Did Chacha teach you the clicks, and that's why you can talk with *N!ki'ka?*'

'The clicks are the same, and some words, but the two languages are hugely different. I was sure Chacha's name was somehow wrong, and I asked him to say it, and because my hearing is so precise, I repeated it perfectly, and he was delighted.'

'I'm grateful to him. He may have saved your life and Robbie's, but it's not a friendship signal. It's more complicated than that.'

'Explain, please, Sam.'

Sam had to think for a minute. 'I can't find the right words. I'll say what I believe it conveys. It means, *"I-might-look-like-a-human-but-I'm-related-to-you-so-I'm-harmless"*. Your arm is like a rudimentary trunk. The elephant can still attack you, but I think it's more likely that she didn't attack because Robbie is so obviously a child, and you have a female smell. In contrast, the hyena is a traditional enemy. But the signal may have helped.'

Koos interrupted Sam and Melissa while they sat quietly on the stone patio before their tent, not speaking but sipping their drinks. 'Sam, do you mind if I disturb you briefly?'

'Of course not, Koos.'

'Everyone wants to hear the story from you and Melissa. Can you tell the story tonight in the lounge? If you don't, it will become a fairy tale.'

'We can, but we might doctor it a bit, Koos. Otherwise, it's unbelievable to all except those who live here.'

'Sam, you and Melissa can tell whatever story you feel best. And Robbie's parents want to see you both. They might want to give you a big tip.'

'Koos, please tell them not to give us money. Saving that boy's life cannot have a cash value. I would rather they didn't offer. But you can introduce Melissa as an author writing a book about her experiences in game parks and say she will certainly include today's events in the book. Then, ask for your clients' email addresses so she can tell them when she publishes her book.'

'You have it, Sam. I reported what happened to the head office. You and Melissa have free accommodation in Mashatu for life.'

'Thanks, Koos. That's generous.'

'No, Sam, that's nothing compared with what the bad publicity would have cost us if the hyenas had got to Robbie.'

After dinner, Sam and Melissa sat on high stools before the assembly of guests and staff. Koos did the introduction as promised, and Sam started.

'I'll try and keep this short. Mel, kick me if I'm still talking at two in the morning.'

She surprised him, and herself. 'I won't. I'll take my clothes off.'

It drew a roar of laughter and a catcall. 'Sam, please keep talking.'

Melissa was flustered. *Why did I say that? And how did I manage to say it? That's not me.*

She calmed herself as Sam began talking.

'Two separate cultures are listening in this lounge. For the rangers and staff who live at this camp, the story Melissa will tell won't surprise them. It will sound unbelievable for visitors from outside Africa, like a fairy tale. So, I'll try to level the playing field by talking to the visitors first.

'Imagine Mashatu as a small but separate country, with a multicultural population but many rules of behaviour typical in the outside world. The cultures live in harmony with each other and the land that feeds them. If we consider one of those cultures, what rules must they obey for peace to rule in their group and for them not to impact heavily on one another? There are many values that I'm sure you can think of. The first may be to love your children, another to love your family members. A third is to help others in difficulty or share your food.

'Now, think of love and care for your children. Does that mean hating the children of other cultures? I can tell you it doesn't, just as it doesn't in the culture of the outside world, and this love overflows. You may dislike people with a different skin tone, but your heart will go out to a small crying boy, no matter his skin colour.

'The animal population of Mashatu think of themselves as civilised and humans as barbarians, but even so, they don't hate us; they just avoid and ignore us. Harmony relies on avoiding a clash if possible, but that doesn't mean they don't have many human feelings.

'We who manage these reserves and welcome you to visit them want to preserve this part of our planet, not as a zoo to look at, but as an example of how diverse cultures can live together in harmony.

'I'll add, if one of you says the animals kill, I'll ask how many people we kill on the roads each year. If you say the animals eat what they kill, I'll say we do too, except we have a silly rule that we can't eat people, something that we used to do only a few hundred years ago. If a lion kills you because you're a threat, he knows he's obliged to eat you; otherwise, it's a waste.

'If we made a rule that if you kill a pedestrian, you must eat him, I'm sure accidents would drop.'

When the laughter died down, Sam continued. 'So Melissa will tell you what she did, and because she's lived many months in game reserves among the cultures you'll encounter here, she doesn't think there's anything magical about what she did. She received help from one of the residents in our community who feels the same about children as we do. Thanks.'

Melissa told her story, but she changed the beginning. As one in ten thousand, she knew they would not understand perfect pitch.

'I climbed onto the anthill by the camp entrance. I knew I couldn't hope to see Robbie in the bush, but we disturb things whenever we walk in the bush, and birds may fly up suddenly. Three or four birds that take off can show that a person is walking along a line drawn through them. I saw the birds, guessed where Robbie would be, and ran. When I was almost there, I saw his tracks and the hyena tracks that covered them and followed the hyenas as they went in a straight line.'

After her story, there were many congratulations, lots of handshakes, and more drinks. Robbie's parents, Tom and Gwendoline, thanked Sam and Melissa.

Tom said, 'Koos told me not to offer you a tip. I'm grateful because I would have no idea how much to offer, but I was amazed to hear you were authoring a book, Melissa. When you're ready to publish, please get in touch with me. Here's my card.'

Sam took it. The company logo was a well-known publisher. 'Tom, could you do something for Melissa?'

'Of course, ask.'

'Can she send you one chapter from her book and ask for an editor of your choice to do a copy edit, showing changes with comments? I'm not an editor and think her work is perfect, but I know there are rules she should follow, and I don't know what they are.'

'That will be a pleasure. Send it to me at the address on the card as soon as you can.'

'Sam, are you determined to make me a famous author? If so, why?'

'Yes to the first. And second, I fancy having a famous girlfriend. Besides, you deserve to be a renowned author.'

His reply left her confused about her feelings. *How do I answer that – does he think I'm his girlfriend?*

'Sam, this is the first time we've slept in the same bed.'

'Think of it as two beds much closer together.'

'Okay.'

'And tomorrow, you can tell me how you learned to speak the San language.'

...

'Sam.'

'Yes, Mel. Can't you sleep?'

'I was thinking. I'm glad you made me change my condiments to ones with no perfumes. Those elephants smelt me.'

'You mean cosmetics, Mel.'

'That's what I said.'

'No, you said condiments.'

'Maybe I had a thought of the hyenas eating me.'

'Sleep, Mel.'

It could have been Sam, not the hyenas.

During the night, while asleep, Melissa moved. Unaware of her subconscious memories that revived feelings of being in bed with her father, she was beside Sam by morning.

10

· · · · ·

SAM WOKE BEFORE MELISSA WITH THE SCENT OF HER HAIR IN his nostrils. He turned. She was lying against him, her head in his armpit, his arm stretched above her. He lay looking at her. *She's the weirdest mixture I've ever met. At first, she wouldn't sleep in the same room, but now she's in bed cuddled up to me. She can hear things I can't and can pronounce San clicks as if she was born to the language but didn't want to admit it to me. She's frightened to say things, yet she fearlessly saves Robbie from hyenas and walks into a herd of elephants.*

Sam paused his thinking, examining her face, twenty centimetres away, and remembered her smile. *Not only that, but she's beautiful and utterly unconscious of it. I want to kiss her, but Mel's a client, and I must obey the rangers' rules. Not unless she asks.*

Then Sam remembered. *She did ask me to kiss her at the Shashi confluence.* Sam leaned forward and kissed her gently on the lips.

He slipped quietly from the bed and went outside. He didn't see the smile spread on Melissa's face. On the table outside was a tray with morning coffee in a metal teapot with a spirit burner below it to keep it hot. He poured himself coffee while he listened to the bush waking up, the coo of a dove, the *Gwaaaay* caw of a lourie, and the morning chatter of guinea fowl assembling for the day's foraging, peace again in his heart.

He heard Melissa leave the bed and go to the open-air bathroom.

'Sam, are you out there?'

'Yes, Mel, coffee's on the table.'

'Can you come in here, please?'

Sam went through the room into the bathroom.

Sitting on the toilet, Melissa had her knees together and her nightie bunched up on her lap while she watched something in the shower. She turned to look at him, her eyes wide. 'There's a scorpion.'

Something is appealing about this. Sam dragged his eyes away from her to look at the shower and saw it immediately. 'It's a Kalahari burrower, not a big one; they're active at night. It must have fallen into the pan and can't escape.'

'Is it poisonous?'

'The sting can be painful; it's like a wasp. It's not lethal. Remember to check for the nocturnal nasties when you rise in the morning.'

'Can you take it outside?'

'I will. Stay there. I'll fetch a sample box from the Landy, and we can give it to Koos.'

Sam captured the scorpion while Melissa watched, quiet and still. 'Thanks, Sam; I'll come for coffee before it gets cold.' She smiled at him as he left.

Sam, for some reason feeling foolish, seized on a fact to clear his mind. *Now I know she doesn't panic when she sees bugs.*

Once outside, Melissa took gulps of her coffee, then said, 'You wanted to know where I learnt to speak some San words.'

'I thought we might talk about that at breakfast; I'm mentally trying to rearrange our schedule.'

'Pooh to the schedule. If it takes three months, it doesn't matter.

So far, I've had more fun than in years. But why?'

'Well, yesterday was unexpected, and I haven't taken you to see the mopani worms. If we do that today, we don't have enough time to go as far as I had planned, so we would have an extra night here if a tent is available. There's another area on the way, but it might mean a night camping. So either we stay here and drive two hundred kilometres tomorrow or go today, and it's a hundred kilometres, a visit to the mopani worms, a night camping, and then drive on.'

'I think we should go. If we can find your mopani worms on the way, that'll be great, but I'm sure we'll see them somewhere else, and camping with you doesn't frighten me. I'll tell you why at breakfast. I'll go and check for scorpions, then shower.'

'Okay, that was my first choice as well. We'll be a burden to the camp here, but I'll ask them to prepare a box of food for lunch and a camp dinner and breakfast to collect at the main camp. That scorpion reminded me I must show you something in the Landy. Remind me after breakfast.'

Sam showered after Melissa, and they walked to the dining area. 'Mel, ask if the internet works. If it does, you can send the mongoose chapter to Tom.'

After filling their plates at the buffet breakfast, Sam said, 'Now you can tell me.'

'Sam, I made four trips to the Serengeti over two years following the migration. The last one was in the south at Ngorongoro, where we met Chacha. By then, I had learnt a bit of Swahili. I can't speak it, but I did learn many words describing what I saw, and the more common ones, like numbers, man, woman, child and things like that.'

'Then we should try to speak it together. I might have learnt more than you because I worked there for two-and-a-half years. Go on.'

'When I heard Chacha speak, I felt Chacha wasn't his real name, so I asked him to say his name in his language, which I learnt later the Hadza people spoke. His name has two vowels and two different clicks, like you would say, "Klah-kleh". With the "K-L" as clicks, Europeans can't duplicate them without practice. I heard and repeated it almost perfectly, and he was delighted.'

'So he taught you more?'

'No. On the third day of my stay, he asked if I would like to visit his people. I said yes, and he took me in a beat-up old pickup to find his family.'

Sam thought what she said was odd. 'Why did you say "find"?'

'They're still nomads, hunter-gatherers for much of the year, so he didn't know where they were, but they leave signs for others. I read about them afterwards.'

'But that doesn't explain how you can speak a San language.'

'I can't. I can try to explain. I stayed with the family for two weeks until my clothes wore out.'

'Mel, I'm confused, but go on with the language explanation.'

'The Hadza speak Swahili as well, so it was easy. They could tell me the name of something in Swahili, then in their language, and so I learnt many words, all with clicks. The language is straightforward. There's no written language, and the future and past tenses are not tenses, just senses. I couldn't learn those.'

'Senses, Mel?'

'Yes, if you say, "I'm happy", I can tell if you are, or you said it when you're sad. It's just tone. The San use that tonal change for the future and past. I can hear the tone, but it doesn't come naturally.'

'Okay, go on.'

'So it's simple, just say "boy and goat". If a boy approaches you with a goat, you understand what we might say. "There's a boy with a goat coming towards us."'

'Fine, I understand, but what about your clothes wearing out?'

'Sam, I felt part of a family for the first time since I was nine. The men mostly ignored me, but the women accepted me as a sister the moment they heard me trying to use clicks, and when the night came, I slept with the women and children under their shelter.

'Then the days passed without me counting. I had one change of clothes and a towel in my backpack, so they wore out and were torn, and by the time I left, I was half naked.'

'Did Chacha take you back?'

'No, Sam. He left after the weekend. When I said I wanted to return, a man showed me the way to the road, and I waited until a pickup came, and the driver gave me a ride. There were no goodbyes.'

She must have thought me a fool when I asked if scorpions would frighten her. I'm sure there's much more I don't know about her.

'Did they call you Melissa?'

'No, Chacha gave me a name. It has three clicks, so you would have difficulty saying it, but like many Hadza names, it's also the name of an animal. It means Vixen.'

'A female fox?'

'Yes, because the bat-eared fox has acute hearing; they can hear an insect moving underground.'

Sam had an odd feeling, *I would be happy to be her dog fox.*

'Mel, why did you call me to remove the scorpion this morning?'

'Because there were no shower pans when I was with the Hadza. A wash was a wet cloth. If there was a scorpion, we brushed it away with a bunch of grass, or if it was edible, we gave it a quick smack. I had nothing with which to catch it, and I didn't know whether it was poisonous or edible.'

'So you ate the scorpions and insects?'

'I had to, Sam. Either that or leave. They don't carry food stocks when they travel. The Hadza collect for the next meal, stop when they have enough and eat. Sometimes raw, sometimes cooked. The women carry little bags of herbs and plants to make things tasty because insects are almost tasteless, although they feel crunchy or squishy.'

'Why didn't you say something when I told you about the horrors of travelling with me in a luxury vehicle by road.'

Melissa grinned at him, 'You seemed so keen on scaring an Englishwoman I had to let you try. You were terrific!'

Sam cringed. *You deserve that, Sam Daniels. Melissa is always ahead of you – no wonder the elephants didn't terrify her. I doubt there's much that will frighten her.*

'Did you write it all down?'

'After I left, Sam, I didn't have enough head space to remember everything, so I wrote everything in handwritten notebooks. I can record in the field. I did write it as a story when I returned to London.'

'Mel, we must start. We can talk as we go along.'

She said it was the first time she had a family. I want to know about that. I know how destructive loneliness can be.

'Before we go, Sam, what must you show me?'

Sam walked to the rear, then opened the door and the cooler box. He took from it a small carton. 'This is scorpion venom antiserum. It only works against the most poisonous scorpions, but they are common in Botswana and aggressive. Look in the cubby at the book with pictures. There's a five millilitre phial and a syringe to inject intravenously into the person stung.'

'Do you know how to do that, Sam?'

'Yes, every ranger must pass a course of first aid in the bush, and the course includes stings. Do you know how to do such an injection?'

'I've never done one, but the lifesaving and first aid course I had to do at the swimming club included it in case of an epileptic fit in the water.'

'Neither have I done one, so we're equal on that score. There are two phials. I replace one every six months, although it lasts a year. If I use one, I check the dates and use the oldest.'

Sam put the antiserum back, and they drove off.

The winding drive through the mixed acacia thorn bush, following the tracks made by the Landy the day before because the Landy tyre tread pattern differed from the Safari vehicles, took only half an hour. At the main camp, they had the first hiccup.

Gordon met them, 'Hello Sam, hello Melissa. We received your message, and we don't have what you need, but Tuli does, and they said if you drop in, they'll have it ready for you. You're welcome to come in for a drink, but if you do, you'll have many questions to answer.'

'Gordon, we'll do so the next time. We must reach Pepe to camp, and we have a stop if we can find Mopani worms.'

'That's a comfortable drive, Sam; there should be some game near the lake at Pepe.'

'Thanks, Gordon; I hope we can revisit you soon.'

As Sam drove away and Gordon waved, Melissa did too and said nothing as she pondered Sam's words, *That's new; Sam said we would revisit them soon. Am I now a fixture in his life?*

Later, as the road closed with the river, Sam stopped beside a nyala tree.

'I'll make a fire; you find the coffee, mugs and kettle.'

Twenty minutes later, they sat in their folding chairs near the fire a few metres from the dry riverbank, and Sam said quietly, 'Mel, turn slowly to your left and look at what's there.'

Melissa did and saw nothing except another nyala tree thirty metres away with a thick acacia bush surrounding it. Equally quietly, she said, 'There's nothing there, Sam.'

'Look *inside* the bush.'

She did, and the bush jumped into sharp detail as everything else faded. 'Sam. There's a massive kudu bull in there looking at us.'

'Count the twists in his horns.'

'Three, Sam – at least the horn I can see.'

'Then he's a rare one, about seven years old. Can you see the females?'

'Only as shadows, two or three of them. The bull has turned away. Will they leave?'

'Probably not.' Sam looked at the smoke rising from the fire that drifted slowly to the left and said, 'They have some green leaves to eat there, but when they leave, if we don't make too much noise, they'll walk along the riverbank in front of us.'

'How do you know, Sam?'

'They will leave when the acacia becomes bitter. Acacia raises the tannin level in its leaves when something eats them. The odour drifts downwind and warns other acacias to do the same. The kudu will walk upwind to find an un-warned bush, and the fire's smoke shows the wind direction.'

'Sam, I'm just beginning to learn how wonderful this place is. Thank you.'

Forty minutes later, after a second cup of coffee, Sam whispered, 'They're coming.'

They watched unmoving as the bull, followed closely by the three females, walked majestically along the riverbank only twenty metres away and disappeared.

'Sam! That was marvellous. That was a magnificent beast, so majestic. Why didn't they run?'

'Because we appeared harmless. The kudu knew we had sighted them, but they knew they could ignore us. Let's go.'

At Tuli, Melissa packed the food the lodge gave them into the Land Rover's fridge box and the dry food into a small tin trunk. With farewells and wishes for a good journey, Sam drove onto the road going west.

'Where are we going now?'

'Along the bank of the Limpopo to a branch road going northwest. I want to take you to the saltpans, but to reach them, we must go to Selebi Phikwe and then north to Francistown. No roads lead north along the Shashi from the Tuli Block; offroad would take days.

'Along the branch road, it's much drier, and we might find mopani and some worms.'

The road sometimes left the river and then returned. The countryside varied between the acacia veld Melissa had seen at Mashatu and the riverine nyala and fever tree forest by the Limpopo.

As Sam drove, Melissa looked out the window. 'What are we looking for, Sam?'

'A mopani tree covered in caterpillars. Unfortunately, we're beginning the dry season. The Tswana people harvest them by the millions in December; they strip the trees clean, so it's unlikely one is close to the road. If there's a tree further away that the gatherers didn't spot, we might be lucky and find a second crop. It'll be too far away for you to see the caterpillars.'

Melissa hid a smile; *I won't tell him.*

11

· · · · ·

AT THE MOTLOUTSE RIVER CROSSING, THE DRY RIVERBED FAS-cinated Melissa. 'Is there water here often, Sam? It looks like it's been dry forever.'

'There's some rain every year, but it's not dry; water is still under the sand. If we drove along the riverbed, we'd find places where the elephants have dug a hole to find water.'

Sam had an idea. 'Mel, I'll turn off here and take you to Solomon's wall.'

'What's that?'

'It was once the dam wall across the river, completely natural; it's a basalt dyke. On either side is the same flat ground. Imagine sticking a cardboard sheet into the ground, leaving just a little punching up. But the dyke has eroded until there are only thirty metres above ground and a few missing bits.'

'Okay, you can photograph us with the Landy and wall as a background.'

When they reached the wall, Sam parked the Landy and said, 'Take a look at it, Mel; I'll fetch the camera and tripod mount.'

'Okay, I want to look around.'

'Be careful. I can see some devil thorns in the vegetation; if thorns are on the ground, they can pierce a shoe. Here, come with me; I'll show you one.'

'That looks more dangerous than a hyena. Do the thorns puncture tyres?'

'Bicycles and badly worn car tyres, not the Landy tyres. They don't pierce my boots. When we reach Selebi, we must buy you a pair of boots; I should have thought of it in Gabs.'

She wandered away and disappeared between the bushes at the base of the wall. After thirty metres, looking for a place to relieve herself without occupying nasties, she spotted a rock python. 'Hello, python, you're a baby. Enjoying the sunshine?' About to leave it alone, she picked it up gently on an impulse and returned, smiling.

'Sam, I've brought lunch.'

Sam looked up and saw the one-and-a-half-metre snake and Melissa's smile.

She's lovely. 'Mel, if you insist, we'll eat it, but we have food, and you've heard my rules: don't kill what you don't need to eat. Have you eaten a snake?'

'Yes, with the Hadza, but I agree: I'll let it go where I found it, but let's take the photo together.'

Sam did, running the camera with his remote, and then she disappeared again.

'It was a friendly little python, Sam.'

'At that size, yes.'

'This is a surprising place. We can go now.'

'And you're a surprising woman. Just don't bring a lion the next time.'

Seventeen kilometres later, Sam turned north. 'We're heading into empty Africa, Mel, keep your eyes out for mopani.'

Fifteen minutes later, Sam drove off the road between some acacia and stopped atop a low rise. It gave them a better view of the countryside.

After a minute, Sam said, 'Mel, let's have our picnic, and then we'll go and look at something.'

'Have you seen something, Sam?'

'Climb out and come to this side. I'll point it out to you...

'Do you see that big acacia over there?' He pointed with his head next to hers. 'About a hundred and fifty metres, I guess.'

'Yes.'

'Well, there's a dark green bush at the bottom of it.'

'Yes, I can see it.'

'Well, I'm sure several lions are on the ground under the bush. We'll eat, then walk over and introduce ourselves.'

'Are you so fed up with me that you'll feed me to the lions?'

'Mel, I'll never be fed up with you; you're marvellous.'

First, Sam calls me a whatsit, and now he thinks I'm marvellous. I'll risk telling him.

'What's special about that bush?'

'It's not the bush; the leaves tell me there should be lions, although not the usual kind of lions.'

'The leaves with the white streaks?'

Silence followed...

'Sam?'

'Can you see the leaves?'

'Yes, I focused.'

She can look far! 'Explain, please.'

'It's what the Maasai do. One of the central Serengeti trackers told me about it when I couldn't recognise the animals at a distance. He pointed them out to me, but they were just blobs. He told me to look only where he pointed and move my head slightly. At first, all that happened was I saw more blobs, and then suddenly, I was looking down a black tunnel, and I could see what they were. I looked it up on the web later but couldn't find an explanation. I can do it if I try, but the Maasai do it without trying.'

Sam turned to her, wrapped his arms around her and said, 'Mel, you're not just marvellous; you're gorgeous and incredible.'

Melissa hugged him, 'Sam, it feels like you're hungry, but I don't want you to eat me. Let me prepare the meal.'

An hour later, sitting in camp chairs on either side of a camp table with a tablecloth under the sunshade that rolled out from the roof of the Landy, a coffee cup in her hand, Melissa said, 'You camp in style, Sam. This beats Hadza camping hands down. I know you can focus. Can you tell me how you learnt and how it works?'

'It was a Maasai tracker who told me, like you. The Serengeti is a vast open space, and I think generations of people who live in such places, like desert nomads and the Inuit in the frozen north, have never lost the habit. In contrast, those who live in closed cities and work in offices without horizons have lost it. I call it "looking far", what you call "focusing". There is a scientific explanation.'

'What's that?'

'You know what a pixel is?'

'A dot on a computer screen.'

'Okay, my camera has forty million pixels; your eyes have six hundred million. Your brain converts those pixels into a picture you see in your mind, but that's a vast amount to convert, and it takes time, so as you move your head around, it converts only a selection of them, and the brain uses guesswork to fill the picture. So the explanation for the moving head thing is that when you move a little, the pixels converted pick up various parts of what you see, and the picture fills in. I noticed long ago when I saw a bird in the sky far away, and it disappeared, I saw it again after I moved my head.'

'I've noticed the same thing, Sam.'

'The black tunnel comes if you can convince your mind to ignore everything around you. It's hard because *not ignoring* is a survival trait; we need to be aware of as big a picture as possible in case there's a predator somewhere. If you can, you use all the brain's conversion power to convert the group of pixels you concentrate on to give a detailed picture. I couldn't do that at first.'

'How did you learn?'

Sam stood up, went to the driver's door, searched the under-seat box and returned, 'I made this.'

'It's just two cardboard tubes joined together.'

'Binoculars without lenses that gave me the black tunnel. It worked, and my brain learnt what I wanted to see. Now I don't need it.'

'Smart, Sam.'

'Okay. Let's go and look at the lions. We'll need some ants.'

'Where do we find ants?'

'Right here, I dropped a bit of sugar on the ground beside my chair, and already a dozen ants are at work.' Sam took a tiny can from his pocket, bent down and scooped up the ants, then he and Melissa began walking to the bush.

'What are the white streaks, Sam?'

'That's where an insect resembling a dragonfly has laid eggs. The eggs hatch into larvae that fall to the ground and bury themselves. They need fine sand, and the fine red sand of this area is ideal. We call it Kalahari sand. It has smooth, rounded grains. Okay, here we are.'

'What are the conical pits under the bush?'

'They are the homes of the larvae called antlions. It's an ancient name. The Americans call them doodlebugs because of the way they make those conical pits. One of the larvae is at the bottom of that cone. Here, sit on the ground, and we'll play.'

They sat, and Sam said, 'Take this grass straw and push a grain of sand from the top of the cone so it rolls down to the bottom.'

'Oh, wow. The bug popped up straight away but disappeared.'

'Okay, let's try an ant. I'll open the can, and when an ant comes out and falls, you can watch what happens.'

An ant fell. Sam capped the can, and they watched, fascinated, as the ant struggled to climb out of the cone.

'It's going to escape.'

'Wait.'

The ant almost managed it, but at the last moment, an avalanche of fine sand carried it down to the bottom, where it began to struggle again.

'I can see the antlion; it's throwing sand at the ant.'

The sand thrown by the antlion started a mini avalanche and brought the ant close enough for the pincers of the antlion to grasp it, and seconds later, the ant disappeared below the sand.

'That was fantastic. What happens to the antlions?'

'They grow until they pupate below the sand and emerge after the metamorphosis as look-alike dragonflies.'

'What happens if something destroys their cone?'

'It pops out and makes another. Scrape a heap of sand together, then push it into a cone to see. Check there's a live antlion by using the grass stem first.'

Melissa did, and they spent twenty minutes watching antlions making new pits.

'They're fascinating and determined. Can we film them?'

'I have a film sequence I took months ago; I can give you a copy.'

'Okay, but take some with me sitting here surrounded by the antlion pits, so it's personal.'

'I'll fetch the camera, and then we must go.'

'We'll reach the camping spot in time to set up camp.'

'Do you have a tent, or do we sleep in the open?'

'Alone, I might do so, or at least with most of me under the Landy, but the shade we used for lunch unrolls to the ground in front and has button-on sides. We can sleep in that; I have two camp beds.'

Sam found a camping spot fifty metres from the Thune Dam, near the dam wall, with a view over the water, and unrolled the shade. 'Mel, unpack the food and gear; I'll collect some firewood and start a fire.'

Forty minutes later, Sam buttoned the sides to the shade and decided, *We make a good team. Mel knows what to do and does it. She's put the table in front of the fire outside the tent.*

Melissa heated a can of peas beside the fire and cooked a pot of instant mash. Sam grilled the pieces of chicken. She had a surprise for him, 'Sam, there's a half bottle of wine in the cooler, so I've put two wine glasses on the table.'

They sat at the table and silently ate as the sun went down to the west over the lake, listening to the night sounds building. 'Sam, thanks.'

'For what?'

'For bringing me here. This trip is nothing like the other trips I've made to lodges. I feel an unusual contentment.'

'Me too. Camping in Botswana is not new to me, but having someone with me is completely new.'

'Can you tell me about yourself, Sam? Start as far back as you remember.'

'I can, but only if you promise to tell me about yourself.'

'I'll tell you tomorrow night; this is your night.'

Sam emptied his glass, and Melissa poured some more wine. And then he began.

'I haven't told this to anyone else; it may be a bit mixed up. I was five and terrified, so I can't remember much. Most of what I know comes from the file Social Services gave me when I turned eighteen. It says that my father was a salesman and my mother a clerk, but I've never tried to find out more.

'They put me in a children's home. I can't remember where it was, but it didn't help. There were kids from everywhere. Some were violent and frightened me, and others, like me, just hid from them, but we didn't talk to each other. I can remember we had lessons about reading. I hid away and read everything I could.

'When I turned eight, they sent me to a boarding school. The kids called me Silent Sam. Two of the teachers had dogs, so I became interested in animals. I remember I read all the time, primarily textbooks, because that was all they had, so in my last year, when I turned eleven, I earned a scholarship and entered a high school for boys, a boarding school in Buckingham.

'Once there, I told a teacher I didn't want to return to the care home for the holidays. One of the teachers arranged for me to spend my holidays on a farm where I looked after the animals, and when I grew older, I spent my holidays working and living at Whipsnade Zoo.

'I didn't participate in team sports, but all the boys had to do something, so I joined the judo group and ran.

'I still read textbooks a year or more ahead of my year, so I won a scholarship to Harper Adams University in Newport, Wales, and graduated with masters' degrees in entomology and zoology.

'I had to escape the crowds. I applied for a job at a game lodge in the Serengeti and spent a year there, then six months at each of three more. There, I began to emerge from behind my shield of silence because I had to talk about the game to the visitors. I registered for a doctorate through research and applied for the job at Likesedi.'

'Thank you,' she said, smiling. 'I think there's more you can tell me ... but let's go to bed. I've put the camp beds side by side so it's easy to wake each other if there's an intruder during the night.'

Sam couldn't suppress his thought. *I liked it more when she cuddled.*

Melissa didn't go to sleep; she was reviewing their day and, after a few minutes, whispered, 'Sam?'

Half asleep, Sam mumbled, 'Yes, Mel.'

'I think you're like an antlion.'

'Why?'

'Because you hide. And you said you wanted to eat me. Then, now and again, you pop out and have a look and sometimes grab.'

Not fully awake, Sam replied, 'You have some weird ideas. I don't feel like one.'

'I doubt they do either. Do I risk you grabbing and pulling me into your lair?'

'No, that's against the rule the lodge imposes: "Don't take clients to your lair".'

'Never, Sam?'

'Only if they ask.'

Melissa thought about this for a long time, then said, 'But you did hold me and kiss me.'

'You asked.'

Melissa felt disappointed, then remembered the early morning kiss. 'But not the second time.'

'I thought you were asleep, and I wanted to.'

Melissa felt a warm glow. 'Good night, Sam.'

12

•••••

SAM WOKE TO THE SOUND OF BREAKING STICKS; THE CAMP BED beside him was empty. He rose, slipped on thong sandals, and pulled aside the front canvas wall to see Melissa, in panties and bra, wearing sandals, her hair unbrushed, preparing a fire. *She looks lovely like that.*

'Good morning, Mel. Do you need more firewood?'

'I will do, Sam. Can you fill the big three-legged pot with water? I want to warm some water for us to wash.'

Sam rolled up the canvas and returned with the pot of water, 'I'll fetch some more firewood.' Melissa looked at him when he left, naked, but for Y fronts. She smiled and called, 'Sam, you'll scare the lions.' He didn't look back, just waved, and Melissa wondered, *I've never said something like that before!*

When he returned with a load of firewood, the pot was on a crackling fire, and Melissa had removed the canvas sides of the tent, moved the table and chairs forward, and folded the camp beds. 'Let me do that, Mel.'

'No, you can pack the beds and one of the side canvas sheets into the Landy. Spread the other where we can wash so we don't have muddy feet.'

'I have a heavy plastic sheet for that; I'll fetch it.'

'Put it over there, Sam, then put the pot next to it; the water should be warm enough.'

Sam was surprised after he put the pot down. Carrying a toiletry bag with a facecloth, a bar of soap and a sponge, Melissa kicked off her sandals, stepped onto the sheet, dropped her underwear onto the sandals, dipped the cloth into the pot and began to wash. Sam couldn't move. *I thought she was shy, and now she's standing naked in the open in broad daylight.*

'Sam, stop gawking, put a chair next to the sheet so I can wash my feet, and hand me the yellow towel on the table. It's not polite to stare at a Hadza woman washing.'

Sam averted his gaze. He waited a few minutes, listening as she used the sponge to rinse, glancing to check that she was ready before he handed her the towel.

Melissa wrapped the towel around her, sat and said, 'Add a jug of water and reheat the water for yourself.'

Twenty minutes later, Sam, who felt he'd lost control of the situation, washed while Melissa dressed and combed her hair. She brought him his blue towel and said, 'Sam, if you're going to walk around in underpants in the bush, you should buy boxers.' Then she turned and began preparing eggs and bacon.

As they ate, Sam remarked, 'You're not afraid to strip; that's unusual.'

She smiled. 'Out here, there's no one to hide from except you, and I don't think I need to. I felt the same when I lived with the Hadza. They all stripped; it was the only way to wash.

'Besides, nakedness only draws attention when it's hidden. You should see my Hadza clothing; the women gave me an outfit when I left.'

'I'd love to see it.'

'You can't. They told me I can only wear it for a special man.'

'How does one become special?'

Melissa grinned at him. 'I don't know. One is just oneself, and one day, one becomes special. What's our plan for today?'

'Well, we need to buy supplies, and we can purchase them in Selebi, so the first stage is to drive there and find a place to stay. It's about a hundred and twenty kilometres, a pleasant drive. We should arrive there for lunch. I'll go shopping, and you can draft a story.'

'Which one, Sam?'

'That's up to you. Have you made a list of those you should write?'

'Yes.'

'Then look at them, decide which ones will be short, and write one of those, and then a longer one, and if it doesn't want to flow, do another short one.'

'Okay, Sam, I'll try. Let's pack up.'

Two hours later, Melissa asked for a stop. 'Sam, find a good place for a coffee; I must borrow that "axe-thing" you have mounted on the back.'

Five minutes later, he pulled off the road on the rise. 'This should do for you; that dead tree will supply firewood. Do you want me to check for anything dangerous?'

'No, Sam, I know what to look for.' She walked off holding the combination hoe-axe over her shoulder and a toilet paper roll in her other hand. Sam watched until she disappeared. *She's the first client I've ever had who would do that, and I'm not worried!*

Melissa was back in five minutes. 'I feel much better, Sam. How's the coffee?'

'One minute, the chairs are on the other side, with the valley view.'

They arrived in Selebi at 1 pm and found that Sam's first choice, the

Hotel Brickhouse, had a room. And after handing over the contents of the Landy fridge box for cold storage and a quick tour of the facilities, they went for lunch.

'Sam, a juicy steak and hot fries is all I need to melt, This is fantastic.'

'I've heard the expression that the road to a man's heart is through his stomach. I didn't know it applied to women as well.'

'It does to me, Sam; it does to me.'

'You can connect to the internet here and find a table near the pool to work. I chose this hotel because it's near enough to the town centre to walk there. I'll go when we've had a coffee. We need food. Do you need anything?'

'First, we must go to the room and arrange to wash our dirty clothes,' Mel mused. 'Buy a small packet of washing powder so I can wash clothes if necessary. Buy some rice, much better than synthetic mash, and a small pot, between one and two litres, for cooking it. Where are we going to camp?'

'I planned to look for mopani around Robelela. There's a dam close by on the border with Zimbabwe – we might be lucky there – and then drive up the border road to Francistown. So that would be a one-night camp, but I always allow an extra night.'

'What do the people do in Selebi?'

'It was a mining town: nickel and copper from 1980, but the mine closed in 2016.'

'What did they do in their leisure time?'

'Like all mining towns, I guess, play sports and party. But they have an artificial lake they stocked with fish, largemouth bass if I remember, and parties at the lake on the weekend were well known for getting wild.'

'Now the mine has closed, has it changed?'

'Yes, it's less party and more serious fishing from visitors. Many anglers come to Likesedi for tigerfishing in the Chobe River and to see the game, and several have told us about fishing at the lake here.'

'Have you fished for bass?'

'No, all the rangers have fishing licences so that we can take our clients, but I've only been twice, and that was for tiger. There are rangers with far more fishing experience than me.'

Melissa wanted more information. 'Is the lake like the one at Pepe?'

'It's much older. It has more vegetation around it. We can pass by; it's not far off our route, and it's the same river we crossed at Solomon's Wall.'

'Then I want to see it tomorrow. I don't suppose you have fishing rods and stuff.'

'Mel, rangers must be prepared for their guest's requests, no matter how crazy they might be. The long tube on the opposite side of the tent has two tiger rods inside.'

'You're a marvel; let's fetch the washing.'

After handing in their clothes at the laundry, Sam filled the Land Rover's water tank and walked to the supermarket.

After shopping, he returned to the hotel, packed everything in the Landy and went to find Melissa. She was beside the pool, wearing a bikini, with her notepad on the table. Sam stood and watched her for a few seconds, noticing her facial expressions as they changed. *The deadpan is her way of hiding*, he realised.

Melissa looked up, 'Sam!'

'Hi. Have you been swimming?'

'Only twice, when I felt hot.'

'Then I'll fetch my shorts and swim too. How's the story coming along?'

'Badly, I'm all messed up.'

'Okay, don't worry about it. We'll swim and talk about it over a beer.'

Sam learnt something new when she joined him for a few lengths of the pool.

'Mel, you're much faster than me. How did you become such a good swimmer?'

'I'll tell you later,' she laughed. 'I'll swim breaststroke so you can keep up with me.'

Fifteen minutes later, they sat on their towels, a beer and an Appletiser before them, and Sam asked. 'Now, why are you all messed up?'

'I don't know. The Mongoose story came together easily, but the monkey one won't come right. I did it the same way, but it doesn't sound right.'

'I had the same problem when I started drafting theses. But one of the lecturers told me how to develop a methodology.'

'How?'

'He said, "First, list the facts you know and want to include, in any order, like 'the leaf is a variegated green.' Then sort the facts into an order that seems right, then explain where each fact came from."'

Melissa was interested, 'And then?'

'Add a background at the beginning, like relevant facts and historical events, but only ones that help the reader understand why the research is important. Read it to check that it's grammatically correct and everything joins up smoothly. Add something if it doesn't.'

'So you follow that methodology.'

'Not completely. I list all the facts first, and then, after adding the first few events, I explain each fact. But that's me. Then, when I've finished, I add links to a bibliography. A moderator caught me once: I listed scientific papers I hadn't read.'

Melissa laughed, 'Sam, for once, you seem human. I did have a method, but you messed it up when you suggested including you as "my guide".'

'Just call me your partner in crime.' He smiled directly at her, and his eyes sparkled.

A waiter interrupted them, 'Sir, a man with boots is looking for you.'

'Please tell him I'm here.' Sam turned to Melissa. 'I asked him to bring them.'

'What are they for?'

'They have thick soles to walk on devil's thorn. I want you to choose a pair.'

Melissa smiled at him, 'You remembered.'

'I want to keep you in one piece.' He smiled back. Melissa felt an unusual buzz inside as she read his expression. *He cares about me.*

After Melissa selected a pair of boots, Sam said, 'Let's have dinner and an early night. You promised to tell me about yourself.'

As Melissa came from the bathroom, Sam said, 'I like these double beds.'

She snuggled close to him, 'Me too, but don't look at me while I talk.'

'Okay.'

'Must I tell you everything?'

'No, only what you want to tell me, but it will make it easier to understand you if you tell me as much as you can. Will it help if I put my arm around you?'

'Maybe.' Sam did.

To Sam, it seemed that Melissa was thinking about where to start, but most of the time, she was thinking about his arm and how she felt. Sam wondered, *does she need me to ask a question?*

Eventually, she began, 'My mother took me to a hearing specialist when I was four.' She told him the doctor prescribed earplugs to block out the noise. 'My hearing was super sensitive, and I heard everyday noises so loudly it hurt. I wore earplugs until I was twenty-three, but they weren't perfect. They resembled hearing aids, so people would think I was deaf and shout at me. I hid from all the noises. Until she died, my mother would speak to me in a whisper. Dad soundproofed our house and my room.

'Eventually, the sensitivity wore off, but habits die hard, Sam, especially when I had no experience with everyday life. I continued to wear them until Mrs Drew, first my nanny and then our housekeeper, made me take them out and gave me cell phone earbuds so I didn't feel naked. I intentionally left the earbuds behind when I came on this trip.'

Sam said nothing, shocked; he wanted to hold her tight but lay still.

'I was nine when my parents died in a plane crash. They were flying back to England across Egypt. When the authorities declared the plane missing, my Aunt Jane moved into our house. It was a week before we learnt the plane had crashed and all on board had died. That week, I spent hoping and praying that they would return, and as each day passed, my fear of the future grew, and I withdrew into a shell.

'Then, because my aunt was busy running a shop, she employed a nanny, Mrs Drew, to live in the house. I called her Nana, and she took my mother's place, and I saw Aunt Jane only occasionally. I usually felt alone, and it was hard for me to make any friends, boy or girl, because they believed I was deaf, so I buried myself in books. I read every minute of every day that I wasn't in a school lesson or doing homework. When I was eighteen, I went to university.'

'And the swimming?'

'Oh, I had severe acne when I was thirteen. Mrs Drew took me to a dermatologist, and he asked me what sports I played at school, and I had to say none. Then, he gave me a bunch of medicines. He said the acne would worsen unless I exercised and suggested swimming.' Melissa frowned and sighed. 'He must have understood I didn't want to do team sports.'

'I hated team sports,' declared Sam.

Mel laughed. 'I started swimming at a heated pool daily and had a trainer for lessons. I never tried to join the school swimming club; it was safer to hide behind my books. I couldn't have managed rejection. The only friends I had were my aunt's cats.'

'Where did you go to uni?'

'London University. I did two degrees in English. I didn't want a job where I would have to talk to people, so I decided to try writing.

'I was finally growing up, Sam. A librarian told me I should visit the places I wrote about, and when I saw a movie about the Serengeti migration, I decided to see it and write about it. I did see it; it took four visits over a year and a half. I've notebooks full of what I saw, but when I tried to write, what I wrote was rubbish, so I decided to try Botswana, and here I am, still trying to write.'

At that moment, Sam remembered the chapter she'd sent to Robbie's dad, so he asked, 'Mel, have you checked your email?'

'Not since we left Tuli. Why should I?'

'Check tomorrow morning. Robbie's dad owes you one.'

13

WHEN SAM AND MELISSA HAD BREAKFAST, THEY HAD NO IDEA that events in London would interrupt their idyllic journey. Mrs Drew, now retired and living with her sister in Clapham, never failed to visit Melissa's retired aunt on Sundays, when she cooked a healthy Sunday lunch and baked a sponge cake for afternoon tea.

Sam drove out of town, and once on the road to Robelela, he asked. 'Mel, did you receive an email from Tom?'

'No, I don't expect to hear from him for at least a week. He must find and brief an editor. The story will then take at least two days to edit.'

'Why that long?'

'There aren't many editors who are zoologists; the editor will probably ask someone else to check that it's technically correct.'

'Okay, do you still want to visit the bass fishing dam?'

'We should, if only for a quick visit. I'm unlikely to come here again.'

Sam felt a jolt at her words.

He sighed. 'Okay, we can see the dam from the Mmadinare bypass road.'

'Don't you want to visit it?'

'Not really; I would rather spend longer at Robelela.' He sounded oddly evasive.

'Why?' she asked, puzzled.

'It's not the fishing season. You'll see: Mmadinare has many peo-ple living near the dam. They were the mineworkers and their fami-lies and settled there because of the water, where they could con-tinue their traditional way of life with water for their goats, cattle, and growing vegetables. They've changed the countryside, and the wildlife has gone. Robelela, in contrast to this dam, is like Pepe, a lake in a pristine wilderness.'

Sam was stressed in Gaborone; now, at the thought of crowds, he's stressing again. Is he still trying to escape the crowds? 'Okay, let's do what you suggest.'

As they passed Mmadinare, avoiding goats and chickens on the road and three stops to allow wandering cattle to cross, Melissa ex-claimed, 'I can see what you meant; there must be thousands of peo-ple with little houses and plots of land.'

As they passed the dam, she said, 'It doesn't look that attractive after all, especially with all those dead trees in the water; why weren't they removed?'

'I don't know, perhaps the cost, but it could be that until they rot away, they provide breeding grounds for little fish.'

They saw no animals for the first hour, but as they drew closer to Robelela, they saw several small herds of impala beside the road. Suddenly, Sam braked sharply and parked on one side of the road.

'What's up?' she asked in surprise.

'Fetch your binoculars and come round to my side.'

'I can see a herd of impala down there in a clear patch, but they look no different from the others we've seen.'

'Watch them; tell me if you see anything different about that herd.'

Melissa watched for five minutes while Sam fetched his camera.

'What have you seen?'

'Not much. There's a big male to one side. Is he the guardian, keeping a lookout? He hasn't grazed like the others, so maybe he's worried.'

Suddenly, all the herd raised their heads, and after a pause, they returned to grazing.

'Was that because of us? Did we startle them?'

'No, we're too far away to worry them. That's alerting behaviour. There's a predator around. Watch the lookout. Is he looking around or always in the same direction?'

'Looks like one direction.'

'Then it's not lions; there would be two or three lionesses in different directions. It may be a cheetah or hyena, but the male impala doesn't know if it's something harmless, like a jackal or warthog. The male is trying to spot it. Keep watching; there will be more alerts if it's a predator.'

'How do you know that?'

'The stalker must move forward, then wait after each alert. The twitch of an ear, the waving of grass, whatever the lookout can see. Sometimes, the predator does it on purpose. Watch for the next alert. See if an impala looks up later than the others.'

Another five minutes passed, and then the herd raised their heads again. 'Mel, the one on our side, to the right, I think that one was late.'

'I noticed him too, a young male. Only a fraction later. Why does it matter?'

'The watching predator will know that the young male will be a fraction slower to start a run, giving the predator an advantage. That's why sometimes they purposely twitch an ear that the lookout can see. It'll wait until the impalas calm down and then creep forward.'

Another five minutes passed, and suddenly, a yellow streak shot from the grass straight towards the herd. Every animal appeared to turn and burst into flight. It wasn't a stampede; the impalas leapt forward with graceful bounds, touching the ground every ten metres.

Sam said with urgency in his voice, 'Watch the cheetah; she has her eyes fixed on the impala she wants, and she'll run to one side of it.'

Melissa asked, 'Why one side?'

'She knows that if the impala turns away, she can cut across the curve. Even if the impala zigzags, cutting the curve each time shortens the run.'

'It's hard to watch.' But she couldn't look away. 'She's catching up to the impala!'

'Only a few seconds more.'

The cheetah appeared to Melissa to hit the impala from the side; it fell, and seconds later, as a cloud of dust drifted away, she could see the cheetah astride the downed buck. 'What will she do now?'

'Grip the impala by the throat until it suffocates, then drag the carcass away. If the cheetah has cubs, she must haul her kill to her den before the hyenas, vultures, and jackals arrive. A lion could also come and steal it from her.'

'That's a shame after all that effort. How did the cheetah speed up without the buck seeing?'

'Cheetahs can reach a hundred kilometres an hour in three strides; it's like they have a powerful wound-up spring inside their bodies that suddenly breaks loose. It was already close to the clearing before it ran.'

'She killed a lovely young male, Sam. I wish it had been an old one.'

'That's nature for you. A weaker male has no life to lead because the females know he's weak. He would never mate, so he was redundant, and the cheetah knew it.'

Mel was momentarily silent as they watched the cheetah leaving the killing field, dragging the impala carcass. *Am I redundant, too?*

Then she said, 'That was a stroke of luck. I've seen cheetahs in the Serengeti several times but never seen them hunting.'

'That's because most clients don't have time to wait for a kill. When I saw the impala alert as we were driving, I stopped because we were alone and in no hurry, and if it happened, you would have something new to write about.'

They drove on towards the Dikgatlhong Dam. Eight massive elands stepped elegantly across the sandy track moments before they caught sight of the water.

'You were right, Sam. This is much better, wilderness Africa. Where will we camp?'

'We'll go past the dam wall. A turn-off to the left leads to two campsites. If there's someone at the first, we'll go to the second.'

'Are you feeling anti-social today? First, you wouldn't stop at the bass fishing dam; now, you want to avoid a camper.'

'I suppose so, but I don't want to share you with anyone else, especially when you wash!'

Melissa laughed, delighted. 'Then I must put on a special display for you.'

'That would be like dangling a beefsteak before a lion.'

Melissa grinned, 'Well, if I were naked, you wouldn't have to remove a nightie to eat me; where would you start?'

Sam grinned, 'I know exactly where to take a big chunk out of you.'

'Ouch, I'll have to be careful not to be too enticing.'

It must be Sam. I can't imagine talking like this with another man.

After a slow drive past the dam wall and half a kilometre up the slope after it, Sam saw a turnoff to the right, braked and turned into it.

'Sam, you said left.'

'Yes, that's further ahead, but there's mopani along here.'

He stopped under a fever tree only metres from the riverbank, overlooking the sand-filled watercourse, and said, 'That's Zimbabwe on the other side.'

'It doesn't look any different.'

'Not for many kilometres. The wildlife crosses here for food and water. Let's look for mopani worms. I'll take my camera.'

They didn't need to go far: fifty metres later, Melissa said, 'There, ahead on the right, that mopani looks different; I think there are worms on it.'

'Yes, that's them. There's quite a few, and they've about eaten everything.'

Melissa picked one off a leaf and let it walk on her hand, 'They are beautiful, the colours are gorgeous, and they are the most enormous caterpillars I've ever seen. Why don't they turn into beautiful butterflies?'

'No one knows. I think it's because they've evolved in these arid conditions. There's little moisture, and instead of making the chrysalis on the tree with no protection, they learned to do so underground. The moth hatches at night, so bright colours are a handicap. Unlike most moths, they don't eat and live only for a week or two. Shall we collect some worms?'

'Sam, we aren't hungry. Let's leave them to become moths and make more beautiful caterpillars. Now that I've seen them, I'd like to return when the moths hatch. It must be lovely to see them.'

'Thanks, that's how I feel too.' *Now she wants to return. That makes me feel better.*

'But take some photos of the caterpillars and me, so I've something to remember them by.'

As they reached the Landy, Melissa said, 'Let's sit on the riverbank. This place is so quiet it soothes the soul. We'll watch and listen for a while.'

They sat, legs hanging over the sandy edge, Sam gazing straight at Zimbabwe. Melissa beside him sat sideways, looking downriver.

'Are you comfortable like that?' he asked. 'You can lean back against me.'

She leaned slightly backwards against Sam and put her head on his shoulder. 'Is that alright?'

'Mmhmm.'

They sat silently for a while, and then Melissa said, 'I'm sure I can hear three different cricket sounds.'

'There may be more; the species in an area depend on the vegetation. What can you hear?'

'There's a high-pitched whistling, the same note, but because many link up, there's a varying volume, like a background wave. Then there's another short sound, a scritch-scritch-scritch. The last is more distinctive, like one of those whistles with a little ball with water in it.'

'That's fantastic. When we arrive at Likesedi, I'll play the individual sounds I've recorded for you to name.'

Sam caught movement to his left and glanced that way. 'Mel, turn slowly to look upriver, on the other side.'

She did and whispered, 'Those are elands; they've seen us.'

Sam, conscious that Melissa was now half on his lap with her head against his chest, still had an arm around her as he whispered a reply. 'A bachelor herd, with some massive old ones, weighing near a ton. It's the heaviest antelope in Southern Africa. They want to cross the river, so they must check us out for danger while they are in the open.'

Two minutes later, the first of the bulls jumped down the low riverbank, followed rapidly by the others. Sam said urgently, 'Look at the last one.'

'It's limping; it's injured its front left leg.'

'Life is over unless it gets better in a day or two.'

'Why so short?'

'For two reasons. Firstly, predators like big cats have an uncanny ability to recognise injured animals. Some can identify the tracks of an injured animal by the spacing of its prints, or they watch the herd.

'Second, nature is logical. When an animal can't keep up with the others, it gives up the struggle to live within days. There are no nursing homes in nature. By sacrificing themselves to a predator, the dying supply food and help prevent the death of other younger members of their species.'

'Is that an indictment of humanity, Sam?'

'No, although in many cases there's a parallel: when an aged human parent becomes a burden and is of no further use, the children or state often shunt them into a living death in a nursing home. Nature's way is more humane.'

'People used to look after their elderly at home, though. Only the poor ones without families went into almshouses.'

'Oh, that's where "alms for the poor" comes from. Part of me is glad I don't have old people to worry about.'

'My aunt is elderly. Anyway, Sam, let's make camp and lunch at the dam. Can we stay all day tomorrow? This quiet atmosphere is what I need to sort out the monkey story, and I must start Robbie's story.'

'Okay, Mel.'

14

·····

SAM TOLD MELISSA, 'WE'RE GOING TO MY PREFERRED CAMPSITE; as the water level is down a bit, there'll be a clear beach between the bush line and the water. It faces south, so we'll have the sunset from the west and sunrise from the east, and the bush will be behind us.'

'Sounds great. I'll help set up camp, take my notebook out of its bag, and edit the monkey story. Sam, why are you so different from other rangers?'

'I don't think I am, Mel. I might know a little more than they do from a scientific viewpoint, but I'm not different.'

'Well, I feel you are. I've met rangers at the lodges in the Serengeti, and you seem quite different.'

'You're saying what you feel; it may not be what others feel.'

'Then why do I feel you're different.'

She's a terrier when she gets stuck into something and won't let go.

'Mel, could it be something simple: just that I like you?'

'Do you?'

'Mel, I've already said I think you're fantastic and adore you. I've never had a girlfriend, been in love, and never said as much about myself as I have told you. I don't know why or have the words to describe how I feel. In a way, you frighten me.'

'I frighten you?'

'Not you directly. I think I'm frightened to come out from behind the barrier that has kept me safe from everyone since I was small, and you're dragging me out.'

'But I'm not trying to, Sam.'

'Mel, I've never worried about what others think of me. I've never tried to make people like me. Since I held you in my arms at the airport, I've wanted you to like me, and I've wanted to make you happy. I don't know why, except that it must be you. Since we met, I've been fascinated and interested in you. Am I the first ranger who has tried to make you happy, and that's why you think I'm different?'

'Not just the first ranger, Sam. You're the first man to make me happy, and you've succeeded. Thank you.' *And does he love me but doesn't know it? Just like I don't.*

Sam slowed as the Landy rolled onto a deserted beach, then turned and parked with one side against the top of the beach beside the bush.

Melissa looked around. 'Your campsite is perfect. Do animals come here to drink?'

'They did the last time. I'll take a short walk and look for tracks.'

While Sam walked to the water's edge and along it, Melissa began unrolling the roof shade. When he returned, he said, 'Some eland, two kudu tracks, and dozens of impala, plus lion signs only three days old.'

'Can we stay here?'

'Of course. We know we must keep an eye out for the lion, but he may be miles away by now, and I think with the abundance of prey, he'll be well fed. Most lions are no danger to humans unless they are surprised. I'll collect a big bundle of firewood. Acacia burns slowly, and we can keep the coals hot all night.'

'So why do they have the label of man-eaters?'

'Only the old males rejected from the pride, who can't hunt alone, although they prefer goats or cows.'

'Okay. I'll set up the beds. You do the fire and make us lunch.'

An hour later, with coffee in her hand, Melissa said, 'Sam, your steak was better than the Selebi Hotel, and the onion and tomato sauce delicious. I'll award you three Michelin stars.'

'Don't tell anyone. If you do, there'll be so many diners you won't have anything to eat.'

'It's our secret, Sam. Now, I'm going to write.'

'And I'll collect a load or two more of firewood. If we stay tomorrow, we'll need it.'

'Okay. I want a shower in the morning, and we have a whole lake of water.'

'Then I'll set up the shower and fill it with water.'

'Sam, I've finished the monkey. I think it's even better than the mongoose. The monkey has character.'

'Read it to me.'

'No hurry. It's almost sunset time. Move the chairs. I'll fetch drinks.'

Melissa sat listening to the growing whistle of the night while the last blush of red faded over the flat western horizon. She felt she was in heaven. Sam didn't say anything. He was happily looking at the stars. Even after years, they still filled him with wonder.

'Sam, the stars are marvellous tonight.'

'I'll take you to Namibia, to the Namib desert. The air is so clear you can see twice as many, and the wildlife is different. While the kudu, I feel, is majestic, the oryx is beautiful.'

'That would be exciting. I'll hold you to that promise, but I'm hungry. I'll make dinner.'

They ate slowly, without speaking, smiling at each other until their plates were clean.

'That was great. I'll wash up. But first, I must call Peter to tell him where we are.'

Sam fetched his satphone from the dash holder and called, 'Hello, Peter.'

Melissa could hear Peter's voice.

'Hi, Sam, you're the only person who rings me from a satphone.'

'We're beside the lake at Robelela, Peter. We'll stay here tomorrow; Melissa wants to write. We'll stop at Francistown for stores and then Orapa for the night on Tuesday.'

'Okay, Sam. How's it going? I'm glad you haven't chopped your client into pieces and fed her to the lions.'

'Peter, you may learn: I'm the one that may not return. So far, she has made friends with a herd of elephants, wears snakes draped around her neck, and discusses when to eat us with leopards.'

Melissa heard Peter laughing and said severely. 'Sam, let me speak to Peter.'

'She wants to speak to you, Peter.'

'Hello, Peter.'

'Hi, Melissa. I feel Sam likes you. What do you think of him as a guide?'

'He's okay, Peter. He does know his stuff but limits his cuisine to barbecued beef, and he's rude. I can't stop him from peeking when I undress to shower.' Melissa could hear him laughing, so she grinned in response. 'Don't worry about him, Peter. If I don't keep him, I'll give him back to you in one piece after I've sorted out his problems.'

Still chuckling, Peter said, 'Thanks, Melissa, have a great trip. Good night.'

'Good night, Peter.'

As Melissa handed the phone to Sam, he said, 'I'm not rude. I'm human, and I know you like me watching.'

'How do you know that?'

'You wouldn't have offered to put on a special display for me.' *And I hope Melissa keeps me!*

Melissa smiled, 'Thanks for reminding me. You can do the washing up.' Then, as she reviewed her conversation with Peter, she added wonderingly, 'That's the first adult conversation I've ever had with a man other than you.'

'Adult means what?'

'Sort of personal, not distant.'

Sam sensed she was thinking and remained silent until he heard her sigh, then asked. 'Are you going to read me the monkey story?'

'Not tonight, maybe tomorrow.'

'Are you reluctant to read it to me?'

Melissa had to think about his question, and Sam watched the expressions on her face.

'Yes, but not because it's you. After writing the mongoose story, I'm hesitant to learn that I've gone backwards.'

'Mel, can you believe I was the same? Halfway through my first thesis, I had severe doubts about the rest.'

'What did you do, Sam?'

'The professor explained something to me. He said that when people write, they often don't write everything because they know it so well it seems trivial and unnecessary. After a while, the writer wonders if they have explained everything correctly. He told me to ask other students to read my thesis and tell me only what they couldn't understand. Not to tell me what was wrong with it. I'm only your first step. After me, you must ask others to read your work and tell you the same thing. If you know that people will understand your story, the rest is your art. Authors must learn that readers have a different view from theirs when they read it.'

'Okay, Sam. I'll read it to you tomorrow. Let's clear up and go to bed.'

15

. . . . .

SAM WAS AWAKE AT 4:30 AM. HE STOKED THE FIRE, ADDED some wood, set the kettle to boil, switched on a portable light and laid out the coffee and mugs. Melissa joined him two minutes later, clutching a tissue. 'Sam, I need to pee. Is the lion around?'

'Take the light and go to the front bumper of the Landy. This is peak moving time for the game, so don't leave the Landy. Something dangerous might mistake you for a tasty breakfast.'

Sam switched the kettle for the big pot of water, added wood, poured the coffee through a filter and had two mugs ready when she returned minutes later and sat beside him. After they had both taken several sips of coffee, and the first pink blush of dawn rose from the horizon, Melissa said. 'This is heaven, Sam. I don't know if it's the country, you, or both, but in one week you've changed me in ways you can't understand. Now I must learn if it's limited to when I'm here with you, and I'll revert to what I was like if I leave.'

Sam said nothing but was pleased she said if and not when.

Sam stood as the sun signalled its presence with a pinpoint arc of blinding light. 'I'll carry the hot water to the rear of the Landy. Fetch your toiletry bag and join me. I'll show you how to work the shower.'

Melissa joined him as he placed the cauldron beside the open rear door of the Landy. 'Mel, this little valve controls the hot and cold water mix. Keep it warm, but use as little hot as possible, for there's not as much hot water as cold. The spray unit has a button; press it for water.'

Sam pushed down his Y fronts, pulled them from his feet, kicked off his thong sandals and stepped onto the plastic sheet. 'I'll set a starting temperature.' He started with cold, raised the temperature until he felt it warm, then turned, saying, 'Here, shower.'

He said nothing more because Melissa, already naked, kicked off her thongs and stepped onto the sheet. 'I'll call for my towel when I'm clean.'

Sam fetched the towel, then stood, the towel hanging over his arm, watching her. She grinned at him, 'See, I told Peter the truth.'

'I'm an art lover. You're a far more spectacular sight than the dawn.'

'Right, pass me the towel. Your turn.'

Melissa dried herself, put on fresh underwear, and brought Sam's towel. She watched. Sam grinned but didn't speak; he would save that for later. Melissa thought, *He would make a magnificent thunder god, Thor, in a movie.*

Melissa made eggs and bacon while Sam, whistling, toasted some bread. They ate, exchanging smiles, and Sam thought, *we are talking, but with smiles. I've never done that before. Is this love?* Melissa sensed Sam was happy, and she felt euphoric.

Then the satphone – in its dashboard holder – rang.

Sam stood and reached in to take it, glanced at the number, and then turned to look outside while he answered. A survival habit – don't let anything distract you from watching for danger.

'Yes, Peter?' Melissa stood up, picked up the plates and went to wash them behind the Landy so she didn't hear what came next.

'Sam, I've had a call from London from a police inspector. Melissa's aunt is ill, and he's trying to find her. He wouldn't say anything else but asked me to persuade her to call. Can you ask her? I'll send the name and number.'

With a tight feeling in his gut, Sam gave a brief response. 'Okay, Peter.'

Melissa returned with the clean plates and mugs, saw his face, and asked. 'What's wrong, Sam?'

'Mel, fetch your book and a pen. I need you to write down some numbers.'

Melissa stopped smiling, fetched them, and sat down.

'Write down my satphone number. It's – 870455382946.'

'Now write down Peter's number – plus 267764573639.'

'And my portable number – plus 267763484724.'

The satphone pinged. Sam looked at it.

'Now this number, the name and number on the screen.'

As she finished, Melissa asked. 'Who's Jared Williams?'

As he replied, she felt the blood drain from her face and her shoulders hunched.

'I don't know, only that he's a police inspector trying to find you because your aunt is seriously ill. Peter asked if you could please phone him.

'Shall I dial for you?'

'Please, I'm shaking.'

Sam sat beside her, took the phone, punched in the number, and handed it to her when it rang.

'Inspector Williams, good morning.'

'Good morning, this is Melissa Grouwer.'

'Miss Grouwer, I'm so glad you called. Do you know a woman named Mrs Drew?'

'Yes, she was my nurse for many years and still visits my aunt every Sunday for lunch and tea.'

'Well, yesterday, she did but could not access the house. She called the police, who had to break down the kitchen door. Emergency services found your aunt unconscious and took her to Guys Hospital. I'm in charge of the case. We found no signs of forced entry. The emergency physician said she shows no sign of abuse, so we have classed it as a sudden illness. We'll secure the back door before removing the police officer from guard duty.

'Have you followed that, Miss Grouwer, or shall I repeat it?'

Sam saw Melissa beginning to shake and reached over and put his arm around her.

'I've understood, inspector.'

'Can you write down the hospital number to call for medical information? Use my name to prove your identity.'

'Five seconds, inspector. Please give the number to my colleague. I'm shaking too much to write.'

Sam took the phone, pen and book. 'Sam Daniels here. Go ahead, inspector.'

He wrote down the number, repeated it, and then asked, 'Inspector, you mentioned Mrs Drew. Do you have her number? We're in the heart of Africa with only a satphone for communications.'

He wrote that down and said, 'Thank you, inspector. Melissa will call the hospital immediately.'

Sam looked up to recheck the surroundings, then hesitated and checked his pistol was accessible in its holster. 'Mel, take the phone and climb in the Landy, please. Move over to the far side.' His calm, firm tone steadied her, and she followed his instructions. Sam kept watching. A smell had warned him, and he saw some buzzing flies. A lion stepped onto the track to the Landy about fifty metres away. It padded forward a few metres, then lay down on the shady side to watch them. *At least it's not hungry. The lionesses must be out hunting.*

'Okay, Mel, return to my side.'

'What was that about, Sam?'

'We have a visitor, just up the road.'

The sight of the lion overrode the worry building in her mind. 'Oh, what do we do?'

'Nothing. He has as much right to be there as we have. Dial the hospital number and find out what you can.'

It was the ward sister who answered, and after establishing who was calling, she said, 'Your aunt is stable, Miss Grouwer; I can't tell you more. I'll transfer your call to Doctor Reddy, her physician.'

Melissa looked up at the lion while the phone buzzed and beeped. The lion stood, and Melissa, angry at an attack by two things at once, yelled at it, 'Shoo, go away, you mangy beast, I'm busy.'

The phone crackled, and she heard a voice that asked, 'Who's the mangy beast? Me or someone else?'

'Sorry, doctor, not you: the lion.'

'Miss Grouwer, *where* are you?'

'In Africa, doctor, and he's about forty metres away.'

'Good God! Can you talk, or must you escape?'

Melissa saw the lion moving away. 'It's okay, doctor. He seems to have heard me and is leaving.'

The doctor forgot the lion; it would be something to tell his colleagues about at tea.

'Miss Grouwer, your aunt is unconscious but stable. We have given her the medical treatment necessary to ensure continued stability. I've spoken to Doctor Niewoudt, a neurologist, who has ordered MRI scans and an encephalography. It will be two or three days before we know the cause and longer before any prognosis is possible.'

'But what happened to her?'

'A stroke or an embolism that reduced blood flow to the brain. That's what we need time to discover. I can tell you that your aunt will be incapable of looking after herself for several months, if not forever, and needs someone to arrange her ongoing care. The police have told me you're the only person they have found who can do so.'

'Thank you, doctor. I'll call to find out how she's doing as soon as possible. In the meantime, if my old nurse, Mrs Gladys Drew, wants to see her, can you authorise access?'

'Certainly, Miss Grouwer,' Doctor Reddy had a sense of humour, 'and give my regards to the lion. Goodbye.'

'Sam, did it go?'

'Of course. You told it to.'

'Then, for God's sake, make me a coffee.'

'Sam, I must go. I don't want to, but I must.'

'I know, Mel. I'll arrange everything. Will you return?'

'I'll try my best to return, but I don't know what will happen. It might be a month or three months. I'll call you once I know.'

'Call me even if you don't know. Hearing your voice will cheer me up. Remember, I'm waiting to hear the monkey story and the rest. Now let me call Peter.'

An hour later, Peter had a seat on the Ethiopian Airlines flight leaving at 14:00 the following day, and JJ de Vos, Sam's friend, owner, and manager of the Ranzi Eland Guest House, a few kilometres before Palapye, had promised a room and a taxi into Gaborone in the morning. All Sam had to do was drive to Ranzi by dark that night.

'Why by dark, Sam?'

'Driving at twenty kilometres an hour in a park at night is okay, but you can kill yourself at eighty when something massive steps into the road ahead. I sleep, then drive at dawn.'

They quickly packed up and began the drive. Sam slowed fifty metres before reaching the road north to Francistown, 'Mel, look over on my side, twenty metres away.'

Beside an eland they had killed, a male lion and two females were gorging themselves.

'Is that our lion?'

'It must be. Lions from different prides don't share a territory. Look at the eland's horns; it was a big one. We can assume it's the injured one we saw yesterday.'

'Wouldn't it have run?'

'Of course, away from the others. Sacrificing itself so they could live.'

They refuelled in Francistown, had a quick meal, and arrived at the Ranzi Guest House at 7 pm.

'Melissa, this is JJ de Vos, one of the few men I can call my friend. JJ, this is Melissa, my favourite girlfriend and author.'

They shook hands. JJ noted the lack of makeup, the week's suntan already turning brown, and the attractive smile and decided Sam had excellent taste. 'Sam, you're in cottage three. Come for dinner when you've sorted yourselves. Service has just started, so please be quick.'

'What time is the taxi coming?'

'It's not. You take my pickup. You said you'd be back by 3 pm, so that's the safest. It's full of gas. You can leave anything you wish in the Landy tomorrow, lock it, put the alarm on, and leave it in front of my house. I'll fill it up while you go to Gabs. I've ordered breakfast at 6 am and coffee in your room at 5 am.'

'Thanks, JJ. Mel, let's go.'

It took only a few minutes to extract Melissa's bag, shoes, computer and file, then Sam said, 'Mel, you've taken everything from the Landy. You can pack your case after dinner. Let's go. We mustn't keep Martha waiting.'

'Martha?'

'JJ's wife. She runs the place.'

Over dinner, another Botswana steak and some ice cream for dessert, Melissa learnt that JJ was short for Johannes Jacobus. She learnt of the tie between him and Sam after dinner.

'JJ has a son who went to Johannesburg to college, went off the rails and became mixed up with the wrong people. JJ learnt about it, drove to Joburg, knocked a couple of his son's pals unconscious, broke the arm of one who drew a knife, then bundled his son into his pickup and drove him back here. He asked me to teach him to be a ranger. It wasn't easy, but he's become a good ranger. JJ never offered to pay me, and I never asked. Good friends don't; they help, and JJ finds a solution when I need things made for my Landy.'

'You're more than a nice guy; you're generous. That's rare.'

'Mel, I know you're going because you must. Have you anything else to tell me about our week together?'

'Sam, you must be tired and have more driving to do tomorrow. Let's go to our room. I need to pack my case ready for the morning. Let's finish that and go to bed. I'll tell you then.'

'Sam. I won't take my new boots. Can you keep them for when I return?'

'Of course. They'll have a place of honour on my lounge table.'

He put Melissa's boots in the box under the Landy seat. He would never remove them; he couldn't. Doing so would mean he didn't believe she would ride in his Landy again.

After preparing for their departure and taking a shower, for fast driving had thrown up clouds of choking dust on the dirt road, they settled into bed, and Melissa snuggled. 'Sam, there's not much to say. The woman I was a week ago has changed, and I hope I won't change back. With your help, I'm learning who I am, that I can be proud of what I've achieved, and that I can do more. But I must be honest: it's due to you. I don't know what love is, Sam; I've never loved or had the chance to do so, so I've nothing to compare how I feel with any other experience. If I had the choice, I would stay with you until you told me to leave and, hopefully, I would learn that my feelings are love. So I'll say, hold on, I'm going to return, and we can restart our journey together right here in this bed. If, for any reason, I think it's impossible, I'll tell you and regret it for the rest of my life.'

'Mel, thanks for saying that. You've changed me, too. I'm no longer as silent as I was. I feel the same. I'll never let you go after you return.'

'Kiss me, Sam. Then we'll sleep.'

They reached the airport in time for Melissa to check in. Then Sam said, 'When you reach London, buy a smartphone, install WhatsApp and send a message to my number. We may only be able to talk when I'm in the lodge or my cottage, but it's better than nothing. Otherwise, call my satphone.'

After an extended kissing session, Sam watched as she went through passport control and then disappeared to the departure gate. There was no point in waiting as he could not see her board, so he left to see Peter.

There was a duty-free electronics shop in the departure lounge, so Melissa stopped thinking of Sam and bought a phone. She closed the deal moments before boarding, for she wanted to know all about the different phones they had on offer. Another passenger, a woman she judged was about sixty, convinced her. 'Miss, you don't need a big screen. You need a small phone to carry in your bag. Big ones grow heavier as the day passes. Look at mine: it's simple to use and has lots of memory.'

16

·····

'HI, SILENT. NO PROBLEMS?'

'No, Peter, Melissa's in the departure lounge. I won't stay long. JJ has a late lunch for me, and then I'll drive on. Do I still have a job at Likesedi?'

'They keep asking for you, Silent, but I've sad news. Carl is leaving on Thursday for Johannesburg. He has a medical problem and is going for tests.'

'Any idea what it is?'

'No, neither does he, but he has lost weight.'

'Yes, we all noticed. I assumed Carl was working too hard. Who will be the manager?'

'As you were in the sticks with Melissa, the directors asked me to step in. I've agreed to three months max, so I'll fly up on Monday, the late flight. You can hold the fort for three days. As we didn't expect Melissa to leave suddenly, we won't have an exclusive for you for a week, so you'll be doing the usual duties. I've told the directors that you're my choice for the manager if Carl doesn't return.'

'Thanks, Peter.'

'Where are you sleeping tonight?'

'I'll fill up in Francistown and try to make Lion Sands before dark; otherwise, a place in Nata. I can camp anywhere if necessary.'

'Shall I give Lion Sands a ring? Coenraad should be there, and he owes me a favour.'

'Yes, never thought of it. If Coenraad has no room, call JJ; he can tell me.'

Peter felt Sam was depressed at Melissa's departure. 'When I called yesterday, I felt you and Melissa were closer than I've ever known you with a client. Are you sorry she's gone?'

'Peter, she's the most amazing woman I've ever met. I would never let her go if I had more to offer than a ranger's life.'

'Silent, never let that hold you back. I had the same problem, and Sally proposed to me. I told her what you've just said, and she replied that there was nothing more valuable than a ranger's life. I guess Sally believed she could do something with me, and she did.'

'Thanks, Peter, but I'm not sure Melissa will return. She has a book to write. I must start moving.'

'See you next week, Silent.'

'Looking forward to it, Peter. Bye.'

Sam left, and as he drove out of Gaborone, he saw to his left the Ethiopian Boeing climbing out on its way to Addis Ababa and London. Knowing Melissa was in it was painful.

He ate lunch with JJ two hours later, then drove to Francistown. The straight road, which was in good condition, had light traffic, primarily trucks going to or coming from Zimbabwe and Zambia. He kept a steady speed with only an occasional need to slow down before passing a heavily loaded truck. He drove automatically, his mind reviewing every detail of his week with Melissa. He revived his memory of her expressions, her eyes when she laughed, and his feelings when he saw her with her head down, her looking-at-her-lap posture, sitting on the toilet in her nightie, washing and showering naked when they camped. And he remembered Melissa yesterday saying, 'Shoo, go away, you mangy beast, I'm busy.'

To Sam, that image, more than anything else, meant she belonged with him.

After the plane took off and the usual hustle and bustle of serving drinks and lunch to the passengers, Melissa plugged her computer into her seat's charging socket and began to write.

One paragraph later, she stopped, erased it, and started again. This time, the first word she typed was 'I'. She stopped again, backspaced and added a line above. 'Dearest Sam.'

The two words opened a floodgate. Melissa didn't write for her book: she typed the words for herself and Sam. She knew she couldn't have done it a week earlier. Melissa had kept her thoughts and feelings to herself for eighteen years, but now they poured out, only for Sam.

She wrote a love letter, like pages in her diary.

She began by describing how she remembered herself before she met Sam and held nothing back. She didn't explain where she'd been or what she'd done, except as a skeleton background. It was all feelings and thoughts.

She described how every time she'd flown to Africa, the flight away from her home and room had terrified her because getting back to where she'd felt safe for years had become a long and frightening journey. She described her fears on arrival, how she'd struggled to control her terror and trembling every time, including her terror as she passed through the arrivals exit at Gaborone, and why the café was irresistible.

Melissa recounted how after Sam had called her a bloody woman, she'd felt utterly lost and had followed him because she had no fear of his attack. Then their words until Sam had taken her in his arms, and she'd fought her terror and almost fainted.

> It was then, Sam, that for the first time in eighteen years, I felt the comfort of a hug and remembered my father hugging me, and suddenly, in your arms, hearing your heartbeat, I was no longer afraid.

She wrote on, pouring all her thoughts and feelings into the computer's databanks, reinforcing her memories and building a reference she could read again. She hadn't considered sending it to Sam; it was for her.

Five hours later, the cabin attendant who had observed her each time she passed Melissa's seat came to her, 'Miss, you've been typing non-stop. You must stop now as we're landing. You can continue in the business class lounge before your next flight.'

'I'm sorry, I don't realise how time flies when writing.'

'That's okay, Miss Grouwer. I do the same when I read a good book.'

In the business class lounge at Addis Ababa, Melissa continued to type for three hours, remembering the meals she'd eaten with Sam, how the food felt while eating when hungry, not the tasteless plastic airline and restaurant food with a planned blandness to suit thousands.

She described her meals with Sam in the tiniest detail.

Sam filled up in Francistown, topped up his water tank in case he needed to camp, took a fresh bottle of water from the cooler, and drove north. He had two hundred and twenty kilometres to Lion Sands. It was 5 pm. Two hours later, he passed through Nata, and fifty kilometres remained to Lion Sands. He decided to continue although the light was fading rapidly. He picked a truck with bright taillights and followed at a safe distance. Although slower, it was far safer than risking a collision with something unseen. At 8 pm, he drove into Lion Sands, where Coenraad came out and met him.

'*Goeienaand*, Silent. Glad you could make it. Peter said you might reach here, and I have a room for you. Park in front, number four, and come for dinner.'

Dinner was again a grilled steak, but not beef. 'Coenraad, are you shooting game?'

'Only when it's necessary. We have an excess of impala. Although I try to stop the villagers from hunting when they need meat, they prefer shooting something to slaughtering cattle. I shoot only the mature males who would be predators' prey and give the carcasses to the villagers. Many lions have moved across the river to Hwange in Zimbabwe because they don't like the shooting. I know the range of those here and hunt far away from them. I'm trying to teach the villagers to do the same, but they don't go far from their villages without transport.'

'How's Annelie?'

'Fine, Silent. She wants to meet you; she'll join us any minute now. Peter told me you have spent a week guiding a tourist.'

'I have, Coenraad. Quite a woman. Unfortunately, she flew back to London. Her aunt is ill, so she cut the trip short.'

Annelie, an attractive brunette with reddish streaks in her hair and green eyes, joined them. Sam didn't miss the discreet bulge of her tummy. He wondered if she was expecting a child.

'Annelie, this is Sam. Sam, Annelie.'

'Coenraad, if I had seen him before you, you wouldn't have had a chance.'

Coenraad laughed, 'Silent, I had to marry her to stop her running off with every ranger that passed through, so don't feel flattered.'

Annelie grinned, 'That's the problem here. For us girls, the men are big, bronzed and handsome. It gives a woman trembling thighs.'

Sam laughed. He decided to ask something that had nagged in his mind during the drive.

'Annelie, will you have children?'

'Yes, Sam. At least two, and I haven't been overeating; the first is due in seven months. It's all Coenraad's fault.'

Sam suppressed a chuckle and tried to put on a concerned face, 'Why, what did he do?'

'He can't keep his hands off me.'

Coenraad decided to defend himself, 'At least half is Annelie's fault, waving her rear end around where I can't avoid it.'

Annelie's answer struck home: 'That's natural; it's what women do when they like a man; if it were only his hands, it would be okay...'

Coenraad had tears in his eyes when he stopped laughing. 'Annelie, you'll give us a bad reputation.'

Sam decided to be serious and asked, 'How did you meet Coenraad, and do you like it here?'

'I met him at a *tiekiedraai*, you know, a traditional Afrikaans dance. He was visiting a farmer outside Joburg, and I was visiting a girlfriend, and we both went to the same function. He was impossible to miss, so I asked who he was and managed to find someone to introduce him to me. He was interesting, and when the evening ended, he invited me to visit him at the lodge in Botswana where he worked.

'I was working in Joburg in advertising and came when I had a long weekend. Before the weekend ended, I knew I wanted to live in Botswana at a lodge, so I packed up in Joburg, and a week later, I was back for good.'

'So it was love at first sight?'

'Love for the place and the life, Sam. Love for Coenraad came later. Peter said he believed you were falling in love with your last client. What is she like?'

Sam described Melissa, and Annelie watched his face. When he stopped, she said, 'Marry her, Sam. You love her.'

'She's on a plane to England, and I don't know when she'll return, if ever.'

'If she loves you, she'll find a way.'

'Annelie, she's English. Although she did live with the San in Tanzania for two weeks, how can I expect her to like the life we lead here?'

'Sam, I came because this place is real. Coenraad is real. He talks only about what matters here, not what others think or do. I love this place and wouldn't exchange it for anything. My life in Joburg was shallow: window dressing all the time with an occasional thrill from a successful advert. The rest was just a hard, tedious daily grind that everyone tried to hide behind falsetto voices and unnecessary talk.'

'What about your children? Will that change anything?'

'No, Sam. Two women here have birthed a hundred babies, and they will birth my child. I'm learning everything I can about treating injuries and ailments, and I have a massive chest of medicines. I'm practising with the local kids already. They all call me Mama. My child will play with the kids here, come to Mama for a sticky plaster like all the others, and hopefully grow up like Coenraad.

'Marry your Melissa, Sam. You and the country will make her happy.'

'Coenraad, I'm sorry you saw Annelie first. You wouldn't have had a chance!'

Annelie laughed, 'Thanks, Sam.'

Just before his 5 am departure the next morning Sam visited the kitchen with a packet of his coffee and sat on the open patio watching the sunrise and remembering Melissa beside him.

Melissa was asleep on the flight from Addis to London. Her sleep was unusually profound for an aeroplane. She woke when the lights came on for breakfast. As she left the customs exit, she remembered she had to buy a SIM card. At the Telecom shop, a boy, whom Melissa didn't think of as a man because he had pimples on his face, asked her to sign a contract after photocopying her passport. He inserted a SIM card and loaded WhatsApp when she asked for it.

'Miss, you can read instructions on the web. Let me show you how to connect to Wi-Fi and use the browser. You must call a Telecom shop with proof of address, like an electricity bill, or the network will terminate your connection in a month. Your number is on the contract.'

17

SAM REACHED KASANE BEFORE 8 AM, REFUELLED, AND stopped in front of his cottage at Likesedi at 9.15 am. Carl walked over to Sam's cottage when he heard the Landy. Carl's deterioration and haunted look shocked Sam.

'Hello Sam. Did everything go well?'

'Yes, a few hiccups, but nothing serious. Peter said you're off to Joburg on Friday. Can I offer to drive you to Kasane?'

'Thanks for offering. Benjy is driving me, then going shopping; you should stay here.'

'Okay, let me empty the Landy, eat some breakfast, and I'll come and see you in your office.'

'Breakfast is still open. The last visitors returned from their game drive a few minutes ago. Empty the Landy after breakfast.'

'Okay.'

After greeting the rangers at breakfast, Sam ate a full breakfast, returned to his lodging for his coffee, and emptied the Landy. Thoughts of Melissa slid into the background as he followed the routine he'd learnt. First, look after your equipment; your life depends on it. He took his Landy to the workshop for a full service and cleaning, then he serviced his pistol and rifle. Finally, he cleaned all his cameras, sound recording equipment, and lighting gear. He packed it all into bespoke cases. Then he showered and changed. He put his washing into a bag for the cleaning service and went to Carl's office.

'Everything sorted, Carl. What can you tell me?'

'Nothing special. You've only been gone nine days. Peter told me about your client's problem. Will she be returning to finish her tour?'

'I hope so; she's an incredible woman. But I'm trying not to get my hopes up.'

'You seem different somehow, Sam.'

'I am, and she's the cause. I had to come out of my shell to help her. It's made a difference to me. I won't be as silent again.'

'That's a good thing. Peter said you might stay with JJ at Ranzi.'

'I did. He's the same as always.'

'His son Riaan has applied for a transfer back here. I haven't decided yes or no because he's your protégé. So it's up to you.'

'JJ didn't mention it.'

'He might not know.'

'Then I'll talk to JJ. Do we have a vacancy?'

'As always, if we don't have a vacancy now, we'll have one in a month. You know that randy young rangers don't last more than a year without long leave to work out the kinks. Riaan's transfer will depend on his current lodge even if you approve it.'

'If we're not short of a ranger for the drives, I'll ride with each of them during the rest of the week and do their assessments. It's been six months since the last.'

'Thanks. I haven't been able to. Peter hopes for an exclusive for you on Monday. He'll email us if it's confirmed.'

'Okay, I'll see you tomorrow.'

Sam took a copy of the rangers' roster and ten ranger check sheets and planned which mornings or evenings he would ride with them for the check. In his cottage, he set up his computer, switched on the

Wi-Fi, and set up his editing studio with two screens. He hadn't forgotten the videos he'd taken with Melissa. He called JJ minutes before lunch.

'Hello JJ, Sam here.'

'Sam. What a surprise. I didn't expect you to call for weeks. Have you heard from Melissa?'

Sam felt a stab of despair, 'No, JJ. If she's home, it's only just. I won't bother her for a day or two.'

'Send her an email to say you returned safely. It's the kind of thing women appreciate. Why did you call?'

'To tell you, if you don't know, that Riaan has applied for a transfer back to Likesedi.'

'I didn't. Has Riaan said why?'

'No, and he won't have a transfer unless he sends an argument saying why. I can tell him, or you can.'

'I'll find out what it's about. Thanks for telling me. Did you see Coenraad?'

'Yes, Annelie is two months pregnant; just showing.'

'Good woman that. I must find a present.'

'She's learning to be a local doctor. Says she'll have the baby there, let it run wild with the local kids, and do the doctoring herself.'

'I'll tell Martha. She'll know what she needs. Thanks for calling. Bring Melissa to visit when she returns.'

'If she returns, JJ.'

'Don't think that; believe she will. Martha and I do. *Totsiens*.'

The rangers usually had two hours between lunch and tea for a snooze because beginning the day before dawn and ending after 9 pm led to sleep deprivation if they didn't.

Sam sent an email.

Hi, Melissa,

This email is to tell you I arrived safely at Likesedi after returning JJ's pickup and sleeping at Lion Sands, where I have friends Coenraad and Annelie de Vos. We have invitations to visit them both when you return.

Sam.

Then a feeling rose from deep inside, and he typed 'Love' before 'Sam'. He returned to the first line, 'Hi, Melissa,' which became 'My darling Mel'.

Satisfied, he sent it, then slept for an hour and a half.

Melissa took the Heathrow Express to Paddington, then a taxi home. She called the hospital for an appointment with Doctor Reddy, then phoned Mrs Drew and arranged to meet her. A visit to a corner shop provided basic supplies, and then Melissa switched on her computer. She forgot to eat until she had finished her love letter at 10 pm. Her last words were. 'I love you, Sam.'

When she read those last words, she concluded, *I don't know if that's true, but I think that may be what my feelings tell me.*

She filed it, named 'Sam', in a directory called 'For Sam'. She hadn't switched on her Wi-Fi.

Then she slept well, feeling Sam was in bed beside her.

Sam met the rangers and their clients for tea and told the rangers he would take a ride with each of them in the next six days. The first assessment ride was with Benjy. He was sure it would take his mind off his sorrow.

Sam said nothing for more than two hours. Benjy knew how Sam worked; he would have an interview and verbal assessment after breakfast the next day.

Sam sat at the same table as Benjy for dinner, still saying little, and judged how Benjy answered his client's questions.

For Sam, it worked. His concentrated attention to myriad details left no time to think of Melissa, and when he went to bed, due to fatigue, he slept dreamlessly.

Sam woke at 4:30 am. His first thought was, *It's 3:30 am in London.* He made his morning coffee and Sam joined Tabansi, one of the older rangers, and his clients, at 5 am, checklist at the ready.

After breakfast, Sam began to edit his films. He only managed the mongoose film that day, converting formats, editing, adding background, initial visual feed into the Tuli lodge and grounds, and cuts. Then, he searched for suitable background music and edited a soundtrack.

It was tedious, but Sam was using the artistic part of his character, which gave him a deep appreciation of the sunrise and the music of the veldt. It took longer than he anticipated, for he had to replay the video several times, and Sam stopped it each time it showed a scene with Melissa, then stepped through the frames with an ache in his heart. Finally, he played it through, and at every scene change and jump, he selected a transition: sometimes a fade, sometimes an overlay or a cut. Then Sam wrote the narration. This alone took two hours. He recorded it and overlaid it onto the soundtrack. Satisfied, he designed an attractive title and added *THE END* before a final fade to the last image and credits.

The Story of Mrs Mongoose.
From the book 'Stories from Africa' by Melissa Grouwer.
Filmed and edited by Sam Daniels.

Sam viewed it from the beginning, then, like anyone proud of his work, felt the urge to show it to the rangers and clients and hear their opinions. But it was *our* work: his and Melissa's. Should he send it to Melissa? He could send the narration text. She could change it if she wished, record her voice narrating, and send it back. The problem went around in circles in his mind until he decided, *I don't want to create a working method with her in London and me here. If that happens, there'll be no reason for her to return, and I want her beside me.*

He took it to the lounge and stuck a notice on the TV.

TONIGHT – Film from the book by Melissa Grouwer.
(After Dinner)

The clients and rangers packed the lounge, and after the show, Sam received a shower of thanks and praise and told every person to post what they thought of Likesedi on the lodge's Facebook page.

Before he finally went to bed at 10 pm, he sent another email to Melissa and attached the MPEG video version.

My darling Mel,

Tomorrow, Carl leaves for Joburg; he's going for medical tests. I'm the temporary lodge manager. If Carl's going away for a long time, Peter has signed up to come as manager on Monday for a maximum of three months, and I'm hoping for a promotion to the manager's job after he leaves.

I'll be busy doing two jobs simultaneously, but I found enough time to edit 'The Mongoose Cook' film today. I've included the video for you. I had to narrate it myself. You can do a new narration when you return, and I'll replace mine. I tried it out on the guests and the rangers. They adored it.

Love, Sam.

PS. I thought of calling, but I wanted to send the video.

When Melissa put on a coat to visit the hospital on Thursday, she remembered the boarded-up back door of her house and put a second key to the front door into her purse. At the hospital, the ward sister showed her into a room where Aunt Jane lay pale and inert in bed, unconscious. She was hooked up to a dozen wires and tubes.

'It's not as bad as it looks, Miss Grouwer,' said the ward sister. We feed her intravenously. The vital signs are regular; on this screen, you have the heartbeat, pulse rate, temperature, blood pressure, breathing rate and blood oxygen.

'We have sedated her, and the other screen shows low brain activity, but there *is* activity. The encephalogram is this afternoon, and the MRI is tomorrow morning. The doctors will examine the results and the chemical blood analyses. We hope that by Monday afternoon, the doctors can determine what problem she experienced, and the neurologist can provide a prognosis for her recovery.'

'What do you think, sister?'

'I don't, Miss Grouwer. I've seen patients who've had a stroke walk out of the hospital in two or three days, and others take months to recover. But don't hope for a miracle. We have no idea how long she lay in her bed before emergency services reached her. It might have been less than an hour; it might have been twelve or more. We all know the longer it takes for help to arrive, the less likely recovery will be total.'

She had to wait to see Doctor Reddy, who had to deal with an emergency. He could add nothing more.

Melissa took the train to Clapham, met Mrs Drew, and took her to lunch at a restaurant near her home. Mrs Drew said what Melissa expected.

'It was such a shock, Melissa. She was such a nice lady. Always firm but fair. Can I go to see her?'

'Of course, Nana, she's sedated now. I'll let you know when she's awake. I have her key to the front door, so please take it. The police will give me the spare key they took. You had a key to the back door, but the police boarded it up, and I must have it replaced. If you want to stay in the house because visiting Auntie Jane is easier, please do so.'

'Won't you be staying then?'

'I hope not, Nana. I've something to do in Africa after I've sorted out Auntie Jane's future.'

'Do you have a *beau* out there?'

It was the first time anyone had asked. Melissa had to think about how she considered Sam. Mrs Drew studied her and the changing expressions on her face. The question wasn't out of place to Melissa, who had confided in her nanny for years. 'I think I might have.'

'Good man, is he?'

Melissa smiled at her memory of Sam. 'Yes, he's kind, and somehow he makes me feel alive but safe.'

'Then listen to me, my girl. You return there as soon as possible. Men that make you feel like that are hard to find. I know; I only found one, and he was already married.'

'Thanks, Nana. I know you mean well.'

Back at the house, with the weight of worry hard to bear, Melissa fetched her swimming gear, went to the gym, paid for a two-month membership, and swam. Fifty lengths of the pool later, she went home and switched on the Wi-Fi.

After dinner, she booted up her computer and received Sam's first email. She read it with a happy smile.

It took her five minutes to decide how to start her reply.

> My dearest Sam,
>
> I can't say I was worried about you returning to Likesedi, but knowing you did so safely is a relief. Thanks.
>
> My aunt is in hospital, sedated. The ward sister doesn't think she will die. They are doing scans today and tomorrow. I hope the doctors can tell me what went wrong and what their prognosis is on Monday or Tuesday. Until then, everything is in limbo, except that I've lots to do. I must find an artisan to replace the back door, search the house for all my aunt's papers, and read them for all the information I need. I don't know anything about her affairs. So wish me luck. I think of you all the time.
>
> I did what you told me to: I bought a phone and a SIM, and I've loaded WhatsApp so you can call me.
>
> Love, Mel.
>
> Tel: +44 7702 096012

Melissa filed both in the 'For Sam' directory.

She switched off seconds before Sam clicked send for his email with the Mongoose video.

18

· · · · ·

WHEN SHE WOKE THE FOLLOWING DAY, MELISSA DECIDED SHE had no option but to go shopping for groceries. Despondently, she estimated she would need at least one month's supplies. However, carrying that much shopping was a problem unless she made several trips. Melissa thought about her little leased car and wished she'd kept it. It was four years old when she went to Botswana, and with the lease about to expire, she returned it. Now, she needed another. After checking on rental cars, Melissa selected Heathrow as the collection and drop-off point, happy in the thought: *That's where I shall depart from for Botswana and Sam.*

She fetched the rental and did her shopping at a mall near Heathrow. She popped in to visit her aunt for half an hour; there was no change in her aunt's condition, and she left when the nurses wheeled the bed out for the MRI scan.

When she called a maintenance service to fit a new back door, the company said they would send an artisan to quote that afternoon. It blocked her from leaving the house, so she checked her emails and found Sam's email about the mongoose. She opened it, filed the mongoose video in her 'For Sam' directory and watched the mongoose film. She felt Sam's voice deep down in her heart. She didn't reply immediately because another email arrived, the reply from Tom, the publisher. Excited, she read it.

Dear Melissa,

Thank you for allowing me to read the most beautiful short story I have known amongst the thousands I've read. As Sam said, there is little to correct from the perspective of a copy editor, but more for the proofreader. The attached document labelled *Style Guide* is the one we use. I suggest you read it carefully. A proofreader alters the text and punctuation according to this style guide (or any other the publishers insist on.)

The second attachment is your annotated text. The style guide dictates the corrections. Study what the editor did, then accept them.

There are other changes not listed in the style guide; they are rules approved by publishers, and in each case, there is a comment explaining what, why and a suggestion. None are grammatical errors; you may ignore the editor's recommendations.

Let me assure you, if you had worked to the guide, your work would be outstanding, as are the story and the language already.

My regards from us all, Tom.

As she couldn't leave the house, she studied what the editor had done, then forwarded Tom's email to Sam with a header section.

My darling Sam,

Attached is Tom's reply. I'm studying it while waiting for the door repair people. You were quite right; what Tom sent will improve my writing.

I've looked up care homes; most are in the country. I've rented a small car to visit them and to use for shopping. My search of the house for Aunt Jane's papers may take four days.

All my Love, Mel.

Then Melissa corrected and filed the final mongoose manuscript.

The repair man arrived, gave her a quote, and she signed it. He said he would order a door and schedule the fitting for next week.

As it was still early enough, she went swimming, then returned to begin a search for her aunt's papers.

She watched the Mongoose video four times before bed, waiting for the right time to call Sam.

Sam woke at his usual time, had his regular coffee, and joined the rangers. They had delayed the morning drives, for they were all waiting by the office for Carl's departure.

Benjy arrived with a pickup, loaded Carl's suitcases, and left with Carl after everyone had said a gruff goodbye. Sam felt sure that none of the rangers expected to see Carl again.

Knowing Melissa was busy all weekend, he expected no emails and drowned his thoughts about her through work. He spent the day in the office with the accountant. Sam didn't want to hand over to Peter if Carl, in his feeble state, had overlooked anything. Carl hadn't cleared his inbox of several invoices, and when the accountant showed him how to access the lodge's incoming emails, he found Carl had answered nothing for four days. Sam verified and approved the invoices for the accountant and answered the emails.

At lunch with the rangers, he said, 'One thing I noticed from the accounts is that the shop sells nothing to the rangers. It's your shop. Say so if you want it to sell chewing gum or gun oil. We can buy it cheaper, and you'll only pay the cost.'

Benjy called from the end of the table, 'Silent. How about condoms and KY jelly? Not for me, for the clients who run out.'

Sam grinned, 'Benjy, a promising idea. I'll tell the shop. Good thing that it's not for you; we can't buy your size.'

The laughter that followed pleased Sam. He felt they were a family.

He did another check ride that evening and sat alone on his veranda after dinner, wondering if he wanted the manager's job that Peter had mentioned. Sam would have said no ten days ago, but Melissa had changed everything. He felt Melissa would not marry a ranger, no matter what Annelie had said, but a successful lodge manager would be more attractive. He reviewed what he could do to make his promotion more likely, something Peter could point to in a recommendation.

Then his phone rang, and he rushed into the cottage to answer.

'Hello, my darling.'

'Sam, I had to call. I've watched the mongoose video four times, and hearing your voice made me yearn to talk to you.'

'I'm glad you did, Mel. Hearing yours brings you closer. Did you like the video?'

'Darling, I adore it and will listen to it every night. What have you been doing?'

Sam told her. Then, he added he was thinking about what he could do to ensure his promotion.

'You said everyone liked the video, Sam. Can't you do some more? Or assemble a presentation of photos of a species and talk about it? You did so well at Mashatu that you'd be a hit.'

'I'll think about that, Mel. What have you been doing?'

'My email told you. I'll be sorting papers all weekend. You won't sleep enough if we don't cut this call short. Go to bed and think of cuddling me.'

'I will. I do. Every night. Good night, darling.'

'Good night, Sam.'

After their call, Melissa slept with a smile and a memory. And so did Sam.

Sam spent the next day working on the monkey video. He knew what he would narrate.

Initially daunted by the challenges she faced, Melissa took a deep breath, made up her mind and said to herself, *I won't allow anything to delay my return.*

She searched each room, discovered cupboards she'd never opened, and found piles and boxes of documents and invoices. By the time she heated a hamburger patty and baked beans, three more rooms, including her aunt's bedroom, remained for her to search. The documents were on the floor of each room. Then she visited the hospital. Aunt Jane was still the same, so after a half hour holding her aunt's hand, she went to a stationery shop, bought a dozen box files and a paper punch, returned home, and searched the last three rooms. Then she carried all the documents to the lounge floor and began methodically going through them, but sorting a lifetime of papers was a mammoth task. After three hours, Melissa decided that the job would take her weeks. She called the number of a secretarial agency with temporary staff for hire.

'Thank you for your call. The agency has closed. Please leave a message at the beep or call on Monday morning after 8 am. Thank you.'

Melissa left a message, 'Good afternoon, I'm Miss Grouwer. I need a secretary and a filing clerk. Please call 7702 096012. Thank you.'

She ate, sorted, ate, and then, tired and discouraged, Melissa went to bed.

Her aunt was unchanged on Sunday. Feeling lost, for it was a week since the fateful phone call and Botswana and Sam seemed like a dream, Melissa decided she couldn't spend another day sorting papers. She went to the zoo for the day. *The animals will refresh my memories.*

She was in the spider walkthrough, looking at a golden orb, remembering how many she'd seen when walking with Sam, when a voice next to her asked, 'Do you find them fascinating, miss?' Melissa turned to see a young man with two chin pimples looking at her curiously.

'Why do you ask?'

'You have a suntan; maybe you know some I don't.'

'I'm sure I won't. A week ago, I was walking in Botswana, and these golden orbs were everywhere. You can't walk without pushing through their webs. I ignore the spiders and insects unless they are good to eat, and they ignore me.'

'I'm James. I'm studying entomology. Spiders fascinate me. Which ones are good to eat?'

'I don't know. If someone showed me a spider or insect to eat, and I ate it, then if I saw another, I would know it was good to eat, but I wouldn't want to know its name. It's better that way.'

'Why?'

'If I knew its name, it would be like eating a friend.'

James had a doubtful expression. 'I suppose so. Will you come to look at insects with me? I'll tell you about them, and if you recognise one to eat, tell me?'

Amused, Melissa said, 'Okay, James, but I imagine the zoo won't allow us to eat them, so I'll buy you a burger at lunchtime. I'm Melissa.'

When she reached home, she felt far more cheerful.

19

PETER ARRIVED ON MONDAY EVENING, AND ON TUESDAY, SAM handed over the reins and told him what he'd done. Impressed, Peter felt that Melissa had changed him, thinking, *I hope it continues and he doesn't regress.*

Melissa began the week hoping the neurologist would tell her that Aunt Jane, who was still in the same condition, would recover fully and she could return to Sam.

The neurologist, Dr Neufeld, was a half hour late for the appointment – by then, Melissa's hope had leaked away, replaced with dread. Dr Neufeld was tall, thin, white-haired, grave and, to Melissa, entirely negative.

'Miss Grouwer, I've looked at the scans and analyses and consulted with another specialist. Your aunt suffered an ischemic stroke, and the MRI shows the remains of the blood clot that has dissolved because of the medication she received on arrival. She's healthy, but the carotid artery has a fat build-up. A lack of blood flow and oxygen seriously damaged her brain. Without brain activity to monitor, I cannot risk an operation. The most I could do is a carotid stent, which carries the risk of an immediate stroke. Neither procedure will restore damaged brain cells and the carotid fat build-up will cease with the proper diet.

'I've studied the encephalograms. We'll progressively reduce the medication keeping her unconscious, so she'll wake in about three days. Wednesday evening or Thursday morning.'

'Well, that's some good news, doctor.'

'I'm glad you think so, but reviewing the possible consequences of the brain damage, I must tell you my prognosis. Your aunt will have paralysis on her left side and impaired balance. Walking will be dangerous. At best, she must use a wheelchair, but with one arm, she will need assistance to move.

'She's unlikely to have complete control of bowel and bladder functions. She may manage to feed herself with her right hand and arm.

'The good news is that her brain's speech and memory areas appear unimpaired. However, she may need to relearn to speak because her paralysis may affect her lip movement. At first, she'll mumble.'

As he spoke, Melissa felt sorrow, pity, and then something worse: pity for herself. Doctor Neufeld could see it reflected in her face.

'Miss Grouwer, I suggest you don't waste time hoping. There are care homes that cater for cases like hers. Few will have space available at short notice, but you *must* find one because you *cannot* do it. She'll need *trained* assistance and care for months or years. Ask the hospital advice bureau for a list of registered care homes. You may find one outside London.'

'And what is her future, doctor?'

'She'll improve her speech with time and training, but one day, after years, she'll have another attack and final release. Until then, she'll be happy and serene. Let the new care home environment and staff take care of her, and continue your life; you do not have the skills and training to do more for her.'

'Thank you, doctor; I've much to think about.'

'Miss Grouwer. I hope to see you here and learn about your ar-

rangements. You'll need a report from me for the care home application. Let me emphasise that the hospital is short of beds. The admin-
istration will pressure me to release her as soon as possible. If you
cannot find a care home in time, they will ask social services to place
her in a suitable institution, one which, I dare say, you'll not like.'

'How long do I have, doctor?'

'I cannot estimate a date until after I see her conscious, but it
could be as soon as the end of next week.'

Melissa went to the advice bureau. The woman behind the counter
asked for the patient's name, accessed Aunt Jane's file, and read the
neurologist's remarks. 'Miss, I'll give you the category C list.'

'What does that mean?'

'A is homes that take only mobile patients. B does, too, but accepts
wheelchair users if they can operate the wheelchair. C is the next,
and D takes bedridden patients.'

Melissa was shocked, and the young woman on the other side of
the desk could see it. 'I know what you're thinking, Miss Grouwer;
your aunt will be put in a box with many others in the same condition.'

'Yes, I did think that.'

'Unfortunately, there are more old folks every year, and the state-
subsidised homes can't cope without streamlining the care. It's a
form of triage.' The woman looked back at the computer. The patient's address was in a wealthy London suburb.

'Miss, could your aunt pay for private care?'

'I'm sure it's possible.'

The young woman took a card from her desk drawer. 'Then look
up this association on the web; they may be able to help.'

Melissa returned home to call the secretarial agency but remembered the neurologist's report and the consequences. *I need to see my lawyer.*

She made an appointment for the following day and called the secretarial agency.

'Good morning. I'm Miss Grouwer. I left a message, but no one has called back.'

They promised to send two women, a secretarial assistant and a filing clerk.

'It won't be before lunch tomorrow, Miss Grouwer. They can start when you wish by mutual agreement. I'll email you our contract and rates; please sign and return it.'

Feeling depressed and lost, she went swimming again – the mindless and exhausting back and forth brought detachment.

When she finally climbed the ladder, a voice said, 'You're a powerful swimmer, Miss Grouwer. Lots of practice.'

It was the gym trainer she'd seen a day or two ago. 'How do you know my name?'

'I asked the desk. Mine's Tyron Banks.'

'To answer your question, yes. I must go; I've much to do.'

Tyron watched her. Melissa sensed his eyes on her and thought: *Twenty-two, a gym trainer on the prowl, and unattractive.*

Melissa cooked and ate her dinner. Feeling better, she switched on her computer to look at the website address the advice bureau woman had given her. It was an association providing advice and assistance for people looking for a care home. What interested her was the button 'Apply for advice and assistance'.

The form to fill in was extensive, and the red highlighted text before the box labelled 'Patient condition' was daunting.

> A doctor's report is necessary for any recommended care home application. Please do not under or overstate the patient's requirements for us to choose the right homes to apply to. Doing so will lead to the home rejecting an application when the doctor's report differs.

Melissa gave up.

She closed the web page and returned to the file directory 'For Sam'. Melissa felt as if she was drowning and needed Sam's voice to rescue her, and there were tears in her eyes when her shaking hand clicked the mouse on the file 'Mongoose Video.' The shake was enough; what opened was the file 'Sam'.

She had to wipe the tears away with her knuckles to see what it was, and then she read it.

When she read the final words, 'I love you. Sam,' she felt something new, something she hadn't felt before, *And that's true. So, get into gear and sort out the problems so I can feel his arms around me again.*

Melissa returned to the website and the application page and filled in every line. In the final line, where it asked, 'Why are you applying to us?' She wrote a simple cry for help.

> Because I have no family or friends to help me find a care home for my aunt, and I don't know what to do.

Then she clicked send and, feeling better, viewed the 'Mongoose Cook' again. Sam was with her. As always, pouring her problems onto paper helped, so she emailed Sam.

My darling Sam,

I would like to hear your voice again, but a disembodied voice won't be the same. If the internet at Likesedi could manage a video call, I would call every night. But I'm a writer; I've written pages in my diary every night since I learnt to write, so I shall write to you whenever I've something to tell you, if only to write 'My darling Sam' again.

I went to the Zoo yesterday. I felt I had to see the animals again, and I met a young man studying entomology. We talked about spiders, and he cheered me up until this morning.

I finally saw the neurologist; what he told me was terrible. I'm feeling depressed, even after swimming fifty lengths in the pool. My aunt may recover consciousness in two to three days. The doctor says she will only have one usable arm, won't be able to walk, and may have no control over her bodily functions. He told me to find a care home for her. The hospital gave me a list of care homes; there are over three hundred in and around London, but I've applied for assistance from a care association. I've asked an agency for two temps to help file Aunt Jane's papers; she never threw anything away and didn't file them, so I have a mountain of paper to sort and file.

I have an appointment tomorrow to see my lawyer. I'll let you know what he says. The mountain to climb is growing, not shrinking.

I'm trying, Sam; I want to return. Please tell me you are waiting for me. It will help.

Lots of love, Mel.

Sam had returned to his cottage as soon as dinner ended, for he wanted to make notes on ideas to improve the lodge. When he finished, he filed the document and checked his email. There was nothing, but Sam went to the bathroom instead of closing the email page and prepared for bed. Five minutes later, when he came from the bathroom, he saw a pop-up on the computer screen and read, 'You have email.'

He sat in his pyjama shorts and read Melissa's email and her first words again.

> I would like to hear your voice again.

I would, too, he thought and called.

Melissa was in her bathroom, a few metres down the corridor. She'd undressed, ready for a shower before bed, and heard the phone. She ran to the bedroom, forgetting she was nude, and picked up the phone. She was just in time to say a breathless 'Hello.'

When she heard Sam ask, 'Is that my darling, Mel?' Her legs felt weak, so she sat on the dresser chair. 'Yes, Sam, I had to run from the bathroom to answer your call.'

'Darling, tap the video button; it's late and might work. I want to see you.'

Forgetting her nudity, she replied, 'Okay, Sam,' and tapped. A few seconds later, she had Sam's image, head and shoulders, on her screen.

Melissa smiled, 'Sam, you look just the same; why are you naked?'

'I'm not. I was about to go to bed.' Sam moved the phone away so she could see he was wearing shorts.

'Sam, that's disappointing; you look good enough to cuddle.'

'You do too, Mel. Who's in your room?'

Surprised, she said, 'No one – look.' She stood, turned the phone, scanned the room before rotating it so she could again see Sam's face, now a wide grin.

'See, I'm alone. Why did you ask?'

'To check if you still look the same. You do, just like when you showered at Robelela.'

It took Mel two seconds to remember she was naked, so she sat down with a bump and brought the phone closer.

'That wasn't fair, Sam.'

'Well, I know you haven't changed. I've read your email, and you have so much to do it will be ages before you return; just looking at you makes me realise how much I want you to return. Shall I come and help you?'

'Sam, before I wrote that email, I had to fill in a form to apply for assistance from the care home association, and I gave up. Then, I accidentally opened the text of what I wrote on the plane returning. It was about you, and I knew I couldn't give up, so I returned to the form and filled it in. I must do this and learn how the world works to help my aunt. Sam, it's hard, but if I don't, I'll hide away from the world again. So no, call me when you can, and tell me you're waiting for me.'

She saw Sam smile as he said, 'I'll try calling you every night when you shower. Then you'll know I want you here. Take things one at a time and tell me what you're doing.'

'Okay, you need your sleep, and so do I. Good night, Sam.'

'Good night, my darling.'

20

· · · · ·

AFTER LOOKING SADLY AT HER MOTIONLESS AUNT THE FOL-
lowing day, she stepped out the hospital room door and found a
handsome man with a white coat and a name tag blocking her way.

She glanced at the tag. 'Sorry, Doctor Trumper, I wasn't looking
where I was going.'

'No apologies necessary, Miss Grouwer. A common hospital hazard we learn to avoid is people who are temporarily elsewhere.'

'How do you know my name?'

'I'm treating a case next door to your aunt and asked. I can understand if you feel depressed. Can I offer you lunch to talk about it?'

'Thank you, doctor, but I have a legal appointment and two inter-
views on my agenda.'

'Then I'll try to catch you another time. Have a good day.'

Her lawyer, Terence Grant, was pleased to see her. 'Melissa, it's good
to see you looking so well. What have you been up to?'

'Writing a book, or at least trying to, and wandering in Africa for
background.'

'So why have you come to see me? You have full control of your
trust. Do you want to remove my remaining powers?'

'Not at all. I need your help.'

Melissa told him everything, and while she did so, he studied her
and felt happy at the change in her since their last meeting.

'Melissa, there are two steps we must take, and as soon as possible. It would be best if your aunt signs a power of attorney, witnessed by her doctor, giving you legal guardianship. Then, I suggest you sign a document giving me the full power of attorney over her affairs and a power of attorney to act on your behalf in absentia. I'll prepare the documents immediately.'

'Please go ahead. I want to return to Africa.'

'Do you have the neurologist's number?'

Melissa gave it to him, and he called. After a short conversation, the lawyer passed the phone to Melissa.

'Hello, Miss Grouwer. I just need *your* confirmation that I should send the report your lawyer has asked for.'

'Please do, doctor. Without authority, I can't take the steps you recommended.'

'I'll email it in the next hour. Send a courier to collect the original after lunch.'

'Thank you, doctor.'

Melissa returned the phone. Her lawyer pressed a call button, and a young man entered the office.

'Melissa, meet Tim Barry. He's working here for experience before registration. Tim, please take Miss Grouwer to your office and fill out a power of attorney for her aunt to sign, appointing Miss Grouwer as her legal guardian for medical reasons, and then obtain all the supporting documents you'll need for court certification. The doctor will send a report.

'Melissa, do you have your aunt's birth certificate and other documents?'

'I'm sure I must, but I've eighteen years of documents to sort through. I've asked a clerk to help. She's coming this afternoon and tomorrow. I'll ask for more help if necessary.'

'You *must* find it, or a passport, even an expired one. Applying for a new original will take at least a month before we can certify the legal guardianship. When you've filed everything, Tim will send a courier to collect them all, including your documents.

'Tim, fill out a power of attorney giving me full rights, in absentia, to manage her aunt's affairs and Miss Grouwer's affairs. Miss Grouwer will sign it.'

Melissa went to Tim's office and left half an hour later with a list of documents to find. Although Tim was friendly, she was sure a lawyer-client relationship barred anything more than polite conversation.

She had a quick lunch on the way home,

The first temp, the filing clerk, rang the doorbell at 2 pm. Melissa judged she was fifty years old and overly formal, but when Mildred saw the pile of papers on the lounge floor, she asked. 'How long do I have?'

'Five hours to find a birth certificate and a week to file everything.'

'Then we need another person. Can I call one?'

'Please.'

Two minutes later, Mildred spoke into her phone. 'Gloria, I have a massive job. Can you come and help?'

Melissa began to sort documents into two piles: invoices and the rest. It was backbreaking work, so she sat on the floor and crawled around to do it. Gloria and Mildred at the table sorted Melissa's 'the rest' pile into categories: bank, legal, and others. They had to extract documents from folded envelopes, but a few minutes before 6 pm, Gloria said, 'I have an envelope that has what you want.'

They examined the papers together: A birth, baptism, and marriage certificate. An inner envelope contained divorce papers.

'Ladies, thank you; you may have saved my life. Let me drive you home, and we can have something to eat on the way.'

'Miss, that would be nice, but look at your dress. The floor is dirty. You'll need to bathe. Let's make it another evening.'

Exhausted, Melissa slept well.

Melissa had a simple but hurried breakfast, for the secretary was to arrive at 8:30 am. When she saw the piles of documents, she remembered how dirty she'd become sitting on the floor. *I'll invite Sam here one day, even if it's only to submit his thesis or my book, but I can't bring him here with my house in this state. It needs cleaning.* Just thinking of Sam made her feel better.

At 8 am, she called Tim Barry.

'Good morning, Tim. I have the certificates and docs you wanted.'

'That's marvellous, Miss Grouwer. Is there an original bank statement with your aunt's address?'

'I'm sure there is. I didn't ask. Why an original?'

'When the court clerk stamps the power, we must show the originals. Then we'll store them at the office. I'll send a courier shortly. If there are other financial documents about investments, I would like those as well.'

Melissa looked through the pile labelled 'bank', selected the most recent statement, and added it to the envelope with the certificates. She then looked for and found other financial documents to add.

Jacqueline, the secretary, arrived. After a short interview, Melissa decided she liked her and said, 'Jacqueline, two women, Gloria and Mildred, are coming to sort and file the documents in the lounge. Let them in when they come; we were here last night. A courier is also coming to collect the envelope on the table marked "certificates"; I'm going to the hospital. Finally, this house needs cleaning from top to bottom. Everything except what's in my room can go. Can you look at everything and organise it?'

'I'll see, miss. Can I have your Wi-Fi details? I have my computer in my bag.'

'Thank you. The Wi-Fi's name is Elephant, and the password is Cheetah, all lowercase.'

Shortly after Melissa entered Aunt Jane's hospital room, a nurse she judged to be young and pretty came into the room, carrying a tray with a glass of water.

'Sorry, miss, I didn't know you were here.'

'No problem. Aunt Jane doesn't mind. Are you looking after her?'

'Yes, miss. I'm Rachel. She's an easy patient. I'm only a junior nurse, so I still have the dirty jobs.'

'Do you like nursing?'

The young woman looked at her momentarily. Melissa felt she was trying to decide something. 'Yes, miss, but we must learn to avoid *common hospital hazards.*'

The three words with the touch of emphasis rang a bell in Melissa's memory, so she asked, 'Like what?'

'All kinds, miss. Like male staff whose wives are at conferences.'

The memory clicked into place, 'Are you trying to tell me something, Rachel?'

'No, miss. Not me. We're told not to talk about the staff.'

'Thanks, Rachel, and thanks for looking after my Aunt Jane. There seems no change, so I'll go now.' *I've just learnt something worth knowing about the world.*

'Mildred, I suppose I could burn all these old invoices?'

'No, Melissa, we'll file them. Your Aunt Jane could burn them, but you can't. We'll put those over five years old into a burn pile.'

Melissa went for a swim and had to fend off Tyron once again. He offered her fruit juice at the gym bar, but she shrugged him off and returned home.

After the ladies left, the door contractor called and asked if he could install the new back door in the morning. Immediately after, Tim called and said the powers of attorney were ready for her signature. Melissa went to sign and fetch them. Then she called the neurosurgeon and explained that if Aunt Jane was conscious, she had to persuade her to sign a power of attorney. She asked if he would witness it.

He agreed to meet her at the hospital and said, 'That's not an unusual request, Miss Grouwer. I'll be pleased to do so.'

Melissa knew Sam would be on a game drive and couldn't answer a call, but she had things to tell him, so she sent an email.

> Dearest Sam,
>
> I didn't realise I had changed, but I have. I've three women and a lawyer helping me. Two searched the pile of papers and found the documents my lawyer wanted. I have a power of attorney document for my aunt to sign, hopefully tomorrow, and I've signed one, giving my lawyer full authority to do everything for Aunt Jane and myself.

My secretary, Jacqueline, is trying to find out how to clean the house. I didn't realise how old and neglected it had become until I thought of what you would feel if I brought you here.

Tomorrow, the new back door is due. So everything is in progress. I hope for a reply from the care association soon.

I feel much better; you should too because I want to tell you I've played the mongoose video nightly before sleeping. Not to watch it but to listen to your voice, which I heard when lying beside you.

Sam, some things may change, but the most important ones don't.

All my Love, Mel.

Melissa was in the bathroom again when the phone rang.

'Darling, how do you do it?'

'Do what, Mel?'

'Call when I'm in the bathroom.'

'Oh, that's easy. We have an existential rapport.'

'A what?'

'A connection, Mel. I just sit in my room and remember watching the sunrise over the Robelela lake, waiting for the moment when you step onto the sheet to shower, then I call.'

Melissa laughed, 'Sam, you'll have to delay calling a bit; I still have my clothes on.'

'Then it must be my fault. So have I. I'll undress the next time I read your email. Do you think your aunt will sign tomorrow?'

'I don't know, Sam. I hope the doctor will help me persuade her.'

'Mel, I don't think you've changed; you dared to visit Africa and walk into an Elephant herd. You'll do the best for your aunt. I'm proud of you.'

'Thanks, my darling; your confidence is what I need to continue. I must shower and sleep; tomorrow is a long day.'

'Good night, my darling.'

21

. . . . .

MELISSA OPENED THE DOOR FOR JAQUELINE AND WENT TO THE hospital. At the ward desk, the sister said, 'Your aunt woke last night, Miss Grouwer. She's sleeping now but should wake again in an hour or two.'

'That's marvellous; I'll wait until she wakes.

'I met Doctor Trumper last Tuesday, and yesterday, something reminded me of a woman I met at a book launch, also a Doctor Trumper. Are they related?'

'I don't know Miss Grouwer; he might have a sister. If her name was Elizabeth, she might have been his wife. She's in Obstetrics.'

Melissa smiled and said, 'I'll go to the coffee shop. Can you call me when my aunt wakes?'

'Of course.'

In the coffee shop with a double latte, Melissa checked her email on the phone and found a reply from the care association.

> Dear Miss Grouwer,
>
> Re: Your request for assistance with your aunt:
>
> The first piece of advice is something you should know, but from your application, we suspect you don't.
>
> All frail-care beds are in short supply, and most homes have waiting lists. Often, months or years will pass before a bed in a specific home becomes available.

Private institutions, especially the more expensive ones, have shorter lists.

First, one must be precise. You should request a bed for a fixed date and accept the terms that specify that fees are due from the reservation date if the place is vacant, whether the patient occupies it or not. In your case, I would suggest you state that you require the accommodation early, for beds become available when incumbents pass on. Unfortunately, this is impossible to forecast, so it is better to pay for an empty bed than have it occupied by another.

Second, in the case of a private institution, persons in your situation often find that an offer to pay for one or two years of care in advance will allow you to jump the queue. Waiving the right to a refund in the case of a death in the pre-paid period will further enhance your chances.

Do not pre-pay for care unless we approve the institution.

Should you consider such steps possible, please reply with the earliest date you expect occupation, and we shall send you a list of approved homes to call by return. One of them may offer a visit, an encouraging sign.

We wish you luck in your endeavour.

Director

As she drank her coffee, she decided, *I'll accept that advice; all I need is a date.*

The phone rang, and she heard the Ward sister say, 'Your aunt's awake, Miss Grouwer. Give us ten minutes. Then, you can see her and give her breakfast.'

'Hello, Auntie Jane.'

The wan face on the pillow turned towards her.

It took half a minute for Aunt Jane to recognise her and when she did her aunt's eyes seemed to light up, and a crooked smile appeared on her face.

'You've been very ill, Auntie Jane.'

Melissa understood the mumbled words, 'You – came – back.'

'Of course. The moment I heard you were ill. You looked after me when I was small; now I'll look after you.'

Melissa thought her aunt tried to protest, so she said. 'Auntie Jane, you'll improve, but the doctor says it will take many months. After you leave this hospital, you'll need specialised medical care for a long time, and I'll organise the best there is, so don't worry about it. You'll be fine.'

Her aunt seemed to relax and said, with difficulty, 'Where – have – you – been.'

'Just listen, Auntie, and I'll tell you.'

Two nurses came in with a tray, helped her aunt to a slightly more vertical position by cranking the bed, and put a stand over it to hold a bowl of porridge. 'Miss Grouwer, can you feed her a small spoon at a time? We'll be back, but you can press the call button if you want us.'

'Auntie Jane, this will be good for you. I'll talk while you eat.'

For Melissa, feeding her aunt a spoon at a time was easy, for she told her about Botswana, the animals, and Sam. Her aunt listened, and Melissa was sure she was interested. Lost in her memories, she stopped when she found the bowl empty.

'There, Auntie Jane, you've eaten it all. See, you're going to improve. I'll call for the nurses.'

The nurses came and cleaned up, and Melissa asked, 'Do you want to lie back, Auntie?'

Jane shook her head, so Melissa continued her story about Robbie's rescue. She was sure her aunt was smiling when she finished, so she said, 'I need you to sign a paper for me, Auntie, so I can pay for the hospital and arrange your specialised care.'

Melissa understood her mumbled reply, 'What?'

'It's a power of attorney, Auntie Jane, to sign things on your be-half. You can cancel it when you're better.'

Melissa said nothing while her aunt thought about what she had said. Then the neurologist came in with a nurse, and Melissa had to step back while he examined her aunt and did some tests. Then he said, 'Mrs Delvers, you had a stroke, and you're lucky that Mrs Drew called the police before the effects were irre-versible, but it will take many months of medical care for you to recover your normal function. Melissa has told me she'll arrange it. I think I can discharge you from the hospital in a week if she has made the arrangements.'

Melissa ensured her aunt heard her when she said, 'Doctor, I need my aunt to sign this document and for you to witness it before I can sign for her care. Please tell me if you can witness it.'

The doctor took the document from her, read the standard clauses, and turned to Aunt Jane. 'Mrs Delvers, this is a standard power of attorney allowing Melissa to act on your behalf as your guardian. She needs it, and I recommend you sign it, and I'll witness it. Do you understand what I've said?'

Melissa felt relief when Aunt Jane mumbled, 'Yes.'

The doctor turned over his clipboard, placed the document on it, removed a pen from his pocket and held the board where she could see it; he put the pen in her right hand, and she had to fumble to grasp it, then pointed to where she should sign. 'Sign here, please.'

Melissa could see it wasn't her familiar firm signature; it was more of a scrawl. But then the doctor took it and wrote on the bot-tom. 'Signed in my presence after verbal confirmation of satisfactory comprehension.' Then, he added the date, the hospital name, signature, and his professional status.

'Mrs Delvers, I'll visit you daily and hope to release you in seven days. Thank you.'

He gave the document to Melissa and left. The nurse said, 'Miss Grouwer, I think you should leave now so your aunt can rest.'

'Can I return tomorrow?'

'Of course.'

'Aunt Jane, I'll go, but tomorrow I'll tell you the rest of my story.'

She went to the coffee shop and replied to the email. It was short and simple because she was unused to writing emails on the phone.

> Dear Sir,
>
> Thank you for your most helpful reply. I agree to all your suggestions and inform you that I will pay for accommodation from next Thursday. I await your list of recommended homes.
>
> Melissa Grouwer

Then, she took the document directly to her lawyer's office.

Her lawyer met her in the reception, took the document, gave it to the receptionist and said, 'Make copies and give this to Tim. Melissa, come with me; we'll go to lunch. It's a long time since I had lunch with a lovely woman.'

To the receptionist he said, 'Marjorie, call the Savoy – and a taxi, if they have a table.'

'Mr Grant, I'm not suitably dressed for the Savoy.'

'Melissa, one advantage of expensive hotels is that you can wear whatever you want. Wait with Marjorie while I fetch my coat.'

Melissa dashed into the ladies. Marjorie followed, and Melissa reappeared with brushed hair and pale pink lipstick.

'This is an impressive hotel, Mr Grant.'

'Melissa, we're not at work; call me Terence. I was sure it was the kind of hotel you would like. It is impressive, old, and has class, but most of all, it's quiet. Compared to restaurants filled with younger people, older people with poor hearing can hear others talk.'

That's nice. Terence considered my hearing. 'It's very kind of you to think of that, Terence.'

'Now, Melissa, tell me everything. You're stressed. We're in no hurry and can dawdle over lunch for two hours or more. I want to listen.'

Melissa told him everything, including about Sam.

Terence did the ordering and watched her slowly relaxing as their meal progressed and she talked. The first dishes she'd eaten mechanically, not noticing what she ate, but Terence was pleased when, as Melissa neared the end of her story, she said. 'This dessert is delicious. What is it?'

'Yak Dar Behesht, the name means "Ice in Paradise". It's a Persian rice pudding with many spices.'

'Well, I shouldn't, but I'll have another and then a coffee. Does the restaurant have Kenyan coffee?'

'I'll ask. Now, Melissa, I want to say something important to you. You have done everything you can; what you have achieved in such a brief time is incredible, and I admire you for doing so, especially knowing your history. As far as money is concerned to support your aunt, there is no problem. You can do whatever you wish. Tim has been through the files you provided, and as you're the legal guardian and I've power of attorney, I shall recover your aunt's investments, and I'm sure their income alone will cover her ongoing costs. Now, I want to say something more personal. Before your departure to Botswana, you were a sad case. Now, I find you transformed and put it down to one thing. Return to Sam, Melissa, as soon as possible so you don't lose him.'

'Thanks, Terence. I intend to take your advice, but I have a question: if I wanted to, could I buy a game lodge?'

Terence had to think. 'Melissa, you can financially, but it depends on many things. If you learn of a lodge that interests you, send me the details. Most of them are corporates with issued shares, where a takeover is expensive, but it may be possible to buy shares. Others are partnerships; one or more partners often want to sell their participation. Unless the lodge has a single owner, becoming the holder of a majority is a lengthy process.

'But don't hesitate to tell me if a lodge interests you. I'll investigate and tell you what is possible.'

'Thanks, Terence. Now we must go. I want to hear what Jacqueline has uncovered before she leaves.'

She found Jacqueline talking to two men who were fitting the back door.

'Hello, Miss Grouwer. This is Mr Cotton and his assistant. He should have finished the back door by now, but I asked him to check all the house doors, and he says there are three that need repairs, and he'll need to break down the entrance to the basement and replace it.'

'I didn't know there was a basement. Where's the door?'

'He showed me. Behind a cupboard in the kitchen.'

'Then go ahead.'

'The alarm was broken and is irreplaceable, so I've asked for a quote to fit a new one.'

'That's fine, Jacqueline. Go ahead with whatever is necessary.'

Mr Cotton interrupted. 'Excuse me, miss.'

'Yes, Mr Cotton?'

'It's out of my province, miss, but the condition of the alarm wires we pulled out looks dangerous. I suggest you have an electrical contractor look at the house wiring and a gas man look at the gas piping.'

'Thank you, Mr Cotton. I appreciate your concern. Jacqueline will take care of it.'

22

· · · · ·

The secretarial ladies arrived after breakfast, and Melissa left for the hospital.

She felt sure Aunt Jane looked better. She smiled lopsidedly when Melissa said hello.

'Would you like to sit up a bit, Auntie?' When her aunt mumbled, 'Yes,' Melissa pressed the call button, and five minutes later, her aunt was sitting comfortably in a more upright position against fluffed-up pillows. 'Auntie, shall I finish my story?'

Another yes, and she did; it took over half an hour. She could tell her aunt was interested and she had smiled when Melissa told her about Sam. She felt her aunt was tired when she finished. 'Auntie, I'll leave you to sleep now. I'll see you tomorrow.' The nurses returned, and she picked up her bag.

She met Doctor Trumper again in the corridor as she left her aunt's room.

'Good morning, Miss Grouwer. You seem cheerful. Is your aunt improving?'

'I think so, doctor.'

He smiled, 'So, do you have enough time today to join me for lunch? Better though for dinner. Doctors often must delay lunch.'

Melissa was feeling good, so she looked at his smiling and handsome face for a few seconds and realised. *I'm not interested, but he must be successful frequently.*

She replied, 'Doctor, I don't accept invitations from married men.'

Then she swept away, feeling even happier, but when she remembered Tyron at the pool, she felt fear. She frowned and put him out of her mind.

Back at the house, Jacqueline asked what colour carpets she should choose.

'Why?'

'Because the old ones are so old they have holes.'

'Then choose a grey similar to my bedroom.'

'Miss Grouwer, Gloria and Mildred have finished the filing. They would like to see you before they go.'

Melissa thanked them both, 'Ladies, I don't know what I would have done without you. Thank you.' Then she told Jacqueline, 'Call Tim at my lawyer's office and tell him to send a carrier for the files, and please, call me Melissa; it's much easier.'

'I've had a call from the care association, Melissa. The director says you should call a care home in Sevenoaks immediately. I have the number on my desk. You must speak to the director, Mr Carington.'

'Green Gables, good afternoon.'

'Good afternoon. May I speak to Mr Carington, please?'

'May I ask who's calling and what for?'

'Melissa Grouwer, it's about accommodation for my aunt.'

'Certainly, you're going through.'

'Miss Grouwer, James Carington here. The association told me you would call.'

'Mr Carington, my aunt is in hospital in London following a

stroke, and I need to find a care home for her. The doctor says he can discharge her by next weekend.'

'Can you visit us tomorrow, Miss Grouwer, at 11 am?'

'Yes, I can.'

'Please check our website; we're one of England's most expensive care homes.'

'I will do, Mr Carington, and I'll see you tomorrow at 11 am.'

'That's a load off my mind, Jacqueline. At least one home will take my aunt.'

'That's marvellous, Melissa. I was reluctant to tell you what Mr Cotton said to me earlier, but he said a full refurbishment of the house will take three months. He went into the basement and said it was a junk heap. He told you about the gas, but he told me the kitchen and electrical equipment was so old it should go, and the heating system was a dinosaur.'

Melissa reacted immediately, 'I'm not going to stay in London for three months. Would you like the job of managing a refurbishment?'

'I don't think I can on my own, but with the help of my boyfriend, perhaps I can.'

'What does he do?'

'He contracts with interior decorators, mostly offices. If I bring him this weekend, at least he can give me an idea of the work necessary. When must you go?'

'If I can, the week after next.'

'Okay, I'll find out.'

When Sam received a package of thermocouples and other research equipment he had ordered, he decided he must return to research. With a two-day break in his duties, Sam left early that evening for a place he'd found next to a route used by elephants going to the river. Sam wanted fresh elephant dung. He found the track and fresh dung, marked several of the dung piles with pegs, and photographed them. The photos had the GPS position and time added automatically.

He set up his camp under the Landy shade, built a fire, made dinner and then sat with his notebook at the camp table, describing the experiment in detail, his reasoning behind it and its possible outcome. When he finished, he put his notebook away, checked there was nothing lying around to attract an animal, put his trash bag in the Landy, and then slept.

Sam woke as usual before dawn, made his coffee, and walked to his marked dung piles as soon as there was sufficient light. Seeing hundreds of dung beetles around each was gratifying, and he took more photos. He planned to repeat the visit every two hours until sunset.

He cooked his bacon and eggs, toasted some bread, and had just finished breakfast when he heard the chittering of wild dogs, so he sat back to watch for them. The pack of nine seemed to pour through and around the undergrowth like a mini flood. The chittering sounds rising and falling in waves enhanced the impression. Sam didn't move; he knew they never harmed humans, and he'd encountered several packs in the Okavango. They came close, the alpha male and female within five metres, and after a thorough investigation of his camp, the chittering volume rose, and the pack dashed away.

Sam couldn't help thinking that Melissa would have adored this, so with their visit fresh in his mind, he began an email describing where he was and what he had seen. His love of the wild, of the dogs, and Melissa turned it from a report into a story.

He made three more visits to the dung before considering lunch. He didn't expect the wild dogs to return, knowing they spent the hottest hours lazing in shadows, but they returned and decided to lay around in the bush before his camp. As he made his lunchtime salad, a dog would raise its head, stare momentarily, and then drop back to a doze. Sam felt happy with their company. The dogs were still there two hours after the last photos, and he had to return to the dung. Sam picked a route that skirted most of the drowsing dogs, gathered his camera, and walked out. To Sam, it seemed they had decided he was harmless; none of the dogs moved. Thirty minutes later, when Sam returned, the dogs had gone. He had more to write.

When she went to the bathroom to prepare for bed, Melissa took her phone. When Sam didn't call, she went to bed with a niggling worry and slept poorly.

Melissa took the 10:20 train from Charing Cross Station to Sevenoaks in the morning. As the website stated, the number nine bus had a stop fifty metres from the home's entrance. Already, Melissa felt she'd found her aunt's future home.

The matron, a smiling, rosy-cheeked woman in her fifties, put Melissa at ease. 'Miss Grouwer, Green Gables is not a hospital; it's a home, and we try to make it a family home where the residents are happy, and we care for them. So relax and think of the tenants and staff as family members.

'The director will meet you at 2 pm, and I hope you'll join us for lunch. Now, leave your bag in my office and put on this apron. The staff can wear their clothes of choice and have aprons in case of accidents. They wear white coats only when it's strictly necessary. Now, let's walk around the gardens and follow with the interior. We'll visit a resident's room if they're in the lounge; privacy is important. They are not patients or ill; best thought of as wearing out.'

Melissa had already decided but dutifully walked the gardens and visited the kitchens, dispensary, and bedrooms. Then the matron surprised her, 'Miss Grouwer, if you would join the group in the lounge and then go with them to lunch in the dining room, I've some things to do. I'll collect you when the director arrives.'

Melissa was delighted with what she saw and with the smiling young woman introduced by the matron. 'Miss Grouwer, this is Annie. She'll show you around. I must go.'

'Annie, call me Melissa.'

'That's much easier. What are your first impressions?'

'The home is superb, but I'm surprised at the number of men on the staff and that mixed group at the big table.'

'Many of the men prefer male caregivers. Sharing intimate matters with a woman disturbs them. Most of the residents at that table have lost the use of their legs but are otherwise normal. Cerebral palsy, spinal injuries, sclerosis, and stroke; there are multiple causes. They are adults with full mental faculties and upper-body strength. We encourage them to dress for meals and join each other.

'They give lectures about their interests and read widely. We love them, mainly as they help to feed the residents who cannot manage a spoon. Many are volunteer residents, preferring life here to alone with a part-time caregiver in an apartment.'

By the end of lunch, Melissa had found a fascinating gentleman with a fund of travel stories. It stirred her emotions when he talked about the Arctic tundra and the solitude while watching the aurora borealis.

'Miss Grouwer, have you enjoyed your visit?'

'Yes, director, you have a wonderful home here. My Aunt Jane will be happy if you have a place. The question is, when?'

'Miss Grouwer, I offered the visit today because you said you were in a hurry. We have a bed that I expect will be vacant within the week, an advanced case of senility now in a terminal coma. I've looked at our waiting list, and the room would remain empty for two or three weeks before the top of the list took the bed. Juggling life and death is not easy, but another bed may be available for that applicant in time.

'I'll email you an access code to our application form. Complete and return it. I suggest you tick the box "Two years" by the question "Advance payment" and upload copies of your aunt's legal documents and the complete medical report. We also need confirmation that the doctor will sign the hospital discharge.

'Is your aunt capable of acting in a legal capacity?'

'She is. But she has signed a power of attorney, and I'm her legal guardian. My lawyer holds my power of attorney, so there will always be someone in London who can take a decision.'

'Excellent. I shall include our bank details and a reference in my email. Please deposit thirty per cent of the first year's fees, refundable if the directors refuse to accommodate her.

'I'll send the documents to the board. Two are doctors. They will, hopefully, approve the application, and I'll ask you to return here and sign the waivers and final contract. You only need to inform us of the day she must leave the hospital. We'll take care of the move.

We start caring as soon as she leaves the hospital room. We have a white minibus, not an ambulance.'

On the train back to London, Melissa called Mrs Drew. 'Nana, it's me.'

'Melissa, I've been waiting to hear from you. How is your aunt?'

'I've been busy this week, Nana, and have mixed news. Auntie Jane is awake and understands everything I say but has trouble talking. If you can come to the house tomorrow, as you did on Sundays, I can take you to see her. I'll tell you everything before we go. Would you like to come in the morning?'

'I'll take the same train I always did, Melissa. I should be there by 10:30 am.'

When she reached home, buoyed by relief, she went swimming. *I don't care if Tyron is there.* Nevertheless, it was a relief he wasn't. As she left, she wondered if he still had a job, so she asked the desk, 'I didn't see Tyron around. Has he left?'

'No, Miss Grouwer, it's his day off. He's back with his old girlfriend.'

Back home, she prepared for bed, anticipating Sam's call, but when it didn't come, she wondered where he was. The niggle became something else. *Is there a sexy client at the lodge?*

23

MELISSA STAYED IN BED AS SHE COULDN'T DO MUCH ELSE ON a Sunday morning. She needed to fetch the doctor's certificate, which she would do on Monday. She lay thinking of Sam and whether she could return to him. She convinced herself that Aunt Jane would go to Green Gables but began to feel that leaving her only days after she arrived in the care home was like a rat fleeing a sinking ship.

She finally left her bed to bathe and went downstairs to put the kettle on for Mrs Drew's arrival. In the kitchen, she looked around, aware of it for the first time, and decided that Mr Cotton had been entirely correct: it needed complete replacement, and the bleak feeling grew.

Mrs Drew arrived a few minutes late and used her key for the front door. Melissa heard her and called, 'In the kitchen, Mrs Drew.' Then she poured the boiling water into the teapot.

Mrs Drew had a large bag. 'Hello, Melissa. It seems ages since I was last in the house, but it's only been two weeks.'

'It seems ages for me, too.' Melissa asked, 'Do you still have milk and sugar?'

'Yes, but only one spoon. How's Jane?'

'She seems better every day, but that will slow down. Talking is the most difficult thing for her. She has paralysis of the left side, including her face and the left of her lips, but she seems cheerful.'

'When will she leave the hospital?'

'The doctor says Thursday or Friday, but that depends on the care home.'

'You've found one, then?'

'I hope so. It's in Sevenoaks, called Green Gables. If you visit her, I'll pay for the train and bus.'

'I'll visit every week, Melissa, as I've done for years.'

Melissa couldn't help feeling some relief. *That's one person who will visit her.*

'Shall we go for lunch, Nana?'

'No, Melissa, I've your favourite cottage pie in my bag and a cake for tea this afternoon. I'll put it in the oven to heat. I've also brought a can of peas.'

'Nana, you'll make me feel like a young girl again.'

'That's good. You need something to take your mind off your aunt.'

Jacqueline arrived by the back door with her boyfriend directly into the kitchen, so Melissa had to introduce Mrs Drew and Jacqueline, who introduced her boyfriend, Michael.

'Can we take a look around, Melissa?'

'Of course. I should leave the basement until last. I looked, and it's dirty down there.'

'Okay, Melissa. We'll go when Michael has seen enough.' Melissa saw Michael produce a notebook and pen as they left the kitchen.

During lunch, Melissa told Mrs Drew about the care home.

'Nana, it's visiting time in fifteen minutes. We should leave for the hospital. I have a car.'

At the hospital, Melissa showed Mrs Drew into the room first. The pleasure on her aunt's face when she saw Mrs Drew was illuminating. Melissa said hello and kissed her aunt. Mrs Drew took a chair and placed it next to the bed, sat down, and said, 'Now, Jane, tell me all about you, and I'll tell you what I've done since we last talked, like we always do.'

Melissa sat to one side, listening, and half an hour later realised, *I was never part of their world. I knew nothing about what they were discussing. I don't belong here.*

When visiting time ended, Melissa and Mrs Drew left to return for the tea and cake, and Melissa said, 'Nana, you made an enormous difference. I could see how happy she was to see you.'

'Well, we've been talking to each other for eighteen years, Melissa, and we like each other. Do you think she was talking better?'

'Yes, Nana, she was trying and improved.'

'Then I'm going to teach her to talk well. All she needs is encouragement.'

'That was a lovely cake, Nana.'

'You can keep the rest for tea with your secretary. Now, we have something to do.'

Surprised, Melissa asked, 'What, Nana?'

'We must take all your aunt's clothes from the cupboards, throw away what's old and unsuitable for a care home, and ensure that she has nice clothes to wear when she goes to the lounge and talks to the other residents.'

'Nana, I didn't think of it.'

'I'm not surprised, Melissa. You've had many other things to do. Now let's have a look.'

They went through Jane's wardrobe. After a short while, Mrs Drew expressed some concern.

'Melissa, the dresses are too tight, and the buttons will be problematic.'

'Nana, we'll throw all the clothes out. When could you come shopping with me?'

'Tuesday, I'll be here at 11 am. Can you take me to the station now?'

'Of course, Nana. And thank you.'

Sam's Sunday was arduous work. Most visible dung beetles had gone, and the dung was drying fast. After breakfast, he packed up his camp, moved the Landy close to the marked dung, and took out his signal recorder. Its battery would last three weeks. He picked a spot for it under a thick bush, then began to dig shallow trenches from the box of electronics to the dung piles. Into each, he laid a cable and then covered it. He took photos of everything. He sat at the first pile, pushed a flexible metal sheet under it, scraping the ground, then lifted the dung and placed it to one side. With a thin rod, he poked the earth to find holes where it had lain. After checking a tunnel was full of dung, he drilled a small hole on one side to a precise depth. Ten minutes later, he'd inserted one of his new thermocouples into the hole, connected ten wires, and covered the cable trench with a shallow layer of earth. He did the same to another tunnel, then replaced the dung pile, extracting the metal sheet.

Apart from a break for lunch, attended by another visit from the wild dogs, this time interested in what he was doing, Sam finished inserting thermocouples under the flagged piles, coupled them to his recorder in the afternoon, and finally covered it with a waterproof housing and branches to disguise it. He returned to the lodge after sunset.

Sam packed his gear away, completed his document to Melissa, writing about the dogs' visit during his experiment, and then went to join the rangers and guests for dinner.

One of the rangers asked, 'Sam, what were you doing out there?'

'Research: trying to establish humidity profiles of the ground.'

'Did the game disturb you?'

'No. A pack of dogs came to check me out yesterday morning, then left. They returned to lounge around at lunchtime and left after I went to my experimental site.'

'They didn't bother you walking alone?'

'Not at all. It's the dogs' territory, so they came to check me out and then adopted me. After I moved camp this morning, they found me at lunchtime and lay around watching while I worked.'

The guest seated beside Sam, incredulous, asked, 'Do you mean *wild* dogs?'

'Yes.'

'That must be a marvellous experience. I thought they were savage beasts. Are those tame?'

'Not tame, only normal. They don't attack humans unless threatened. You can think of them as a pack, a closely-knit team. You can't threaten one. If you attempt to do so, you're endangering the whole pack, and they are fast movers.'

'We haven't seen any. Do you have photos?'

'Seeing them on a game drive is an accident. They move so fast you can't catch them. I parked in their territory, and they came to me, but it could have been days before they returned. I'll show you the photos tomorrow night after dinner and give a short lecture.'

After dinner, he told Melissa where he'd been and sent his story about the dogs with attached photos.

> My darling Melissa,
>
> I've been in the bush researching since Friday night and have found some friends. Included are the story and photos. You would love them. They talk like birds. As you can do San clicks, you can try to speak to them. I'll be giving a lecture about them tomorrow after dinner.
>
> Love, Sam.

He clicked 'send' and went to the bathroom. Then his phone rang, and he had to dash out naked.

When Sam didn't call after Melissa was ready for bed, she decided to call herself. The thought, like a black cloud, was hurtful. *I must know if he has another woman and doesn't want me back.*

Sam answered, 'Hello, my darling.'

His voice and words banished the black cloud. *He called me darling.* 'Sam, do you have a sexy woman I don't know about?'

'Mel, I've two, but not the human type. I sent an email moments ago to tell you.'

'Tap the video button, Sam; it's my turn to check you're alone.'

He did, scanned the room, and she said, 'This existential thing seems to work both ways; you're naked.'

'You caught me in the bathroom, Mel. Has my email arrived?'

'Hang on, I'll check....'

'Yes, Sam.'

'Then read it and call me back.'

A few minutes later, Sam's phone rang.

'Sam, that's a lovely story; you might be a great writer.'

'It's for you, Mel. You can rewrite it.'

'Only if you'll take me to see them, Sam. Why only two girl-friends?'

'Wild dog packs have three times as many males as females, Mel. I'll explain it to you when you see them.'

'I was worried you didn't want me back when you didn't call. I can't compete with wild dogs.'

'Mel, every day I want you back with me. It gets worse daily. How is Aunt Jane?'

'I'll send an email, Sam. I think everything will be okay, but keep your fingers crossed. Bye, my love.'

'Bye, darling.'

They both slept soundly that night.

24

· · · · ·

FOR MELISSA, IT APPEARED THAT TIME RUSHED BY. SHE LET Jacqueline in at 8:30 am, handed her the key to the front door, and said, 'I've taken the spare back door key. Please take this and have a locksmith make five duplicates. One is for you and send one to my lawyer. I'm going to the hospital to see the doctor.'

She had to wait over an hour before the doctor came. While she waited, she told her aunt about the Hadza and how she'd lived with them.

'You love it there.'

'Yes, Auntie, I do.' Melissa's eyes lit up when she thought of Sam, and her aunt could see it.

'Then you must return, Melissa.'

'I don't want to leave you alone, Auntie.'

'Melissa, I'm an old woman who's lived her life. I'll be happy with the time I have left in the care home, and Mrs Drew will visit me as she has done for years. You must live your life. Go, and send me photographs.

'I'm looking forward to seeing them. Make me proud of you.'

'I will, Auntie, I will.'

The doctor came, checked on Aunt Jane, promised to email a medical report that afternoon and said, 'I'll have to sign a release by Saturday, Miss Grouwer. Can you manage that?'

'I'm sure I will, doctor. I've asked for Thursday.'

Melissa returned to the house, filled in the application form, paid the deposit, and downloaded the medical report, copies of her power of attorney, and her aunt's birth certificate. Then she waited an hour and called Mr Carington.

'Hello, Miss Grouwer.'

'Hello, Mr Carington. I've done everything you asked. Can you check your email and tell me if anything is missing?'

'I've already done so. It's complete and will be with the directors tomorrow morning first thing. If you can, allow for a visit to sign a contract on Wednesday. The directors should let me know by tomorrow night.'

'Certainly, Mr Carington. Thank you.'

Mrs Drew came on Tuesday as she promised, and by the day's end, they had bought a suitcase and filled it with new clothes.

'Is that enough, Nana?'

'I'm sure it is. Jane won't need shoes, and we have warm socks and slippers, vests to keep her chest warm, blouses and cardigans with Velcro on the front so she doesn't have to pull them over her head, woollen skirts with an elastic waistband and panties big enough to wear over a nappy.

'I've done this before, Melissa; for my mother and a neighbour.'

Melissa reflected, *I still have lots to learn. I would never have thought of this alone.*

'Nana, is there anything else I should do?'

Mrs Drew frowned, then said, 'Melissa, if she can have some decorations and photos in her room, you could take them to the care home. Why not ask Jane what she wants?'

'I'll do that, Nana. Thank you.'

Melissa went to Sevenoaks on Wednesday, signed all the papers, and asked. 'Now, when can you collect my aunt?'

'The incumbent passed on last night, the funeral services have the room today, and the cleaners will sterilise the room tomorrow. I suggest Saturday, for there's less traffic.'

'Can you call her doctor and tell him? He'll sign the release for Saturday morning.'

'Of course.'

Melissa gave instructions for a bank transfer. *I should be ecstatic. I'll soon return to Sam. Why don't I feel it?*

'Good morning, Jacqueline.'

'Good morning, Melissa, I have an estimate from my boyfriend and the quote for the alarm system. He says all the work must follow a sequence, and because of piping and wiring, the walls and ceiling will need repainting. He said the electrical system doesn't conform to current regulations, so he must replace it. He says four months to completion.'

'I must go to the hospital now. I must tell them my aunt is leaving on Saturday and ask for medicine prescriptions, but when I return, you can show me.'

'Okay, I'm going to fetch carpet samples.'

'Now, Jacqueline, let's look at the refurbishment.'

'Here are the estimates, Melissa. The items are in execution order, starting with emptying the basement. There's a price and time for each.'

Melissa looked down the list and the total price and said, 'I must ask my lawyer to approve this, Jacqueline. I'll do that tomorrow. Are you willing to be the manager?'

'My boyfriend says he'll help, so yes. Can you tell me what colour walls and carpet you want?'

'White, or off-white, with grey carpets and tiles in the kitchens and bathrooms. Do you have the samples?'

Jacqueline lifted a carpet sample book to the table. 'Michael said number six, Melissa. I prefer number seven because it has a black thread.'

Melissa looked through the samples. All were grey. She said, 'I like number ten. It reminds me of an African sky at sunset with the stars shining.'

'It's lovely, Melissa, but you wanted a plain carpet.'

'I did, but now number ten has hooked me.'

'Then that's what I'll buy.'

Melissa sent another email to Sam and told him everything that had happened.

Sam read the email the following morning before leaving on the morning game drive.

Melissa has done everything but doesn't say when she expects to return. Is she hesitating?

When Jacqueline arrived, Melissa had an update for her. 'Jacqueline,

I have my lawyer's approval to proceed with the refurbishment. You can send all the bills to him for payment, and if you want my advice, you can email or call me if I'm not here.'

'I'll have the basement emptied next week. The contractor says he'll do it on Saturday because of the traffic. I'll take care of everything, Melissa.'

'Before that, please see my lawyer. He'll pay your agency fee but expects you to ask for a bonus and something for your boyfriend. Sort that out before you start.'

'Okay, Melissa, I'll do that on Monday.'

'Fine, I'm going to the hospital, but first, I must visit my aunt's bedroom.'

With her aunt once again, she asked, 'Auntie, you're moving to a new room tomorrow, and you can have your decorations or pictures. What would you like me to take for you?'

It wasn't easy prompting her aunt with the list of things she'd seen in her room, but an hour later, she left with a shorter list. As the first item was a recent photo of herself, she had to visit a photographer and left with a framed picture. She then bought two tins of her aunt's favourite shortbread biscuits and returned home.

With her aunt's move looming larger, Melissa placed her suitcase of new clothes in the lounge. Then she went upstairs to collect the pictures and mementoes on her list.

Jacqueline left, and with nothing more to do, Melissa could feel the adrenaline dropping and fear rising. Tomorrow, after her aunt moved, what came next? Could she return to Sam? She looked at her watch and decided to send a WhatsApp message, the first she'd ever sent.

> Hello darling, my aunt is moving tomorrow, and everything is ready. Call me tomorrow night. All my love, Mel.

Her mind released the accumulated fatigue from three weeks of intense effort, and the fear drove her to her bedroom, where she'd hidden from the world for years. She slept – for eleven hours. She'd left her phone in the lounge, so she didn't hear it ring.

Sam read her WhatsApp message when he woke from his afternoon nap and called, but when she didn't answer, he wondered where she was. *She never said when she would be back.*

Aunt Jane moved on schedule, and Melissa followed the white minibus. At the care home, once her aunt settled into her room, the matron said, 'Miss Grouwer, I know you would like to come and see your aunt tomorrow, but we usually advise a new resident's family and friends to delay doing so for a week to give the resident time to become familiar with Green Gables and meet the staff.'

'I may not be in England in a week, matron. Can I stay for an hour and say goodbye, just in case? Her friend Mrs Drew will come in a week on Sunday.'

'Of course.'

The returning weekend traffic was slow, so Melissa arrived home late.

At home, she felt lost, with nothing remaining undone. Fear tempered what should have been euphoria, the fear of new choices and decisions she would need to make. Then Sam called.

'Hello, Sam. Aren't you doing a game drive tonight?'

Sam decided she was tired, 'Hello, my darling, did it go well today?'

'Yes, Aunt Jane is in the home and is comfortable. I'm feeling low and lost now that I've done everything.'

'Then return here, darling. That will cheer you up. When will you come?'

'I don't know. I can't visit my aunt for a week. The home says she must settle in. It might be after that.'

Sam felt a deep pain in his gut. *She's not returning.*

'Darling, you're tired. Go to bed and sleep. Tomorrow, the world will be brighter. Call me when you can.'

'Okay, good night, Sam.'

'Good night, dearest.'

Melissa slept late on Sunday. There was no reason to leave her bed; even the zoo didn't attract her. After lunch, Melissa went swimming.

After thirty lengths of the pool, the millrace in her head had become a tranquil pool. So she climbed out. Tyron was there.

'Miss Grouwer, you're early today.'

'Yes, Tyron, this may be my last time. I've lots to do.'

'Problems with your aunt?'

'No, she's now settled in a care home. They'll look after her for as long as she lives, and her affairs are all in a lawyer's hands.'

'That's a pain and a waste of money. I think the old folks should die off and let the younger people live their lives. They've had their innings.'

His words shocked Melissa. *Tyron's an animal. Worse, he's a selfish animal. He hasn't evolved beyond that. Sam was right: humans are still evolving, but many have a long way to go.*

'Goodbye, Tyron. Remember when you're old to jump off a bridge.'

Then Melissa thought, *Maybe when I'm old, I'll walk out to meet a lion or hyena. But I'll live first.*

25

·····

WHEN MELISSA WOKE ON MONDAY MORNING, SHE REMEM-
bered it had been three weeks since the phone call telling her about
her aunt. She'd done everything possible; her aunt was comfortable,
and Mrs Drew would visit every Sunday. Melissa had to think of Sam
and what she would do. Returning to Africa was a massive magnet,
but deserting the only woman who had come forward to look after
her when her parents died still seemed like a betrayal of something
fundamental.

The idea that she could now write undisturbed made her go to the
library after breakfast. She did have a lingering reflection. *I would
have worked at home before. Do I now need people?*

The same librarian was sitting at the supervisor's desk, with the
little nameplate, 'Ms A Tancred', and email address below it. She
recognised Melissa. '*Melissa!* I haven't seen you in ages. Where did
you get the suntan?'

'In Africa, Ms Tancred. I took your advice and went.'

'And have you written anything for your book?'

'A little, but I had to return because my aunt had a stroke. Now
that she's settled in a care home, I want to continue writing.'

'Melissa, you went because I told you to, so you owe me another
example of your writing. Can you send me something?'

'I do have a story. I'll fire up my computer and send it.'

'Thanks, Melissa.'

Melissa found a vacant chair at a table, sent the now-corrected mongoose story, and then started to search through her notes to decide what she should try next. Nothing stood out, and nothing stirred her emotions. Melissa saw the monkey story, read it through, and decided it needed nothing more. Then, she remembered she'd promised to read it to Sam and drifted into a reverie of memories.

Amelia Tancred had library visitors to deal with, those who wanted to borrow, others to return, and even more who wanted guidance on where to find a reference book. It wasn't until the numbers dropped as lunchtime approached that she had the time to open Melissa's email and the attached story.

No one was watching. If someone had been, they might have noticed a faraway look creep into her eyes, and when she finished reading, they would have seen her staring, unseeing, into another world for several minutes. Then she shook her head and looked at Melissa, a frown creasing on her forehead. She stood and walked over.

'Melissa, have you had lunch?'

After thinking deeply about nothing for at least five minutes, Melissa looked up, startled. 'No.'

'Please come with me. I'm going to the canteen.'

Following orders from an older woman had been a habit since Melissa's childhood. They selected fish and chips with veg from the counter and sat at a corner table.

'Melissa, I need to tell you something. I hope you won't mind.'

'Ms Tancred, you helped me once. I won't mind.'

'Amelia, Melissa. Please call me Amelia; I think I've enough girl left to feel pleasure when someone uses my name, although no one has for many years.'

'Then go ahead, Amelia.'

'I've read your mongoose story. It belongs alongside epic poems that can take the reader into realms that ordinary people rarely reach. I shall read it whenever I feel low for the inspiration it gave me.'

'Thank you, Amelia. Another person has said much the same.'

'Sam?'

Melissa had forgotten Sam was in the story. Startled again, she replied, 'Yes.'

'Then I'll tell you something and ask for something else.

'Return, Melissa, to the place that generates the enormous love you felt when you wrote that story and the man you love intensely, and then write more. Every time you write something, I ask that you send it to me, to an ageing woman who has spent her lifetime in the cool darkness of a library, who has read about people and places but has never seen them. Your story took me to Africa, Melissa. I was there. I felt a warm relationship with the mongoose mother. Before I shuffle off, I want to experience the places and things you'll describe. I shall keep them as my treasures and read them repeatedly.'

'I want to return, Amelia, but I feel I'm betraying my aunt. I returned because she had a stroke. I'm her only relative. She looked after me when my parents died when I was nine. She's now in a care home and will never come out. There's nothing I can do, but the feeling of betrayal is terrible.'

Amelia Tancred said nothing for a minute or two.

'Melissa, feeling like that is understandable. Is it because you're leaving her alone, even though you can do nothing?'

'I think so, although our housekeeper, Mrs Drew, will visit her every week. But Mrs Drew is retired and aged; I don't know how long she'll be able to visit.'

'Melissa, if you return to Sam, I promise I'll visit your aunt once a week, on Saturday or Sunday, check on how she's doing and how the home cares for her, and send you an email update. I shall read her every story you send to me.'

'Why would you do that?'

'I would do much more to receive more stories from you.'

'I'll think about it, Amelia.'

'Hearts don't think, Melissa, they can only do. Heads should follow them. Go.'

Melissa remembered her thought when leaving the pool: *maybe when I'm old, I'll walk out to meet a lion or hyena. But I'll live first.*

That was what triggered the decision. *Botswana is where my heart wants to be.*

Melissa went home and called Peter's home number. Sally answered.

'Hello, Sally Reynolds speaking.'

'Hello, Sally. It's Melissa, Sam's friend; I hoped to speak to Peter.'

'*Melissa!* How lovely of you to call. When are you returning?'

Melissa was surprised. *She wants me back.* 'That's what I want to arrange.

'Is Sam at the lodge?'

'Of course, Peter says he's moping around and is regressing to the old Silent Sam. He needs you – come quickly.'

'If I come now, can we pick up the trip we were doing where we left off?'

'Melissa, you have friends here that you've never met. JJ, Martha, and Coenraad's wife, Annelie, keep asking about your return. So do Hennie at Tuli and Gordon at Mashatu. Between us, we'll make sure it happens.'

'Who is Coenraad?'

'Sam's friend at Lion Sands; you haven't met him.'

Melissa remembered Sam's first email in which he had told her where he had stopped on the way from Gaborone.. *So many people like me?* She was astounded, but it also made her feel warm inside.

'Sally, I'll check on flights. I can try for a seat on one leaving tomorrow and arriving on Wednesday.' Melissa had another idea, 'Could I take a taxi to Ranzi, and JJ could give me room three like the last time? Then we can start exactly where we stopped if Sam arrives by Wednesday night.'

'Call me in an hour. I'll have the info.'

An hour later, Melissa called. 'Hi Sally, I have a seat tomorrow or Wednesday night, arriving at 1 pm the following day.'

'Tomorrow's fine, Melissa. JJ has your room available for Wednesday, and a surprise: Coenraad will be there with Annelie; she's pregnant and visiting the gynae here for a scan. They'll be there on Wednesday. If Peter were here, we'd come too. It should be a great party.

'Peter says Sam will follow orders and drive there to arrive between 5:30 and 6 pm.

'I'll have a taxi waiting for you at the airport to take you to Ranzi.'

Peter walked over to Sam's cottage to which he had seen Sam retreat after the evening drive and dinner. He'd struggled with what to say to Sam and decided not to raise his hopes; anything could happen.

'Hello, Sam. How was the drive this morning?'

'It went well; we were lucky. I took a turn through the wild dog territory, and by chance, we saw them – the same pack that visits me when I camp there on my days off.'

'Are they friends yet?'

'If you judge by the time they spend sniffing around, they are. They come, see it's me, and leave. It's their territory, so they check all intruders. I never leave anything edible lying around to attract them.'

'That's great. If they're friendly, you could add the place to your routes.

'By the way, I have a new client for you, or at least JJ has. He wants you to pick up a client from Ranzi, one who wants to see the Pans and the Okavango.'

'Why me?'

'I asked, and he said you're the only one he knows who's qualified, for the client is not a newcomer to Africa.'

'Do you know any more than that?'

'JJ said he would know after the client arrived. So you're flying blind, Sam.'

'When?'

'Wednesday. I said you couldn't leave today or tomorrow but could drive there on Wednesday. He's expecting you between 5 and 6 pm.'

'Okay, I can do that. The garage can service my Landy tomorrow, and I'll pack all my gear. Is it one or two clients?'

'He said one, and if he's out driving with the client, you must head for cottage three. He said you know which one that is, and he'll put beer in the fridge for you.'

'Okay. I have the drive tonight and a morning drive tomorrow, so I'll need help loading the Landy after lunch tomorrow. Can someone else take my clients to Kasane?'

'Sure, Sam. I'll have the kitchen stock the fridge box and supply food. What else do you need?'

'If I think of something, I'll tell you. If I drive to the Okavango, ask JJ to have my flashing beacon ready. I lent it to him when I passed through with Melissa.' The mention of her name brought a twinge of pain. *If only she would return.*

Melissa had a full day to prepare for her departure. She started by calling Amelia Tancred.

'Hello, Amelia, it's Melissa. I'm calling to tell you I'm returning to Africa and to give you my aunt's address.'

'That's marvellous, Melissa; I know you'll be successful. Send me the address by email; it's safer than copying it onto a scrap of paper.'

'Amelia, where do you live?'

'In a small flat in Ealing. It's a long commute, but I have some countryside nearby.'

'Amelia, my house will stand empty without me, hopefully for years. I've someone refurbishing it. I'll send you the house address and the contact address of the lawyer responsible for it and give him instructions. If you look at it and fancy a bit of adventure, you can live there and look after it. The lawyer will pay all the bills. You don't have to move permanently; you can use it during the week if the commute is shorter.'

'Melissa, it will be fun even if I don't accept your offer. And when you publish your first book, I'll make sure every library in England buys several copies.'

'Thanks, Amelia. I imagine if I do publish, I'll need to spend a week or two in England at book signings. I'll tell you when.'

Melissa packed her case. She left behind most of the clothes she'd bought during the last six weeks in bags in the cupboard. Then she went shopping. Sam's dream lens, with a camera in a leather bag, became her second piece of hand luggage, and she bought some tight shorts and tee shirts. *It's warm in Botswana; I'll try to be brave enough to wear them.*

After handing him a fat envelope, Sam's clients left the following afternoon. He added the contents to his savings for a new lens and continued his meticulous preparation of the Landy and its contents, including his rifle in its secure box and his pistol in his under-seat box, where he found Melissa's boots once again. He almost took them out, but couldn't. Hope still flourished. That night, he sent Melissa another email.

> My darling Mel,
>
> I have another client whom I must collect from Ranzi. Driving through the Okavango will take a week or more. I'll be out of phone and Wi-Fi range. If you need me for something, use the satphone number. My memories of you beside me will go with me every kilometre of the way.
>
> I'm hoping that you have sorted out everything in London.
>
> All my love, Sam.

Melissa didn't receive it; she'd switched off the Wi-Fi.

26

• • • • •

TRYING HARD TO KEEP CALM, FOR SHE FELT MOUNTING EXCITE-
ment, Melissa had forced herself to follow every step on her check
sheet. She'd unplugged all appliances and closed the main water tap
and gas. Mrs Drew would come on Saturday to take all the food and
switch off the refrigerator. Melissa stood in the hallway surrounded
by her bags a few minutes before the taxi arrived at 5 pm. She'd
never felt such emotion. Her aunt had been at the door to say goodbye at each of her earlier departures, but this time, Melissa had no
return date. It felt to Melissa as if she were about to plunge into a
void, but then she recollected, *Sam will be there.* When the doorbell
rang, she whispered. 'Goodbye, Aunt Jane. Thank you. Wish me
luck.'

Sam rose at 4:30 am, drank a coffee, showered, drank another cup,
and then drove out at 5:15. He estimated he would arrive at Ranzi at
5:30 pm, after a break for lunch and a fuel stop in Francistown, plus
a couple of stops for the call of nature. In a heavily loaded Landy, he
felt that was pretty good going.

The flight arrived fifteen minutes early, and Melissa was one of the
first passengers to exit the customs area, pushing a trolley with her
suitcase, three items of hand baggage, and six kilograms of

Ethiopian coffee, a surprise gift from Ethiopian Airlines in response to her complaint about the quality of the coffee on her first flight. She didn't make a beeline for the coffee shop, as the coffee at breakfast was excellent.

Melissa looked along the line of greeters waving placards, trying to spot her name and the taxi driver. As her eyes passed the last one, she saw a tanned woman with a wide straw hat. Her long pants and loose khaki shirt didn't match with an international airport. Melissa looked curiously, then noticed the bulge. The woman smiled broadly. She smiled in return, and the woman stepped forward and, now grinning, held out both hands and said, 'You must be Melissa.'

Then Melissa replied, 'I am,' then, guessing, added, 'Annelie.'

Annelie hugged her as a deep bass voice next to her said, 'No, thank you. I don't need your help to carry the baggage.'

Melissa turned and had to raise her head. At a metre ninety-two, Coenraad, with twinkling blue eyes, had stepped up to intervene when a man with 'porter' on his shirt had taken possession of Melissa's trolley with its baggage.

'Melissa, this is my husband, Coenraad. He looks terrifying but like Sam he's a real softy.'

Melissa smiled, 'Pleased to meet you, Coenraad, and you, Annelie. What a wonderful surprise. Sally said you were here to see the gynae, so I didn't think I would meet you before tonight. How did you recognise me?'

'Sally said, "A beautiful woman with no makeup dressed like me." When I saw you, I knew. Now, let's go to the pickup. We must reach Ranzi before Sam.'

They did, and Melissa learnt that Annelie was an extrovert who would talk about herself, Coenraad, and Lion Sands without a pause.

Melissa asked about the bulge and discovered it might be a boy, but it was too early to be sure. By the time Coenraad stopped before cottage three, Melissa felt she'd come home, and adored both Annelie and Coenraad. Melissa also learnt two important things. The first was revealed when she asked how Annelie and Coenraad had met.

'At a folk dance on a farm. He invited me to visit his lodge, and I went with a girlfriend and found him fascinating. He hardly talked to us, though, although he could talk about the game. All the rangers are like that, big silent men. I couldn't forget him, so I took him up on his offer to visit his lodge. I went with another girlfriend. It was a poor decision for her; she was unwell and cried off the last three game drives, so I was alone with Coenraad. We didn't drive much, walked a little, then sat and watched, not speaking. That was when I learnt that I didn't want to live the shallow, hectic life in a city but lost in the country's peace. When he didn't try to kiss me, I told him to. That was it.'

I told Sam to kiss me. He and Coenraad must be the same.

'I returned alone and learnt these guys don't chase women, at least not in the country. I had to ask him to marry me. We wangled the job running Lion Sands three months after buying a majority share.'

Coenraad added a comment. 'She didn't ask me: she *told* me to marry her, or else.'

The second important thing she learned came when Melissa asked Annelie about raising her child. 'I'll do just like all the local women. It seems to work fine, but I'm collecting medicines and learning how to use them.'

'What about schooling?'

'I've seven years to start a school, so I hope to give my kids a good primary education. After eleven, if we aren't near enough to a high school, they'll be boarders in Francistown.'

Coenraad carried Melissa's bags into the cottage, and Annelie said, 'Sam should be here in less than an hour. Take a shower and be ready to surprise him. Coenraad and I are in cottage nine, but come to the lounge with Sam when you're ready. JJ should be back by 7:30 pm. Martha is preparing a feast for us.'

Melissa put the camera and computer bags on the table, and pushed her large holder bag into the cupboard. She took a shower, her first in thirty hours. Then, instead of dressing, she smiled secretly and sat on the wooden bathroom chair, towel wrapped around her, to think. The butterflies began to swarm in her tummy. While waiting, she replayed her memories of Sam's emails, and questions rose in her mind. *It's so easy to say things in an email. Is it true? Will he be thrilled to see me? Or does he remember someone different and will he be shocked to find I'm different to his memories?* The butterflies began to rock and roll. When she heard the Landy stop in front, she stood, hung the towel on the chair, and stepped back into the shower.

Sam drew to a stop in front of cottage three. When JJ didn't appear, he assumed JJ was out with the client and stepped onto the veranda where he removed his dust-covered veldskoen shoes and socks, and unbuttoned his shirt. With the roar of the Landy engine still ringing in his ears, he had one aim: a hot shower. He pushed open the cottage door, shrugged off the shirt that dropped to the floor, shucked off his shorts and boxers as a pair, stepped forward to the bathroom door – and heard the shower.

Hell, there's someone here. Sam knocked, forgetting he was nude.

'Are you my guide?'

Sam felt struck by lightning. His legs trembled, and he almost collapsed. Then, with a flood of joy filling him, he threw open the door to see Melissa grinning at him, naked under the spray of the open shower. He leapt forward and wrapped her in his arms. With Melissa's head on his chest, they stood for over a minute, and then Sam said, 'You said that after I grabbed you.'

'Well, I wasn't naked or in a shower, so this is different. And you're still good at grabbing.' Then, still holding tightly, Melissa said, 'Turn, Sam, you smell dusty. I'll scrub your back; you can do the rest while I dry my hair.'

Ten minutes later, dressed only in underwear, Sam found beers and Appletisers in the small fridge, opened one of each, and he and Melissa sat side by side on the veranda couch as the sun dropped to the horizon.

When Melissa said, 'Sam, you look handsome in boxers,' Sam answered, 'I bought them because you said I should, but now I like them. Did you take a taxi from Gabs?'

'Annelie and Coenraad met me at the airport and brought me here.'

'They're here?'

'Yes, in cottage nine. Sally organised it. I think they're great. Annelie went to visit the gynae.'

Sam put his arm around her. 'Mel, how's the book?'

Melissa looked down at her lap. 'I've written nothing more. I was busy, and when I tried, I couldn't.'

Sam remembered. *That gesture is still there; she may have changed, but she's still the same underneath.* 'You promised to read me the monkey story. Please read it to me after dinner. How long will you stay this time?'

Melissa remembered what Annelie had said. 'Sam, I asked Peter to send you to complete our original trip. If I can kickstart the writing again, then when we arrive back, I'll stay with you until I finish the book. You can continue to work as a ranger.'

Neither Sam nor Melissa had ever experienced such a dinner. It lasted two hours, and the pleasure the six felt seemed to fill the space around the table. Sam, JJ, and Coenraad spoke little – an answer to a question, an amusing comment, or a hilarious comparison – but Sam felt the love shown by Coenraad when he looked at Annelie, and JJ's pride in Martha when admiration for the food she presented overflowed. He didn't realise they could also see how much he adored Melissa and how they kept looking at each other with surreptitious glances.

Then Martha said, 'JJ, you must hold my hand.'

He replied. 'Why, my love. Do you feel lonely?'

Martha grinned, 'Yes, Coenraad keeps holding Annelie's hand, and Sam hardly allows Melissa to eat. I feel left out.'

It brought gales of laughter, and Melissa thought, *Real people with real feelings. No embarrassment.*

The conversation moved through several subjects. The women talked about the problems they had met living in remote areas and their pride and happiness when they solved them. Sam felt they did so to encourage Melissa. Melissa listened to the stories and thought, *They aren't alone like I was in a city; they love and help each other. I would love to be part of their life.*

Over a delicious dessert that Melissa learnt was a *melktert*, JJ asked, 'When will you leave, Sam?'

'No rush, JJ. If you don't need the cottage, we'll go after lunch. It's about four hours to Orapa. We'll spend the night there and take three or four days to cross the pan to Gweta via Jack's Camp.'

'That's fine. The cottage is empty. Spend another day if you wish.'

Annelie interjected, 'Melissa, Orapa is a giant diamond mine. There's a jewellery shop there. Don't let the bear beside you buy a massive diamond ring. It's the kind of thing they believe they must do, and we don't wear them. Tell him there are far better presents.'

Sam stood up for himself, 'I won't, Annelie. I fancy the present Coenraad gave you.'

Another round of hilarity and affectionate teasing followed.

At 9 pm, the party ended. Melissa and Sam returned to their cottage, and Melissa asked, 'Can we sit outside again for a while.'

'Of course.'

They sat in silence, and Melissa listened. 'There's a fox out there with its vixen.' She paused, then said, 'I learnt something tonight.'

'What?'

'There are places with people who belong in those places. I felt the same thing when I lived with the Hadza. Their piece of the world was where they belonged, as the fox and its vixen belong here, to this land, and each other. Tonight, I felt that everyone around the table belonged and that it brings happiness and contentment that people who don't belong will never feel, no matter how great their wealth or fame.'

'Mel, that's a profound statement. I can only say that having you beside me made me happier than I've been since you left, and you belong here with us. Let's go to bed. You go first.'

After Melissa came from the bathroom in her nightie, the same one he had seen her in when she first arrived, Sam followed. When he came out, she was in bed. He undressed, took his pyjama shorts from his rucksack, and saw her camera bag on the table. 'Mel, this looks like a camera bag on the table. I didn't notice it before.'

'I'm not surprised. I was naked, and you couldn't look at anything else.'

'Why'd you buy it, and why's it so big?'

'That's our next project. But if you want to borrow it for research, you can.'

'What project?'

'I'll return to Baboon Rock and film the baboons settling for the night. I hope you'll come.'

'Mel, did you bring a low-light lens?'

'Have a look. There's a small camera for my use. I'm going to make a nude movie, and you're the star. I should have taken it out before you left the bathroom.'

Sam looked down. He'd forgotten again that he was naked. Excited, he said, 'I'll continue acting and have a look first.

'Mel, this is magnificent. It's the latest version, first available a month ago.'

'If you're pleased with it, come to bed and kiss me.'

Five minutes later, Melissa said, 'Okay, let's sleep. You must drive tomorrow, and I must read you the monkey story.'

Sam fell asleep happy. Melissa cuddled like the last night they had spent in the cottage.

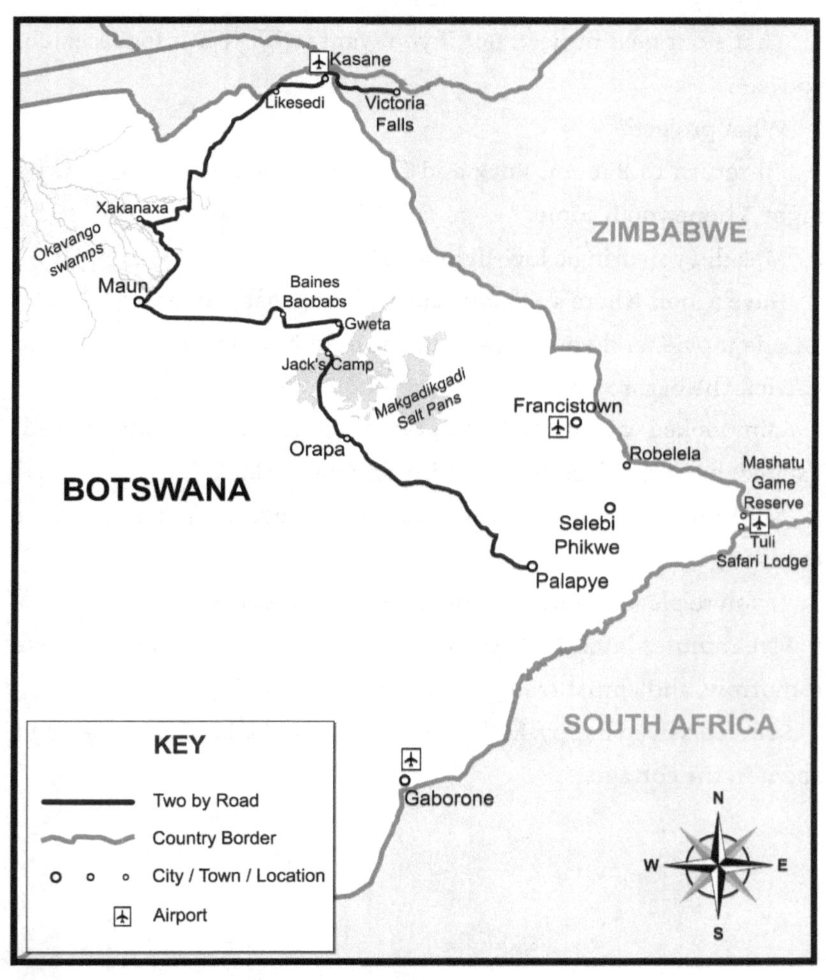

Melissa's Tour of Botswana After her Return from the United Kingdom

27

· · · · ·

AFTER SAM AND MELISSA ATE BREAKFAST WITH COENRAAD AND Annelie, Sam went to help Coenraad load his pickup, and Annelie went with Melissa to cottage three. Melissa knew Annelie had something to say privately.

'Melissa, I'm going to be open with you. If you and Sam have sex, ask him to marry you. I told you these men don't ask. It's because they believe they have nothing to offer. If you aren't involved sexually, I'll extend what I said. The lodges all have a rule: the rangers have orders not to have sex with clients. The instruction exists to avoid inundation by frustrated women looking for sex away from prying eyes. There are only two exceptions. First, a woman must ask for sex directly, and it must be a one-night stand. Second, if refusal could bring negative publicity if she slates the lodge, it's sufficient reason to break the rule.

'I'm telling you this because I know Rangers like Sam well enough to believe he hasn't had sex with you, and he won't unless you ask, although I'm convinced he loves you.'

'Thanks, Annelie. I've wondered why Sam hasn't tried. What you said explains it.'

'Then I'm glad I spoke to you. When you feel it's right, ask Sam to marry you, and then ask him to make love to you.'

Melissa remembered the Hadza. 'Annelie, I lived with the San people of Tanzania for two weeks. They have no choice but to see each other naked every day. A woman makes a minimal bead costume, es-

225

pecially to invite a man when she's ready.'

'Then they are far more civilised than the people in the city. Can you speak their click language?'

'Yes, I know many words, but every clan uses different words, so it's difficult.'

'It's only a few hours from Likesedi to Lion Sands. Please come to see us when Sam has time off. I meet many women but have few friends.'

Melissa was surprised, not at what Annelie said, but at the thought that she was a *friend*, and Sally and Martha too.

After Sam and Melissa waved goodbye to Annelie and Coenraad, Sam said, 'Now, read me the monkey story.'

They sat on the veranda, Sam closed his eyes, and Melissa read. She asked when she finished, 'So, what do you think?'

'Read it once more.'

...

'Okay, it's good, but not as good as the mongoose. Read me the first paragraph.'

...

'Now, describe to me, without reading, the place, the lighting, the shadows, the trees, the leaves, the colours, whatever you want. Shut your eyes and remember: describe it, and ignore the monkey.'

Melissa closed her eyes and, two minutes later, began to speak...

'Mel, what you just said is beautiful and far more than you have in the story. Now close your eyes again: describe the monkey when he lifted the mug.'

She did, and Sam said. 'Stay there; I must fetch something from the Landy.'

Sam returned with a small handheld tape recorder and four batteries. 'Let me put these batteries in, then take the recorder, shut your eyes, remember, and speak into the mike. Tell the story from the beginning, just like you've told me. You can press the pause button each time you want to describe a new scene, and when you've remembered it, speak on.'

'Why do you have the recorder?'

'Before I had the camera and sound gear, I had to record my research observations. Things can happen too quickly to remember the details later. I still use it when I need to.'

Thirty minutes later, Melissa finished, and Sam said, 'Now, use the playback, type it, and correct it. We have three hours before lunch. I'll leave you to do it. I must pack the Landy and see JJ.'

While Sam packed the Landy, JJ came carrying a long pole and a box. 'Sam, here's your beacon. I've changed the stick. It's a collapsible swimming pool brush handle. Much lighter. The beacon is in the box. Shall I put the handle in the fishing rod tube?'

'Thanks, JJ.'

'What route will you take from Orapa? The road to Mokoboxane or the airport track north of the Ryasana pan?'

'The airport track, then north to Madista.'

'Someone from Jack's came through Madista a week ago. He spent three days stuck in the river. They're still closed. I suggest you go to Mopipi, then northeast to Jack's. Are you going on to Baines from Gweta?'

'That's the plan.'

'I called the Diamond Inn in Letlhakane; they have a room for you.'

'Thanks, JJ.'

'Okay, if you go to Xakanaxa, he pronounced it *"Zakahnakha"*, please give my regards to Petrus. It was my old lodge. Are you coming for lunch at 1 pm?'

'Yes, Melissa should have finished typing, and we'll leave afterwards.'

'I've finished. It needs a proofread, but it's as clean as possible.'

'Read it to me.'

Sam closed his eyes and laid back in his chair and listened to Melissa's voice.

When it was over, Sam opened his eyes. 'Melissa, I saw and felt everything in that story but could never have written those words and phrases to describe it. File it as approved by Sam. That monkey loved you. Then do the proofread that Tom told you about.'

'I'm going to send it to Amelia.'

'Who's she?'

'A librarian in England. I've promised her each story. I'll include the style sheet and ask her to proofread it. She's sixty-three and has never left the country. I'll tell you about her later. She'll make weekly visits to my aunt and has access to my house.'

'That's wonderful.' *Mel won't have a reason to rush back to England.*

Then Melissa told him, 'I'm going to keep this recorder available. This is a great method, although I'm not sure it will work with something new. I think I must write at least a framework first, as you told me, all the facts and sources properly sequenced.'

JJ and Martha joined them for lunch and after saying goodbye, they drove out.

The road was boring, and the wild game was sparse, although goats, chickens and dogs were plentiful. Due to the shortage of water and the density of the human population, they passed through multiple small roadside settlements and a few villages, and dipped in and out of Serowe, a small town.

Sam explained where they were going. 'Orapa is the biggest diamond mine in the world by area. There are four other mines there. When it first started mining, it was a closed security area with little water, so businesses supplying the mine opened in a nearby village called Letlhakane, where there was underground water. It's now the principal town where we'll stay. We can buy fresh food there and diamonds.'

'I don't want a diamond ring, Sam.'

'Okay, there's an alternative.'

Melissa was confused when she remembered what he'd said to Annelie.

Two hours after leaving Ranzi, Melissa asked, 'Sam, can we stop for a call of nature?'

'Okay, an abandoned road camp is a kilometre ahead, with a cleared area. We've some time to spare. We'll have a coffee, take a break and as I promised I'll teach you something about getting lost.'

Sam left the road and drove eight hundred metres to the cleared area. While he unpacked the folding table and chairs, Melissa walked twenty metres, checked for nasties, and relieved the pressure. Sam started a small fire, and Melissa boiled the water while Sam walked away. He returned with a stout stick about a metre long, and while she filtered the coffee, he carved one end to a sharp point and then walked away count-ing his steps. He returned after hammering the stick into the ground.

'How far did you go?'

'A hundred and ten paces, say a hundred metres.'

'What for?'

'Once we've had our coffee, I'll blindfold you, and you can walk to the stick.'

'Now, Mel, face the stick. Remember where it is. I'll blindfold you, and you must walk to it.

'Walk! I'll walk beside you. Stop if you think you've reached the stick.'

...

'Stop and take off the blindfold.'

'Where's the stick?'

'Behind you on the left.'

Melissa looked. 'I missed it by ten metres?'

'Yes, let's return. I wanted to prove that you can't walk in a straight line without seeing where you're going. The primary rule is if you don't know where you are and can't see where to go, don't move. The further you go, the further you'll be from where people search to find you.'

'Is there nothing that can help?'

'A compass, or a shadow from the sun that you can keep at the same angle, and at night, the stars can keep you to a straight line. You don't veer off so much if the wind is straight ahead or behind.'

'What about a path or a track?'

'That's worse. Tracks and roads zigzag, and soon you lose all sense of direction. So don't move.'

'That must be hard to do.'

'It is. But sit, wait until nightfall and the stars are there. I have a flashing strobe beacon on a pole. It's visible from about ten kilometres, with white and yellow flashes. If I walk away from the camp at night, I start it flashing. I could return to the camp area using the stars if it's clear, but I might walk past the camp only forty metres away and not see it. Then it's worse; I wouldn't know if the camp was ahead or behind.'

'Why tell me this, Sam?'

'We'll visit the salt pans, where there are no references like hills, and although the visibility is normally superb, if there's heat haze or a whirlwind that stirs up the fine dust, getting lost is possible. And the visibility can disappear in a minute. Remember always – don't move. I'll find you or wait until you see the beacon after nightfall.'

They arrived at Letlhakane. Sam fuelled the Landy at the first station, and then they checked in at the Diamond Inn.

'Wow, this place is super luxurious!'

'Mel, it's my first time here. I usually camp or pick a modest place.'

'So why are we here?'

'For you, to show you the odd places that exist. Socialites worldwide like to flash their diamonds and say they chose them at the diamond mine. So they come here to buy them. Every stone has a certificate saying, "Bought at the Orapa diamond mine", although I suspect most of the cut diamonds aren't from the Orapa mine. Imagine the added prestige when a woman says, "Yes, my dear, Hymie bought me the diamonds at the Orapa mine, and we had them mounted in Paris at the Place Vendome".'

Melissa chuckled, 'I've seen people like that in films. Are they real?

Can we change, go to the cocktail lounge, and see them?'

Sam couldn't help thinking. *I've never met a woman like Melissa: superbly competent in many ways and completely innocent of human behaviour except what she's seen in films.*

28

'SAM DANIELS! OF ALL PEOPLE, I DIDN'T EXPECT TO SEE YOU HERE.'

Sam turned to the speaker. It took a moment to recognise the woman, 'Likewise, Crystal.'

'What are you doing here, Sam?'

'Just passing through. I'm showing Melissa around Botswana.' He turned to Melissa, 'Mel, this is Crystal Turner. She visited the lodge where I worked in Tanzania about two years ago with some friends. Crystal, Melissa Grouwer.'

The women shook hands warily. 'Melissa, are you from England? I hope you're enjoying your *guided* tour with Sam.'

The subtle emphasis on guided made her meaning clear.

'Yes to both, Crystal. I'm looking forward to seeing the salt pans and the Okavango. Did you enjoy the Serengeti?'

'Oh yes, the *game* is wonderful, and the atmosphere is – *so virile.*'

Sam asked, 'Crystal, what are you doing here?'

'I'm here with my fiancé, Herman, who's at the bar talking business with someone. We came to buy a ring. Herman says he'll take me to Paris with him next month. Oh, he's looking for me; I must go. This hotel is delightful, but I can't wait to return to Joburg. Have a *thrilling* trip. Bye.'

Crystal swayed away, and Melissa asked, 'Do you have many female guests like that at Likesedi?'

'Fortunately, no. But there are always a few wives, with husbands away on conferences or playing golf, who come to a lodge to release the stress of keeping a marriage alive. Crystal won't return to the same lodge, but she might visit a different lodge if Herman assuages his libido with a much younger secretary in a few years.'

'Did she come alone?'

'No, with two other women, Jennifer and Sarie, if I remember.'

'Did you have sex with all three?'

Sam laughed, 'No, Mel, I try to obey the rules and stay away, so I don't stand at the lodge bar in the evening and drink with the guests unless it's all male, although if a woman asks, I must be polite, drink a beer, then leave.'

Melissa spotted the gap. 'So, if not all three, which one?'

Sam squirmed. 'Mel, aren't you being a bit too personal?'

'No, Sam, I need to learn these things, and it was long ago. Was it Crystal?'

Sam felt being open was better than lying. 'I tried to avoid it, but the other two women had scored with a ranger and on their third and last night, Crystal invited me for a drink and said quite openly. "Sam, if you don't come to my room and screw me, Joburg will pity or sneer at me. Jenny and Sarie will be too proud of their success to keep quiet. We never say who except that the men were lusty and big in all departments, so we won't mention your name, although I might mention a part of you. Besides, I like you."'

'So you screwed her?'

'Yes, Mel. Only once because they left the next morning. So that you understand, we heard the other two women come in after we went to bed. They shared the other bedroom, and when they went to bed, Crystal picked her moment before we had even warmed up and said loud enough for them to hear, "Sam, oh Sam, harder, please harder."'

Melissa laughed, 'It seems like a movie. That must have shocked you.'

'It did.' Sam congratulated himself that he didn't have to say he'd spent all night in her bed.

Melissa, however, had something else to consider: *I must avoid that line, 'Harder, please harder.' Can I use 'More'?*

She had to squeeze her thighs together before saying. 'Let's go for dinner.'

After thinking of Crystal, it was at dinner that Melissa decided, *I should know about the competition in case another Crystal pops out of nowhere.*

'Sam, can I expect to meet any other old girlfriends during the trip? If so, you should tell me.'

'Crystal wasn't a girlfriend, Melissa. I've never had a girlfriend. You're the first.'

'Then will I meet another woman with whom you've been intimate?'

'Mel, you're the only woman I've told my history to or trusted with my feelings. I can safely say I've never been intimate with any other woman I've met.'

What he said gave Mel a happy feeling, but it didn't answer her question, so she tried again. 'Sam, stop trying to wriggle out of an answer. You know what I mean, a woman you've slept with.'

'Mel, do you want to know about my past sexual acquaintances?'

'No, Sam. That's your past. I know that a man your age may have had many women in his life. I'm only interested in those who might walk up to us as Crystal did.'

'That was a chance in a million, Mel. It might never happen again.'

'Only might, Sam. I'll limit my question to Botswana.'

Sam gave up, *Mel's like a terrier and won't let go when she gets an idea; there is only one.*

'There's only one, Mel, and you're unlikely to meet her. She wasn't a client. Although it was at the lodge, and it was when I first arrived at Likesedi a year ago.'

'Okay, Sam, just tell me. What was her name?'

Sam told Melissa the story, although he left out some bits.

'Carl called me to the office six weeks after I had arrived at Likesedi and said, "Silent, the head office in Johannesburg is looking for publicity to boost our client numbers. They're sending a couple of women with cameras. I think you're the best ranger to show them around. It would help if you took them to places where they can take spectacular photos and some close-ups of animals – scenes from a movie. You must pick up the women in Kasane."

'I went to Kasane to fetch them, and they were vastly different from the usual lodge visitors. I was surprised when Karen MacPherson spotted me with my greeter's board. She was tall, had black hair to her shoulders, and wore a tight jersey knit dress and heels that displayed her figure and walk to perfection, like a film star. At first, I didn't notice the woman several paces behind her with a trolley carrying three suitcases and two large aluminium valises; she had a loose dress but looked compact and muscular.

'I introduced myself as Silent Sam Daniels, and she said, "Sam, call me Karen; this is Jennifer, my photographer." Then she asked how far it was to the lodge.

'I told them and suggested they change clothes because it was dusty and maybe muddy, and then Karen asked if I didn't have a Range Rover.'

Melissa asked, 'What did you say to that? Did it make you feel small?'

'I said I could rent one, but the lodge offers an African bush experience, and it starts at the airport. I said I had brought the safari wagon as they wanted to know what Likesedi was like.

'I can remember thinking, Mel. "She's a spoilt city goddess who expects to view the real Africa through a glass window from an air-conditioned car. Four to one, she asks me to rent one."

'I was surprised when she dumped the camera gear on me and went to the ladies with Jennifer to change.'

'What did they wear when they came out?' *That's important?*

'Karen wore skin-tight khaki shorts, a loose khaki shirt, a coloured scarf and soft suede boots. Jennifer had dressed the same, although her clothes were far less revealing, and she was assembling two cameras. Then Karen asked where the name Silent came from.'

'How did you answer that?'

'With my stock answer. "It's a kid's nickname because I never talked much." Then she said Sam was fine and told me why they had come. I remember what she said because it was something I didn't know.'

'She said, "I'm what the world outside these remote places calls an *influencer*. I have websites and Facebook pages where I talk to people personally, and those who like me can ask questions and see where I go and what I do in my everyday life. I've over a hundred thousand people who connect to my pages. If I eat eggs for breakfast, and an egg box with a visible logo is on the table, sales of those eggs go up. It's the same as TV advertising but low budget, and the egg producer pays for the push.

"I've five days and four nights scheduled, and Jennifer must take hundreds of photos and some video clips. I must rely on you to take me to places where we can take spectacular photos of the countryside with me in them close enough for viewers to know it's me, and pictures of me with animals. You must warn me what we'll see so I know what to wear.'"

'Wow, Sam, that's a tall order.'

'I had to think about where to take them, and it wasn't that easy, Mel. Jennifer took a photo of me and said I was photogenic, just what she needed in the photos and images with Karen.'

'Why, Sam?'

'I remember taking them to see the sunset over the river. Jennifer said, "You look super, Sam, you'll make a good film star; Karen, he's taller than you, well built, and looks like he belongs in the wild. If he stands by the water looking at the sunset, I'll have a great shot; then you can walk into the picture, put your arm around him, and look up at his face to catch the sunlight. Smile, and try to make it look adoring; your fans will be jealous or furious, so they'll return to watch a second episode."'

Melissa laughed. She remembered what Sam was like when she met him. 'I'll bet you were embarrassed.'

'Very, Mel. The few shots with Karen and me together petrified me.'

'So, which one did you have sex with. Or was it both?'

'Mel, for three days, they were very professional. I took them all over the reserve to take super videos and photos of the scenery and the animals. I took them to my special spot, where there's a pool in the rocks. Jennifer taught me about different lenses and backgrounds so that she could edit the images so Karen sometimes looked like she was beside an elephant.'

'Sam, you're doing it again.'

'What, Mel.'

'Trying to worm out of the truth. Out with it.'

'After dinner on the last day of filming, Karen told me she wasn't married and had no boyfriend and asked me to take her to my room. I had a ranger's cottage then, not the assistant manager's cottage.'

'So you made love, Sam.'

'Mel, I don't think so. Making love for me is what two people who love each other would do. For Karen, it was just sex. She wasn't interested in me.'

Melissa grinned. 'Just a part of you. Was that the end of it, Sam?'

'Yes, Mel, although she stayed two days after Jennifer left. When I dropped her at the airport, she waved goodbye, and since then, not even a message of thanks, even when Jennifer sent copies of everything they had taken while at the lodge.'

'Did the publicity work, Sam?'

'Very well, Mel, although the jump in bookings only lasted six months. But it did have a bonus for me.'

Melissa had an idea, 'I read the lodge brochure that says children under twelve are not accepted. Allowing families with small children to visit the lodge would mean a long-term increase in reservations. But what was the bonus?'

'The directors saw my face and learnt I had been the guide, and Carl had asked for a manager for client activities, so they asked me to take the assistant manager job with that portfolio. They also authorised the exclusive guide safaris that brought us together.'

Mel asked, 'So you're a film star, Sam?'

'No, Mel. I can show you the videos she posted on Facebook. You won't recognise me.'

'And she never returned?'

'She was all business, Mel. Although learning about what she did and what Jennifer explained about photography was interesting, I learnt nothing about either of them as people. I suppose it was because they were from the big city.'

'But when we met, I was from the big city too.'

'Yes, and for the first days, I considered you to be a client. It was after you saved Robbie that I realised you weren't a big city person but someone who belonged here, and that was confusing because sometimes what you said didn't fit.'

'Are you still confused, Sam?'

'Not about where you fit, Mel. I know where you belong. I may be confused because I'm unsure where I do.'

'So where do I belong, Sam?'

'In the Botswana game parks, Mel.'

I know, too, but only because he's here. Is Sam wondering if he'll fit into my life? I must find out.

29

· · · · ·

SAM DROVE ONTO THE ROAD GOING EAST AFTER A LUXURI-
ously comfortable night and a gourmet breakfast. Two hours later,
they turned off at Mopipi and two hundred metres later, there was
no track to follow. 'Sam, I've no doubt you know where you're going,
but *I* don't.'

'Into the middle of nowhere, Mel.'

'So what's there in nowhere?'

'Nothing.'

'Sam, any moment now, I'm going to start screaming. I'm a
woman. I must know where I'm going.'

'No, you don't. You're my darling Melissa, and I'm your darling
Sam, and if they're together, it doesn't matter where they're going.'

'Sam, that was in emails. You must be polite, or the emails disappear into censorial limbo, or the PC explodes. Now's different: I can
pull your hair or scratch.'

'Better pull my hair, or you can drive. I'll tell you a story.'

'This better be good. I'd rather drive a tank.'

Sam began, 'Some time ago, a bunch of weirdos....'

'What kind?'

'Scientists.'

Melissa smiled. 'Oh, real weirdos, like zoologists, not fakes.'

Sam smiled but ignored her innuendo. 'Yes, they agreed that if
they could obtain enough DNA analyses and know where the donors
lived, they could ask a computer where humanity began.'

The smile expanded, 'Sounds like that book I read long ago. Did the computer tell the weirdos the answer was forty-two?'

'You're not listening.'

'Okay, go on.'

'Well, they took some shortcuts because they took DNA from people they knew were of ancient origin. Like the San, then they fed the data into their computer.'

Melissa grinned, 'Now you'll say they had to buy a more powerful computer. That's what happened in the book.'

'It has nothing to do with a book, although they did install a much bigger computer.'

She crowed triumphantly, 'See, I told you so.'

Sam grinned but ignored her again.

'Eventually, the weirdos all agreed that the answer given by the computer was pretty good and told the world.'

'So, where did the weirdos say it began?'

'Twenty degrees forty-two minutes south, twenty-five degrees four minutes east, three hundred thousand years ago.'

'Where's that?'

'Where we're going, what you can see now was a wet, green savannah back then.'

'Okay, so you follow the GPS?'

'Out here, that's all we have except a compass and odometer.'

'No roads?'

'Hundreds, Mel. There are tracks in every direction. Follow one, and you might end up where you came from. Unless it's washed out in the rainy season, a vehicle track lasts years.'

'You sound like that book again, Sam. They returned to where they came from. Are we camping there?'

'Only lunch unless there's a delay. Then we go on to Jack's Camp for the night. They're closed, but we can camp there.'

'Great. I'll call the story "The Restaurant at the Beginning of the Human Universe".'

'You've been reading too many books.'

'If you don't stop soon, I'll never read another. Bouncing around in a tank gives my bladder a hard time.'

'Check carefully. Scorpions and snakes like this scenery.'

While she was gone, Sam added a waypoint to the GPS.

Ninety minutes later, as Sam stopped and cut the engine, Melissa asked. 'Is this it, Sam?'

'I think so. Look at the GPS.'

'It says we're at a waypoint called "RABHU". What's that mean?'

'Initials, Mel, work it out....'

Melissa grinned at Sam. 'Sam, I'll move my bed far away from yours tonight. You cheated when I wasn't looking.'

Sam grinned. 'Not at all. I'll photograph the GPS and a panorama from the cairn of stones fifty metres behind you to illustrate your story.'

Melissa spun and looked. 'Is the cairn the marker?'

'I guess so; there's no reason for it being there if it's not.'

'Let's walk to it, and you can kiss me.'

'Why?'

'The boy always kisses the girl in the restaurant.'

'Okay. Then we must have lunch; we have another twenty-five kilometres to Jack's Camp.'

'I'll fetch the hoe-axe thing and toilet roll; I might need it.'

They reached the cairn, and Sam opened his tripod to put the camera on. Melissa said, 'I'll only be a minute or two, Sam,' and walked past the cairn to a small hollow. Sam could see her head as she squatted. Standing only three metres from the cairn, he waited for her to return so Melissa would not be in the panorama. Sam watched her walk back. She passed closer to the cairn than when she went out, and Sam caught movement at the foot of the cairn. A second later, he saw the scorpion come from the cairn rocks.

'Mel, *back off now*. Scorpion!' Then he walked rapidly forward.

Melissa looked down, saw the scorpion and backed away, but the scorpion, for whatever reason, decided attack was the best defence and scuttled forward, its pincers waving, and its sting curled up in attack mode.

Sam reacted. He took two rapid steps and kicked at the scorpion attacking Melissa. She'd lifted the hoe-axe but would have been too late. The scorpion, warned by the shadow of Sam's boot, stopped and pulled back. Instead of impacting its body, the boot crushed its claws. The tail stabbed forward and stung Sam's boot on the ankle. A second later, as Sam stepped back, Melissa brought the axe down and killed it.

Sam sat down and unlaced his boot. 'Sam, are you all right?'

'I hope so. It stung my boot. I must check if the sting went through to me. It was a fat-tailed parabuthus. I felt something.'

He removed the boot, and Melissa could see the red spot where the scorpion sting had gone through the skin.

'Mel, can you fetch the Land Rover?'

Melissa ran and, a minute later, stopped next to him.

'Open the passenger door, move the seat to the rear, then lower the back as far as it will go, and then I'll climb in.'

'That was poisonous, wasn't it?'

'Yes, now fetch that phial of anti-venom I showed you and the syringe.'

'Shall I inject it, Sam?'

'No, keep it in the cubby. I don't think the sting was full depth, and only a little poison entered my foot. If I start thrashing around, pass out, or can't reply lucidly to a question, inject me with the anti-venom. I'll strap myself down, then you drive me to Jack's Camp. At least there will be people who can carry me to bed. I'll set the GPS for Jack's Camp while you put the dead scorpion in the back somewhere for identification. It's up to you when we arrive at Jack's. I should be okay in a day or two. Drive slowly. Even at fifteen kilometres per hour, we'll be there in two hours.'

Melissa didn't forget the camera, hoe-axe, toilet paper or the boot. She threw them in the back.

Melissa found the Landy easier to drive than the safari vehicles she'd tried in Tanzania, but the terrain needed learning. On the drier rises, she could reach twenty-five kilometres per hour momentarily, but in the soft, damp, sticky sand in the dips, she used low range and, at four kilometres per hour, the Landy churned slowly through to the higher ground. Favouring the rises, she didn't follow a straight line but weaved from side to side on the GPS screen, sometimes two kilometres off the GPS track as she rounded a pan. Melissa stopped on a hump every fifteen minutes and checked Sam. After the first hour, she was worried, for he didn't respond to her questions. Melissa thought, *better a live Sam in two days than a dead one tomorrow.* She gave him the injection and drove on.

Sam had not mentioned another camp, and when she went over a low rise, she saw a group of white tents on a dune ahead but to the left. She assumed it was Jack's Camp but it was actually San Camp, five kilometres from Jack's.

Sam had said Jack's had closed, so when she stopped before the highest tent and no one came out, she left the Landy and went in. It looked like a lounge tent, so she went to another and found two canvas camp beds and a simple cupboard. It seemed like a ghost camp.

When she came out, a short man was standing by the Land Rover with a boy half his size, and when she reached him, he said, '*¡Hola!*' Followed by a few more words. Melissa hoped he was asking if they needed help. She put a hand on her chest and said, '*¡Hola!*', then her name, Vixen, with three clicks. She walked to the door, opened it, pointed to Sam, went to the back of the Landy, and threw the dead scorpion onto the ground. The man who had followed her jumped back, looked at the scorpion, turned to the boy, and after a few rapid words, the boy ran away, *fast*. Melissa hoped he was going for help.

He was. An entire San group of fifteen appeared minutes later. They carried Sam into the tent and laid him on a bed. A woman with a wrinkled face and smiling eyes asked something. Melissa sensed more than understood, so she pointed to Sam's foot and used the click word she knew for a foot.

Thirty minutes later, a small fire was burning in front of the tent. Melissa had provided a pot and water and the woman had added a selection of herbs to the water. Melissa held Sam's head up while the woman Melissa had decided was the San grandmother poured her concoction a bit at a time into his mouth until he slept quietly. The woman listened to his heartbeat and then smiled at Melissa. 'The gods are happy.' Melissa knew the expression; it was the same in Tanzania.

It was like being back with the Hadza. They brought three more beds into the tent, and the grandmother and two other young women slept on them. One or the other remained awake all night watching Sam and giving him a few sips of the herb tea at intervals.

Melissa warmed some water in the big pot at dawn and carefully cleaned Sam. She was sure the herb tea was responsible for his continued slumber. Then she stood naked in the tent, wiped herself down, and offered the pot with more water and the washcloths to the women. They did the same.

Feeling hungry because she hadn't had lunch or dinner the day before, Melissa looked in the food store, extracted what she hoped everyone would like, and showed it to the grandmother. She'd chosen well, for forty minutes later, they sat around the big pot with sheets of bark as plates and, with their fingers, ate maize meal mixed with vegetables, chopped-up bacon, and wild herbs.

Sam woke at 2 pm, confused to find himself naked but for a towel, with Melissa on one side and the wrinkled face of a San woman on the other. Puzzled, he asked, 'Where are we, Mel?'

'With a San group, in a tent on a dune.'

Sam had to think carefully. His mind had other ideas, but finally, he grasped what she'd said. 'Near Jack's Camp?'

'Close. When I saw it from a distance, I came here.'

'It must be San Camp. Jack's is five kilometres away. Who's here?'

'Only the San group. They helped me, and grandmother has treated you with a herb mixture, although I gave you the injection on the way here. The scorpion must have shot more venom into your foot than you believed. Just lie there. You can leave the bed a bit later. Do you want a pillow?'

'Yes, but I need the toilet.'

Melissa said something he didn't understand with a half dozen clicks, and the two women helped him up and held him while he walked through the back flap of the tent to a bucket in the makeshift bathroom. Feeling better, the women helped him back to the bed, and Melissa fetched a pillow from the Land Rover.

'Just lay there, Sam. We'll fetch you something to eat.'

At 5 pm, after he'd eaten a delicious soup without asking what was in it, Melissa gave him some shorts and thongs and helped him out of the tent to one of their camp chairs. Two young women were busy around the fire, where grandmother, squatting on her heels near them, was giving instructions. Melissa joined her, squatting with the same easy, fluid movement.

Sam watched. *Mel's incredible. She may not know many words, but she uses gestures, and they understand each other.*

He saw her look up and turn to the west. Then, the others did the same. 'What is it, Mel?'

'A vehicle is coming. It'll be here in a few minutes.'

It was a safari vehicle, with a suntanned ranger and the San man Melissa had first met. As it drew to a halt, the driver looked over the door at Sam and said, 'Silent Sam, of all people. What are you doing here?'

'Hello, Mike. Guiding a client to Baines.'

'A San woman? *!Xhai* said a *Lekgoa* and a San woman had come to this camp. I understood from him a scorpion stung you.'

Melissa heard what he said as he opened the car door and came to shake Sam's hand. She smiled, content to learn that the San group considered her one of them.

'Parabuthus, Mike. It went for my client, so I kicked it, but it stung me before it died. Mel, come and say hello to Mike Tomlinson from Jack's.'

Sam enjoyed Mike's visible surprise when Melissa stood. He knew Mike hadn't noticed her amongst the San. She came around the fire with a smile, advancing her hand to shake. 'Mike, my San client: Melissa Grouwer.'

'Hello, Mike. Pleased to meet you.'

'Likewise, Melissa. But you aren't San!'

'No, but they accept me as one. My name is Vixen.' Melissa voiced the San version.

Flabbergasted, Mike turned to Sam, 'That's a bad scorpion, Sam. I expected to find you unconscious. Are you okay now?'

'Yes, with the anti-venom injection that Mel gave me and the herbal mixture grandmother prepared, I'll be fine tomorrow morning.'

'Would you like to come to Jack's? It's far more comfortable.'

He didn't see Melissa shake her head, but Sam did. 'No, Mike. I'd rather rest here. We'll call by for breakfast. We won't have any food left by morning.'

'I brought some. You can have that too. Have you enough water?'

Melissa replied, 'Yes, we still have half a tank.'

'Then I'll leave you. See you in the morning.'

!Xhai brought the food to Melissa as Mike drove away.

Sam was sure he would never forget the feast that followed. It wasn't the food; it was the feeling.

As they packed up after sunrise, the San disappeared one or two at a time without a farewell. Sam asked, 'How do we thank them, Mel?'

'We don't. If *!Xhai* or grandmother offer you an open palm, place yours against it gently. Their help is a duty and requires no thanks. That sign says, "We are one." I think it's ancient. A sign from early man.'

The five kilometres to Jack's took ten minutes. The breakfast provided two hours for Mike to learn about the Hadza and then talk, as all good rangers do, of the countryside they love. Sam let Mike talk. He couldn't do better.

Gweta was a two-hour drive. There, they refuelled and bought food.

30

'SAM, REMEMBER I NEED TO KNOW WHERE I'M GOING.'

'I haven't forgotten, although you don't seem to arrive there when I tell you where to go.'

'Admit I found better help than you expected, and tell me where we're going.'

'Okay, you did. You're incredible. We're on the road to Maun. I zeroed the odometer, and when it reads fifty-five kilometres, we leave the road and head directly north for six.'

'Just like that? No signpost?'

'And no road. We choose our way through the bush and arrive at the Nxai pan. Then we drive north along the sides of the pan until we reach the first of the campsites, although it's number three because it's furthest away from Kudia Island.'

'And then?'

'We continue to number two, then one, and finally to the island where we're not allowed to camp because it's a famous place.'

'Why?'

'In 1862, Thomas Baines, a painter who became famous, painted a picture of the island baobabs. Ever since they have had the name Baines Baobabs. One fell over centuries ago, but it's still growing.'

'What attracts you, Sam.'

'You'll hear. The pan surrounding it is flat, like a billiard table, and there are no insects. The only sound is your heartbeat, and if you concentrate, you will hear what a client once said is the rumble of mother earth's tummy.'

'Okay, I'll watch for the game. Is there much?'

'It's the beginning of the dry winter season. Most pans are dry, and the animals have moved back to the Okavango, Savuti and Chobe areas, but there are always some all year. In the wet season, there are far more, and the birdlife is incredible. You would have seen them if we had come on the first trip. We'll spend a night at Baines, at our campsite of choice, watch the sunset behind the baobabs from one place on the pan and the sunrise from another, then after breakfast, drive to Xakanaxa in the Okavango.'

Melissa exclaimed as they drove onto the flat white plain that disappeared over the horizon ahead. 'This is fantastic, the end of the world.'

'It does seem like that. Every time I see it, I have the same feeling.'

'Now I know why you told me about getting lost. Alone out here, I wouldn't know where to go.'

'Don't. Stick to me like a leech. Keep your eyes on my Landy or me constantly, and don't wander off to look at something interesting. When something distracts you, you can forget where you are.'

They sat in silence while they drove north across the deserted pan. Melissa felt they were the only people on the planet. She realised Sam hadn't used 'my darling' once in the last two days. He didn't seem as affectionate as on the first trip, and although her return had started well, he was more distant. Was it the pan? She asked herself if nursing Sam had injured his pride but scrapped that because Sam had saved her by kicking the scorpion.

It was nothing particular – Sam was thinking.

Campsite three had no visitors. It had some trees, a waste bin, a long drop with a box on top, two fireplaces with cold ashes, and a view across the pan to the west.

Melissa felt campsite two was better. The facilities were identical to campsite three, but it had west and north views.

Deserted and visibly the most used site, campsite one had a rudimentary fence around the long drop. Its view was Kudia Island and the Baines Baobabs.

Melissa chose it. 'Let's stay here; it's the closest.'

'Okay, let's have lunch, then we'll walk over to the baobabs for a look around, and I'll photograph you lounging on the fallen baobab.'

'Like a film star, Sam? With my cleavage showing?'

'Mel, sometimes you amaze me. Although I'd like the memory, I would never make a revealing film of you that others might see.'

She replied, 'Although you've seen me naked many times, posing naked seems far more intimate than sleeping with a nightie. I'll mark it in my memory as something to do when you deserve it.'

'What must I do to deserve it?'

'I can't tell you, Sam. I'll know when you do.'

It left Sam confused and made his thinking more difficult.

Lunch over, Sam said, 'Let's take the beds and stuff out and arrange them to show we've claimed this campsite, then we'll drive to the island.'

They explored the island and Sam took photos of Melissa lounging on the fallen tree. As the sun neared the horizon, Sam drove two kilometres east onto the pan for the sunset and placed two chairs side by side, facing west, with his camera on the tripod. They sat and as the sun neared the horizon Melissa said, 'Hold my hand.'

The island and the pitch-black baobabs were grotesque alien shapes against the scarlet western sky.

Once the last trace of light had drained from the western horizon, under the canopy of stars, Melissa felt the silence and thought, *Alone, it would be as frightening as a crowd of noisy people.* She squeezed Sam's hand.

Although Sam could have sat there all night with Melissa beside him, for he felt he was in heaven, he mistook the squeeze for a signal to leave and said, 'Okay, the show's over; we'll return to the campsite.'

'It plays every night. Promise me you'll bring me back one day to watch it.'

'I will if you'll come.'

'You'd have to tie me to a tree to stop me from coming.'

Sam felt something deep down inside.

Sam lit the fire, and Melissa removed the food box from the Landy, but as she put it down, she said, 'Someone's coming.'

Then Sam heard it, too: a Land Rover coming fast. It braked to a halt with a shudder, and a man stepped out. Melissa saw a young girl in the passenger seat. 'Please, we need your help. My wife and youngest are at campsite two, and my twelve-year-old son Martin has wandered off, and we can't find him. My wife says she last saw him walking into the pan.'

Sam didn't waste time talking. 'Do you have a GPS?'

'Yes.'

'Then set two or three waypoints for offset tracks from here to camp two, south of the direct route. Separate them by fifty metres, then drive them, hazard lights on, beams on bright, at four kilometres an hour max with the windows open. Stop every hundred metres, hoot twice and listen. If you find him, hoot eight times.

'We'll do the same on the north side. Go.'

'Mel, let's go.'

'Sam, I'll sit on the bonnet with your parabolic birdwatching microphone. I'll turn the amplifier up and listen through the headphones. When you stop, give me enough time to scan.'

Two minutes later, as the other vehicle left, she climbed on the bonnet, headphones on and the microphone with its backing dish in her hand. Sam had erected his flashing beacon and plugged it in. The Landy looked like a Christmas tree. Sam decided that with the amplified microphone, Melissa could hear something more than fifty metres away, so he took the third parallel track.

Sam calculated twenty-three stops before turning. At each halt, he switched off the engine, hooted twice, and waited, silent and unmoving, watching Melissa as she scanned from extreme left to the extreme right, then signalled to go on.

Time seemed to drag, but on the sixteenth stop, Melissa swung the microphone back and forth, then raised her arm and pointed to the left. Sam turned in that direction and drove forward until she gave a halt sign. He switched off, she listened again, then indicated even further left. When she raised her arm, Sam stopped. Melissa jumped off the hood, and Sam joined her. Forty metres further, they found the boy curled in a ball, sobbing.

Melissa was the first to reach him. She lay beside him and put her arm around him.

'Martin, it's okay. You're safe now.'

Melissa could see the Landy Christmas tree and led the way with Sam carrying Martin.

Sam hooted eight times.

Half an hour later, they were at Camp Two, and Martin was safe in his mother's arms. His father, John Rowland, tried to find some material way to thank them, but Sam refused. 'No thanks needed, John. Melissa and I are rangers. We frequently save kids from becoming food, as do all the rangers. Visit us at Likesedi Lodge. We can show your kids things you can't. If you want to help, the lodge has a Facebook page. Post something there.'

'Then please, will you and your wife stay and have dinner with us?'

'That will be our pleasure, John.'

Melissa waited until they returned to their campsite.

'So, Sam, we save kids daily from hungry lions, and I'm a ranger and your wife.'

'You must admit it seems a habit; we make a good team. First Robbie, then Martin.'

'Okay, twice is a habit. What about my qualification as a ranger?'
Mel's not going to let this pass, I can tell.

'I decided you deserved a promotion. I'm a champion of female equality, and you're the first San woman to qualify. Congratulations.'

Melissa smiled. *He's not going to get away with this.*

'Sam, you're as slippery as an eel. How did I marry?'

'I could tell they were strait-laced; they must go to church twice weekly. They would have considered you a fallen woman if I'd said we weren't married. That would be bad for your status as a ranger.'

When she stopped laughing, Melissa had tears in her eyes, 'Sam, what is much more slippery than an eel?'

Sam grinned. 'No idea. Maybe a ranger?'

Melissa considered what he said, 'You may be right, Sam, but you're not off the hook. I think what you said is subliminal: what you wish for – I'll remember that and think of something before we arrive at the lodge.'

Sam thought, *Melissa's right; it's what I wish.*

Melissa asked herself, *If he wants me as his wife, why doesn't he ask?*

They left before dawn and parked on the western side on a small hillock, with the baobabs still invisible, between them and the sunrise. They sat once again, in silence, side by side, the camera beside them on its tripod, while the day crept into the sky. Melissa reached over and took Sam's hand.

Sam was now thinking seriously; he hardly saw the sunrise. First, he had to admit that he wanted Melissa with him forever, which meant marriage. Then Sam had to admit that marriage meant children. He could not deny her children, and children needed schools. Lodges did not have schools, so marriage meant separation, or, like Peter, they would have to live in a town or city. Sam knew he could not, even if Melissa could support the noise. There seemed no solution except to find a lodge elsewhere. He could try South Africa, with schools near enough for children to attend.

He decided he could not ask Melissa to marry him before finding such a lodge. He would start looking when they reached Likesedi. He did ask himself a final question: *Am I terrified she'll say no?*

Once the sun was up, Sam drove west for fifty minutes, then stopped amongst some low bushes.

'Mel, we'll have breakfast here and a shower. In an hour, the park gate will be open, and we'll go on to Maun for lunch and then to Xakanaxa this afternoon. The road to the park entrance is only a few hundred metres ahead.'

At the national park gate, Sam showed the receipt for the fees the lodge had paid, and they drove on.

'Sam, this road is boring, straight, the bush is unchanging, and the game has gone elsewhere. What's at Maun?'

'Maun is the tourist capital of Botswana. The Okavango and Savuti areas are a unique ecosystem. We don't have the time for a full exploration, but it will give you an idea of what it's like. We must return often and spend months there to learn about it in detail.'

What he said confused Melissa – *Does he expect to bring me here often? If so, why do I have that negative feeling?*

'Why?'

'The change in vegetation and animal activity gears to the seasons. The Okavango dries in winter until there are only the open water canals and the land around and between them dries and seems dead. Then the floods return, not the raging flash flood beloved by movie makers, but quite different. I once sat in a chair for a day, watching the water creeping over the bare dusty ground towards me in a slow flood. It's like when someone spills a pot of syrup on a table, and you see the pool slowly expanding, oozing forward in one or more directions. The feeling of certainty and a driving force builds as you watch it. I returned a week later, and the new grass was already centimetres high.

'Then the animals come, everything that can migrate, and the millions of insects, butterflies, and dragonflies that hatch from a chrysalis that has waited for trees and bush to grow leaves the larvae and caterpillars can feed on. It's like watching life burst forth as it must have at the Earth's beginning.

'To see every step in the process, many visits are needed, or you must live at a lodge for a year.'

'I can tell you love the place, but where does Maun fit in?'

'There are no roads, only tracks, and in the wet season, most are impassable. The lodges can accept road traffic for part of the year, but aircraft are the only way to reach them for several months. Some close for months, others keep going, fed by aircraft. Maun is the hub for hundreds of flights to and from the lodges, where everything – people, food and necessities – go into the Okavango.'

'Are we going to fly?'

'No, it's dry enough now to reach Xakanaxa; it's on a waterway but on the outer edge of the Okavango. If they don't have a room, they'll have a campsite.'

'Do we just drive through Maun?'

'We'll fill up with fuel and water, buy food, have lunch, call Petrus and ask if there's a cottage available, and then drive on. Lunch should interest you. Look at the people. You'll find a completely different atmosphere to a regular town of that size.'

'How would you describe it?'

'A pioneer atmosphere, an adventure atmosphere, the spirit that people facing unknown lands must have displayed for centuries.'

'Sam, you're a romantic.'

'I guess maybe I am; I suspect I need to change to avoid the label of an armchair romantic.'

Melissa couldn't help thinking. *Or a good push.*

Two hours later, they drove out of Maun. 'Well, Mel, did you feel it?'

'Yes, and I know something else.'

'What?'

'If you don't decide to leave the armchair, you'll regret it for the rest of your life.'

Sam said nothing. He wondered, *Is she telling me I should propose?*

31

· · · · ·

AFTER FIFTY KILOMETRES, THEY TURNED ONTO A WINDING track, and Sam asked, 'Did you see wild dogs in the Serengeti? I know there aren't many.'

'No.'

'I don't know if we'll see any here, but Botswana has more than anywhere else. I find the best way of seeing them is to park in a convenient spot, relax, have a cup of tea and listen. I told you about the Chobe pack I'm friends with. We'll see them as soon as we return.'

They said nothing for minutes until Melissa decided Sam was dreaming.

'Sam, wake up, Sam. You're half asleep. If an elephant stepped into the road, you'd ram it!'

She saw him shake his head. Then he turned to look at her. She smiled.

Sam felt something he'd never felt before, so he smiled in return, and Melissa asked, 'You were miles away, Sam. Where were you? You'd left me. Were you dreaming of another woman?'

Sam's smile grew broader, and it was Melissa's turn to feel something new. 'No, since we met, that's impossible. I was thinking about my research.'

'I've read the excuses men give their wives and girlfriends in a hundred books; congratulations, you've just added a corker to the list. If you want me to believe it, tell me about it.'

'Do you remember about an hour ago when the road had elephant dung all over it?'

'Yes, Sam, and you said, "A herd must have crossed here, and by the looks of the dung, during last night."'

'That's the place. Then I started thinking of the dung piles.'

He could hear the disbelief in Melissa's voice as she exclaimed. 'Are you researching elephant dung? You're weirder than I thought.'

Sam grinned broadly and chuckled, happy at her reaction.

'I suppose I am, but I didn't say that. I'm researching the environment in and around an elephant's dung pile, preferably a fresh one.'

Melissa had to regain the advantage, 'So you hide behind a bush, shovel and bag in hand, waiting for an elephant to drop a turd. Then you rush out and collect it to take to your laboratory, where, wearing your white coat, with spectacles perched on your nose, you sit and watch the dung evolve.'

Sam roared with laughter. It caught, and Melissa laughed with him. Sam said as the laughter died, 'My darling, you're good for the soul, and I've just learnt what a marvellous storyteller you are.' She blushed. She felt the admiration in his eyes. *He said 'my darling' again.*

'Tell me the truth if you don't want me to believe my story.'

'I will. I'm going to guess, but up ahead, there are trees and bush beside the river. It looks like a suitable place, and I hope we find elephant dung; then I'll teach you about it.'

'I never read a book where a man taught a woman about elephant poop. It's shaping up to become a unique story.'

'Wait and see. If there is some, we'll park under the tree and make coffee first. Scientists must drink lots of it.'

There was dung, much of it, and fresh. So was the coffee.

'Now, let's pack up and walk back to the road to look for a nice dung pile.'

'I've just added another item to my description of you; you won't like it.'

'I'm sure it will be true; what?'

'You suggested, "My guide Sam." I'll extend that to "My guide Sam, who thinks elephant dung is nice."'

Sam gained the upper hand with his reply and his delighted grin. 'Then think of what it says about you when you add "later my boyfriend" to that.'

Melissa felt her reply was weak; the word boyfriend did it. 'You're a *whatshim*, Sam.'

As they walked to the road, Sam, with his camera hanging from a strap around his neck, asked. 'What do you know about dung beetles?'

'I've watched them at work in the Serengeti. The rangers always tell the tourists about them.'

Sam smiled, 'I didn't doubt you had seen them. I asked what you know about them.'

Melissa's boredom dropped away. 'They fly, looking for fresh dung, and prefer herbivores; then they make little balls of dung, roll them to a suitable spot, bury them and lay an egg in them, so when it hatches, the larva has dung to eat. They also eat the dung, and often there are so many that a pile of elephant dung disappears in twenty-four hours.'

'And that's all they said?'

Melisa turned and faced him, 'Is there any more they could say? Watching the dung beetles was fascinating, but only for a while.'

'My opinion of rangers like that is that they aren't doing their job, but that's not your fault. One of my research projects is about dung beetles, and there's much more to know.'

Melissa saw his expression, and her hearing picked up the timbre of his voice, including one of annoyance. She wondered if he was annoyed at her.

In an apologetic tone, she said, 'I'm sorry, are you annoyed with me?'

Surprised, Sam asked, 'Why should I be annoyed with you?'

'Well, I heard the annoyance in your voice.'

'Not with you, but with the rangers who told you so little. But tell me, can you sense my moods when I speak?'

'I can't sense them; I can hear something in the sounds when you speak that gives me a clue.'

'Wow, I must be cautious with you. Would you know if I thought something like "Goddamned *whatsit*" when I said something?'

Melissa grinned, 'Something like that, I'm sure I would, so don't. I might throw elephant dung at you. Now tell me about dung beetles.'

'I don't know if it would make a story for your book, but for me, dung beetles reveal what this land is like.

'We must walk further along the road and find a good pile; I think just off the road with shade might be best.'

Sam cut a sturdy walking stick-length branch from a bush, cleared it of foliage, and sharpened the end to a flat spade. Then, they walked ahead on opposite sides of the road.

After a hundred metres, Melissa called, 'Sam, there's a big one here, and several dung beetles are working on it.'

Sam crossed over, looked at it, and remarked, 'That looks like an excellent example to study, dropped late yesterday. Take the stick, push it in from the side, and try to lever the top half up and over, then tell me what you see.'

Sam filmed her doing so, and then she exclaimed, 'The inside has a hundred little beetles in it. Where did they come from?'

'Describe them.'

'There are lots of little ones, sort of round. They're running around and trying to dig into what's left. They don't like me.'

'I'm not surprised. You upset the beetles. What size are they? And are there others?'

'Less than a centimetre, and there are other bigger ones; they're longer and have stripes on them.'

'Okay, the first lesson: they're dung beetles.'

'Babies?'

'No, all of them are adults, including the ones rolling dung. But they are three sub-families of the same beetle. Before I tell you about the Egyptians, use the stick to clear the dung to one side. I want you to look at the ground under it. So don't scratch the ground if you can avoid it.'

Melissa did so, and Sam filmed.

'There, that's it.'

'Now, take my knife and cut some grass stalks about thirty centimetres long; there's a clump by that bush. Use a stem to poke the ground where the dung was to find a hole.'

Melissa kneeled beside the mark left by the dung. Absorbed in what she was doing and so obviously excited by what she might find, she gave Sam a warm feeling. *She would be a good research assistant.*

'There's a hole here.'

'Push the straw down; find out how deep it is.'

'There's something down there.' Melissa reacted and pulled out the straw, and as it came out, a striped dung beetle shot from the hole, scuttled to the now-moved dung and buried itself inside it.

'It was one of the striped beetles in the hole.'

'Okay, see if you can find some more holes and find the deepest.'

Sam continued to film.

'I've found five: three had beetles, one is almost blocked, with something spongy, and the other is half a straw deep.'

'The striped beetle drills those holes, then they push and compact dung down and lay an egg in it. The blocked one is dung filled, and the deep one is waiting for a load. When a beetle has filled it, there will be several dung sausages, each with an egg and a thin earth barrier separating it from the ones above and below. Some species in other countries do it differently; this is our one.'

Melissa asked, 'Do they all hatch simultaneously?' The question impressed Sam. *She's also quick to grasp the consequences.*

'No, and that's what I'm researching. There are many theories but no proof why the most recently laid top egg hatches before the egg below and in that order.'

'That's fantastic. What have you done?'

'I'll tell you as we drive. Let's look at the big ones, those you can see. They roll balls of dung and bury them. Were you told how they do it?'

'No.'

'Then let's try to find one that's decided to bury a ball.'

It took them twenty minutes to check on rolling balls of dung before Melissa said, 'Sam, I think this one has decided to dig.'

He came to her and said, 'Yes, he's excavating. If the ground is soft enough, we should see it doing something like an ant lion. It's digging a small deep hole under the ball and then keeps widening it, pushing the earth out to the side of the ball, which will settle into the cavity until the beetle can cover it. The egg-laying happens before covering. Some species excavate a cavern and put several balls in it.'

Half an hour later, Melissa said, 'That was worth watching; that beetle had determination. You haven't said how the beetles find the dung; is it by smell?'

'They are nocturnal and fly around at night, trying to smell something. The most fantastic thing about them is that they can navigate by the sun, moon, and the Milky Way.'

'Sam, I may be an innocent woman and a newcomer to Botswana, but I can tell when you are pulling my leg. Tell me the truth.'

'Okay, they all carry a tiny GPS.'

'Sam, I warned you.'

'What will you do? You won't believe me when I tell you the truth, so I'm helpless; I felt an author would believe a story.'

'Is that fable about the moon true?'

'Yes, scientists discovered it when someone noticed that when the beetles roll a ball of dung, they try to do it in a straight line, east to west, so the researchers investigated how they did it. That's another thing we know they do but haven't worked out exactly how.'

Melissa had to think about what he said and asked, 'How did they research that?'

'In a planetarium under a night sky that they could move around.'

'I'm sorry for disbelieving you; you've never lied. I feel terrible.'

'Can I kiss it better?'

'You can try...'

'Do you feel better now?'

'Much better, thanks.'

'Did the ranger tell you that dung beetles eat dung?'

'Yes. Don't they?'

'And that they choose fresh dung so it's easy to roll the dung into balls?'

'Yes.'

'There may be some truth in the latter, but the adult beetles eat the juices covering the undigested vegetation; the juice contains digested vitamins and minerals. It's the larvae that eat the vegetation in the dung. The adults eat the vegetation only if the juices are in short supply.

'We'll return to the Landy and drive on. Those three species of dung beetle make short work of a dung pile because the rollers take and bury the outside, the dwellers dry out the middle, and the tunnellers take the bottom layer down into the ground. It's a cooperative effort by all three species. The remaining traces of dried-out dung can blow away in the wind.'

When Sam drove back onto the road, Melissa was feeling cheerful, and it was visible. She also had far more interest in dung beetles and Sam's research.

'Sam, how are you trying to solve the problem of sequential hatching?'

'I hide behind a bush, shovel and bag in hand, waiting for an elephant to drop a turd. Then I rush out and collect it to take to my laboratory.'

'*Mr Sam Daniels*. I shall never talk to you again.'

'Okay. I won't take it to my laboratory. I set thermocouples to measure the temperature at different depths. My theory was that the deeper ones would be cooler and hatch slower, but the temperatures are all over the place, as some days are cool and others hot. So I started again with humidity sensors. My new theory is that the bottom sausages are the wettest and have more for the larvae to eat before pupation. If it's true, it means the dwellers that dry out the dung are regulating the larvae of the tunnellers. When we reach Likesedi, I must recover the recorder. It will have run for three weeks.'

'That I can believe. I'll change what I said.'

'What to?'

'I'll speak to you only when I want to.'

'Then can I return to my dream girl without you disturbing me?'

'Don't you dare. I don't want to run into an elephant's backside, no matter how much you love their dung. What were you going to say about Egyptians?'

'Only one thing. Four thousand years ago, the Egyptians worshipped the dung beetle as an image of the sun god. Way back then, they recognised their importance.'

Melissa remembered what she'd read. 'Scarabs? Broaches and jewellery?'

'Yes, well worth researching on the Web; the scientific name for the family is Scarabaeidae. The humble dung beetle has been a jeweller's motif for four thousand years.'

32

'SAM, IS IT ONLY ELEPHANT DUNG THAT FASCINATES YOU?'

'Yes and no. It's the only dung I'm studying, but the other animal poo tells stories.'

Melissa smiled delightedly, 'I knew it: you're an ef-ef.'

'Mel, is that an invented word?'

'No, the initials for a Faeces Fanatic. It explains why you decided to study elephant poo.'

'Mel, all the rangers must learn. Fresh poo tells us what animals might be nearby and that we should look for them. Poo is a tracker's signpost.'

Melissa, still smiling, was interested, 'Give me examples.'

'Okay, some simple ones. Rhinos have toilet spots they use repeatedly to mark the boundaries of their territories. If I see fresh poo in a Rhino's midden, I know there's one in the area to look out for. Hyenas have white dung; they eat bones and expel the excess calcium in their excrement, so it's white. Fresh white poo tells me to watch out because there's a hyena around. Giraffes may be massive, but their poo is small balls that scatter when they fall from a height; zebra are like horses, a buffalo like cows.

'I have a theory about poo that's impossible to prove.'

Now serious, Melissa asked, 'What theory?'

'I told you about predators looking for the weak, slow and injured. I think they can smell the difference between the poo of a healthy animal and a sick animal and look for it. Especially hyenas or jackals.'

'Sam, why haven't the rangers I've met told me those things?'

'Can you imagine a ranger telling his visitors that the day's lesson is about crap? Most visitors want pretty pictures to show their friends how brave they are to visit animals in the wild. It's a reason why the five most dangerous species are popular. Few want to learn any detail.'

'So why tell me?'

'You asked, Mel, and you're interested. I don't think of you as a tourist but an inexperienced ranger who needs to know these things.'

That's an admission of note! 'Thanks to you, I'm learning every day.'

'Mel, you belong here and will be the best ranger in the country. You can hear and see better than anyone. All you need is to learn what you're seeing and hearing.'

As Sam approached Xakanaxa, Melissa remarked. 'This is another world, unlike anywhere else we've been to. It looks like it should be a jungle.'

'It was when the water flowed continuously, but as it's now much drier for half the year, the jungle has evolved into what you see: reeds in the shallow water, trees and grass which grow on the slightly higher areas. The lodge is beside one of the eastern waterways.'

'Do we have a cottage?'

'Yes, for three nights.'

'Sam, how do you ask for a cottage for you and your client without saying you're sleeping with her?'

Melissa could see he was embarrassed as he replied, 'I didn't have to; Petrus already knew I was driving you and that we share a room.'

'Sam, be honest, else I'll believe you say, "Petrus, do you have a room for me and my mistress?"'

Sam smiled, 'That would be insulting. If I had to ask, it would be "for me and my girlfriend." But I didn't ask. When I said, hello, Petrus said, "I have a cottage for you and Melissa." I think we've picked up a reputation among the rangers. They talk.'

'So we're a juicy bit of scandal to pass around?'

'No. When I said, thanks, Petrus said, "You're welcome, Sam. I'll be thrilled to meet a woman ranger from Tanzania who speaks San."'

'You made that up.'

'I didn't. You can ask him in about ten minutes.'

Melissa didn't reply. *I don't need to decide if I want to stay in Botswana, where I'm no longer an orphan; a dozen people have adopted me.*

Sam stopped in front of the large main building with a veranda two metres above the ground level. Melissa intuitively knew that the man who came down the steps to meet them was Petrus – *another man from the same mould as Sam and the others, not as tall as Coenraad but just as handsome.*

The two men shook hands, and Petrus turned to Melissa, his hand out, 'Melissa, welcome to Xakanaxa. Everyone wants to meet you, and I have a friend of yours here who was delighted to hear you were coming.' He looked over her shoulder, 'He's just behind you.'

Melissa turned to see N!ki'ka's smiling face.

She reacted with a broad smile and held her arm up with an open palm facing him. '¡*Hola! N!ki'ka.*'

He smiled in return and placed his hand gently on hers. '¡*Hola!* Vixen.'

Petrus watched for half a minute while Melissa and *N!ki'ka* spoke with clicks, then turned to Sam and said quietly, 'That's one hell of a woman you have there. I thought the stories we've heard about you and Melissa were exaggerated, but now I know they are true. Have you asked her to marry you?'

'I'm trying to work up the courage, Petrus.'

'Don't hesitate. Don't waste a moment. Go for it.'

They didn't know that Melissa could hear their baritone voices clearly behind the chatter of *N!ki'ka*. She thought, *At least Sam's trying.*

'Sam, are you driving around tomorrow or want a mokoro?'

'We'll do a late drive tomorrow. It's been a long drive from Baines, and we need the sleep. The day after, a mokoro and a picnic basket for lunch. Say, leave at 9 am and return before 4 pm.'

'Okay, Sam. *N!ki'ka* can go with you on the drive, and I've just the guy for you for the mokoro. I'll organise it.'

'Sam, these are unusual cottages. Why are the windows so small and the roofs come down so low? And there's no veranda.'

'Hippos, Mel. A veranda must be strong enough to carry a walking hippo. That's one reason the lodge is so high up on piling. If a hippo tried to look through a window, it could break it, and the roof hanging down prevents them from approaching. It's also small enough to discourage a leopard from climbing through.

'There are chairs and a small table inside that we can carry out if we want to sit outside.'

'They look vastly different. Can you take photos?'

'I will do, Mel. Let's put our stuff inside.'

Dinner was cheerful and full of laughter as the rangers asked about the stories they had heard. Melissa had to tell the story of Robbie and afterwards, a ranger asked, 'Sam, how do you manage to keep her alive?'

'It's difficult, Cyril. I've learnt to prepare for anything.'

'Why, Sam?'

'The first time, I had to save a Kalahari Burrower from being breakfast; the second time, she disappeared into the bush and returned with a python around her neck. Then she told a lion less than forty metres away he was a mangy old beast and asked it to push off.'

When the laughter died, a ranger asked, 'Sam, we heard Melissa eats insects. Did she eat the lion?'

After several laughs, Melissa smiled, 'No, he was too old, probably stringy, and he left when I told him to.'

Petrus asked, 'What happened with the kid at Nxai Pan?'

Surprised, Sam asked, 'How do you know about that?'

'You should look at the Facebook page. You and Melissa are the superheroes of Likesedi. At least the kid's parents think you are.'

Melissa had to tell that story as well.

33

· · · · ·

THEY ROSE LATE FOR ONCE, DRANK A COFFEE, SHOWERED, dressed, and went for breakfast. As they left the lodge dining area, the unexpected happened. One of the rangers returned early, screeched to a halt before the lodge, and hurried into the office. Sam and Melissa heard his voice. 'Petrus, there's a baby elephant stuck in a mudhole by the riverbank; the adults are trying to extract it.'

'Where? And can we help?'

'By the nyala tree struck by lightning. I don't think we can do anything, but I came to tell you.'

Melissa surprised Sam, for she stepped purposely into the office. Sam could only follow and heard her say, 'Petrus. If you aren't going to help, I am.'

Petrus looked at her, 'We'll certainly go, Melissa, but the elephants will be upset and won't allow us near them.'

Sam said, 'If we're going, we must take ropes and slings. Do you have any?'

Petrus turned to the ranger. 'Go to the store. We have polypropene padded slings and fifty metres of polypropene cord for rescue. Fetch them.'

'Melissa,' said Sam, 'we'll take the Landy; the winch on the front has seventy metres of wire cable. I don't know what we can do, but it might help.'

As they left the office, *N!ki'ka* joined them. He'd come for the scheduled drive.

Five minutes later, the ranger with Petrus led the way with the Landy close behind. When they stopped, Sam stopped beside the safari wagon and estimated they were a hundred metres from a small group of four elephants by the river's edge and a larger group standing further away. Melissa jumped out, carrying their binoculars and climbed onto the Landy bonnet. Petrus, the ranger and *N!ki'ka* climbed onto the safari wagon.

Sam asked, 'What can you see, Mel?'

'Not much, there's a baby in the mud, and there's one elephant with it trying to dig it out. I think the biggest one is the matriarch, she's giving instructions, and there's another half-kneeling on the bank trying to help. The baby is up to its mouth in the mud and breathes through its trunk. I must go closer to see.'

Petrus said, 'If you go closer, you'll be in trouble. They don't like interference when they have a problem and won't run.'

'Mel, these elephants don't know you. The matriarch will charge.'

'Sam, they helped me rescue Robbie. If they let me, I must help them save their baby. I'll watch for the signs.'

Sam knew she was going. As she'd said once, short of tying her to a tree, he couldn't stop her. 'Okay, Mel, I'll come with you, but let me fetch the rope and slings first. I'll carry them.'

Sam turned and found *N!ki'ka* had anticipated the need for the rope. He was tying a loop sling to the rope five metres from the end. Sam guessed why – *two slings with a handle.*

Sam tied another sling to the end, leaving half a metre of rope loose, then shouldered the two slings and walked back to Melissa while *N!ki'ka* fed the rope to trail behind him.

'Okay, Mel, take it slowly.'

Melissa walked steadily forward with Sam half a metre behind her to one side. As Sam expected, the matriarch saw them coming, wheeled to face them, and shuffled towards them, trunk in the air. It wasn't yet a charge.

Melissa didn't hesitate but raised her arm to wave in the friendship signal, and Sam did likewise. The matriarch stopped, and Sam looked and concluded, *That's one puzzled elephant.*

They continued to walk forward, and the matriarch raised her trunk, probing the air for their scents, but she showed no sign of aggression as they approached.

Back at the vehicles, Petrus said, 'I'll be damned; that elephant seems tame.'

The ranger replied, 'She's not, boss. She charged me once when I drove too close.'

Melissa stopped a few metres before the matriarch. Sam did, too; he had no idea what came next.

Melissa had to look up at the enormous elephant to see her eyes. To Melissa, they showed curiosity.

Melissa thought her request to the matriarch. *We have come to help your grandchild. Will you allow us to pass?*

Sam took one pace forward to stand beside Melissa, his heart in his mouth, and his arm still waving. Then the matriarch reached her trunk towards them and shuffled forward until she could brush the tip over Melissa's head. After a moment, she switched to Sam, backed away, swung around and led the way to the stuck baby.

Melissa and Sam followed.

Back at the vehicles, Petrus said, 'I'll be double damned; that elephant is leading them to the baby.'

Melissa heard rumbles between the elephants. She was sure that the matriarch had told them to go when all but one elephant backed away and joined the group of others thirty metres away. Melissa decided, *The one who stayed must be the baby's mother.*

When they reached the river's edge, Sam could see the problem. The river level had dropped. And the riverbank was too steep and too high for the baby. The effort by the elephants to lift it out had created more mud, and the baby was up to its eyes in the bog; only its little trunk kept it alive. It also seemed tired as it was not struggling.

Sam didn't think of the adult beasts; the pitiful baby galvanised him. He dropped the slings, took the end one, and slid over the bank into the mud beside the baby and, holding the free end of the sling, tried to push it under the baby's chest.

Melissa saw his problem. Sam could push the sling through the mud, but the thicker clay mix under the baby prevented him from pushing it out the other side. She sat, slid down the bank into the mire, and then struggled around the baby. Once away from the riverbank, the top layer was thinner as it mixed with river water, and once on the far side of the baby, she said, 'Try again, Sam. I'll try to grab it this side.'

Neither Sam, hidden behind the baby, nor Melissa, with her back to the open river, saw the danger. The mother elephant did, and she was not going to stand by and watch a crocodile attack her child, so she launched herself off the bank in an attack to drive it away. Although she succeeded, the tidal wave she created knocked Melissa sideways, and she disappeared under the muddy water but surfaced seconds later.

Single-minded, after being under once, she yelled, 'Sam, push it now,' and dived.

Sam did the same and pushed the end of the sling as far as he could, feeling relief when the sling pulled from his hand. Melissa hauled on the sling with her knees against the baby for leverage and rose to the surface.

Another two heaves, and Melissa handed the sling to Sam, who immediately tied both ends together with the remaining rope.

It was *N!ki'ka* who noticed the rope to reach the vehicles was too short, for he'd fed it out, then held the end and walked forward so he was forty metres ahead of the Landy. When he saw the mother launch into the water, he instinctively knew that a crocodile was attacking, so he ran to help Melissa. He arrived just as Sam finished tying the knot and saw Melissa was okay, with the mother guarding her and the baby from attack. *N!ki'ka* reacted by picking up the second sling and pulling it until the rope was tight. That was when the matriarch realised he was there, turned, shuffled towards him and would have attacked, but didn't because *N!ki'ka* faced her, lifted the sling and said, with multiple clicks, 'Here, pull this.' Then he added action to his words, stepped forward and threw the sling loop over a tusk.

Whether the matriarch understood or not, she jerked back when the sling landed on her tusk, the rope came tight, and she stood still for five seconds. Then she lifted her trunk, wrapped it around the rope, and began pulling.

Holding onto the sling, Sam came onto the bank with a rush when, with a noisy sucking sound, the baby suddenly came loose and slid up onto the bank. He quickly undid the knot holding the slings and stepped back, looking for Melissa. He couldn't see her.

N!ki'ka stepped forward and, with a huge smile, spoke, with clicks, a word he recognised, 'Vixen', and pointed.

Sam gaped. Walking beside the riverbank in the shallow water, the mother elephant was on its way to a place where the bank would allow her to climb out, and sitting on her was Melissa.

The matriarch was passing her trunk over the baby on the ground, and the other elephants were approaching. Sam and *N!ki'ka* stepped backwards slowly until they were well out of the way to watch the mother carrying Melissa running towards her baby. The other elephants let them pass. They saw Melissa, with a broad, happy grin, slide off the mother, drop to the ground, and kneel beside the baby. The mother caressed her hair with her trunk. Then Melissa stood and walked to them, and the elephants stepped away to let her pass.

'Mel, you enjoyed that.'

'Yes, Sam, I love them. And riding an elephant is fun. We've returned the favour. The baby will be fine once it recovers its strength. Don't you feel good too?'

'Very much, Mel. Incredibly good. We need a bath.'

She laughed and turned to *N!ki'ka*. Sam didn't understand when she said, 'You did a brave thing asking the matriarch to pull.'

Nor his reply, 'The elephant is our friend.'

They began to walk away from the elephants, but halfway to the Landy, Melissa heard an elephant behind her and looked back. The matriarch was catching up. 'Sam, stop.'

The three of them stopped and turned, and the matriarch came close. Melissa held her arm up, palm forward. *N!ki'ka* did too, so Sam followed.

Her trunk passed slowly over each hand and each head, and then Melissa dropped her hand and turned back to the vehicles as the matriarch wheeled and returned to her charges.

As they reached the vehicles, they saw that from the initial two, they had become twelve. No one was talking, although many had cameras to their eyes. Sam asked Petrus, 'Where did everyone come from?'

'News spreads fast, Sam. We'll collect the rope and slings when the ellies have gone. Right now, you and Melissa need a bath. Let's go. We'll talk at lunch. I'll drive you. You can't drive your Landy covered in mud. Benny can drive it.'

When Mel and Sam stood in their bathroom and looked in the mirror, Mel, with a huge grin, said, 'I think we should have a photo of us like this, dearest. You look like a caveman.'

'Darling, you look like a cavewoman. There were so many cameras clicking away. I expect they have taken hundreds of pictures. I'll ask Petrus to collect them. Let's wash.'

Everyone stood and clapped for ages when they entered the dining room for lunch.

Petrus stood up and tapped a glass, calling for attention. As silence fell, he said. 'This morning, everyone here witnessed something that, to my knowledge, has never happened in the Okavango: the rescue of a baby elephant. Unfortunately, Melissa, Sam, and our tracker, *N!ki'ka*, were too busy to take pictures. On their behalf, I'm asking everyone who has photographs or videos to send a copy to Sam by email or WhatsApp. A pile of slips with the details is on the table by the door. You can also use the lodge email address. Now, on behalf of everyone, I'll ask Sam and Melissa to talk to us after dinner and tell us how they managed it. I'm sure you want to know – I do.'

He turned to look at Sam and Melissa and asked.

'Sam, Melissa, will you please tell us?'

When Sam said, 'We will, Petrus. Perhaps we can persuade you that we aren't superheroes.' The applause was a repeat of their arrival at lunch.

During the lunch, the clients asked questions. They asked the lodge rangers, Sam and Melissa, equally, and Melissa had a feeling,

Why do I feel different? A little later, she thought, *I can hear a tone in their voices; it's not what they say.*

Halfway through the lunch, it clicked: *the clients all talk to me as a ranger, and the rangers speak to me as one of them. I'm a ranger! I'm a part of this world. That's why I feel different!*

34

·····

BACK IN THEIR COTTAGE, MELISSA SAID, 'SAM, I MUST WRITE MY notes today before I forget anything, but I can't write them alone. We saved that baby together, and I don't know what you were thinking. Can we write them together?'

'Of course, Mel, although I might reveal things about myself that I wouldn't like to see in a book for the world to read.'

'I promise that if you say anything you don't want in my story, I'll take it out before anyone else sees it.'

'Okay, Mel. Let's do it.'

'I'll write the beginning notes, then when I need your thoughts and actions, I'll ask.'

Fifteen minutes later, Melissa said, 'I've written the notes about arriving here, what you told me about the lodge, the cabins and the hippos, and how we went for breakfast and saw the ranger arrive in a rush, and then what I heard Petrus say, and how I reacted. How did you react, Sam?'

Sam had to think back. 'When I heard Petrus, I felt "what a shame". I know it happens; I've seen a baby elephant carcass in the mud beside a pan. Then when you told Pertrus that if he didn't go, you would, my first thought was, "Shit, Melissa's going to give orders to the elephants, and I'll be in trouble again."'

'Why, Sam?'

'Because there was no way I could stop you unless I tied you to a tree. You said so once, so I knew I was coming with you. What did you feel when I said I would come?'

It was Melissa's turn to think. 'First off, it didn't surprise me, and then when you asked for the ropes and slings, I realised just how much I needed you, and I suddenly felt that I was not alone any more. I had someone who would take risks to help me.'

'Okay, Mel. Now write down your feelings when we walked to the elephants and the matriarch came straight at us. Tell me.'

Sam could see her frown. 'It wasn't the same as with Robbie. Then, I didn't think of myself at all, but of the elephant as someone who would save us from the hyenas. This time, I wasn't sure. I don't think I would have gone on alone, but you were beside me, and if you dared to walk with me, I wasn't going to disappoint you. What did you feel, Sam?'

'It'll sound corny and stupid if I say it, Mel.'

'We're being honest, Sam. Please.'

'I believed you would succeed, Mel. I had to believe that, but I also decided that if the elephant charged, I would step in front of you, and if we both died, at least we would be in heaven together.'

'Thanks, Sam.'

Melissa wrote several lines, but she also reflected on what Sam said. *I didn't know what love was until now, but a willingness to sacrifice himself for me has clarified it.*

When she looked up, her warm smile gave Sam a thrill. 'Now, Sam, when she came forward and scented us?'

'Then I knew that somehow you had sent her the message. Afterwards, I was sure it had her flummoxed because we showed no fear.'

'I felt the same, Sam, and when she turned away, I knew she'd realised we could help.'

'I felt she'd decided we were no danger and was returning to the baby.'

Mel wrote, and then she asked, 'Now, when we reached the baby?'

'I forgot about the matriarch. I only wanted to save the baby. And you?'

'When you slid into the mud and couldn't push the sling under the baby, I couldn't help sliding in, not to save the baby, but to help you, and when the baby's mother jumped in and made the wave that knocked me over, I didn't ask why, I dived down to help you.'

'Thanks, Mel. Did you see *N!ki'ka* throw the rope and second sling over the matriarch's tusk?'

'Yes, Sam. It was courageous of him, but the matriarch smelt him as San, and the elephants probably know the San aren't dangerous.'

'Mel, how did you climb onto the mother's back?'

'She helped me. I had to hold onto something when the baby became unstuck. I held her trunk and stepped on a tusk, and she lifted me. The elephants had rolled around in that mud; we must have smelt just like them by then.'

'That idea never entered my mind. It looked like you enjoyed the ride.'

'I did. What did you feel when we said goodbye to the matriarch?'

'Pride, Mel. Pride in you, pride that I had helped to save the baby, and pride that we had done it together.'

'Thanks, Sam.'

Melissa continued to write while Sam relaxed. Finally, after twenty minutes, she stopped.

'That's it. My notes are complete.'

'Mel, let's rest. We'll be late tonight after dinner. I want to say a few things to you, but that can wait until bedtime.'

They slept and woke refreshed, and Melissa said, 'I'll take another shower. Then, would you massage me with oil? That mud dried my skin.'

'With pleasure, Mel.'

Melissa came from the shower, naked with wet hair, and Sam knew he loved her.

'Sam, rub the oil in, don't caress me, although I like it.'

'Yes, that's better.'

'Sam, go and shower, then I'll massage you.'

She had dried and brushed her hair when he came from the shower and lay on the bed.

'I must be careful with you, Mel. You have strong fingers.'

'It must be years of typing, Sam. I've never massaged anyone before now.'

Sam and Melissa met the guests at a pre-dinner cocktail organised by Petrus, and Sam was delighted. *Melissa's relaxed, and all the guests believe she's a ranger. She belongs.*

After dinner, in the packed lounge, Sam felt *déjà vu* when he and Melissa sat on bar stools in front of the crowd.

As Sam had asked the same favour, Petrus introduced them and said Sam was researching for a doctorate, and Melissa was writing a book. Then Sam began.

'From what you said to us before dinner, I realise you have all heard of Robbie, the little boy lost at Mashatu in southeastern Botswana. What happened there was simple. Melissa found the boy within twenty metres of an elephant, and because two hyenas had also seen him, Melissa had no choice but to ask the matriarch for help. I ask you to think of your feelings if you see a three-year-old lost and crying alone. You won't ask yourself if he's a different colour or dirty; you help.'

A woman in the audience said, 'Of course we do!'

Sam smiled at her, 'That's our survival instinct; we look after children, no matter who they are. We who live here think of elephants as people. As different people, but with the same basic feelings as ours, and when Melissa and a little boy were in trouble, the matriarch helped, drove off the hyenas, and kept them safe in the herd until I arrived with our tracker.

'Today was *exactly* the same, except the baby elephant was in trouble, so it was the other way around, and Melissa felt she had to help. You might think she wanted to return the help she received, but I'm sure it's not. It was a baby in trouble, and she's a woman.

'Before anyone asks how I felt when I went with her, I was terrified, but I had confidence in her ability, and I had to go because I love her.'

Melissa heard it. *He said it in public!* She saw the smiles in the audience.

'Now I'll let Melissa tell you how she managed to win the cooperation of the elephants and ride on one.'

Melissa told the story, but she ended with a warning.

'Please remember this: outside this room, there are billions of people. Very few are our friends, and we try not to upset those who are not. It's dangerous to do so. Sam and I may be friends with two elephants, but we treat the others as people, not friends, and try not to upset them. I beg you to do the same and avoid going too close. If anyone here posts photos of the rescue, please tell everyone we can't rescue foolish people who believe elephants in reserves are tame.'

The applause was long and loud. As everyone left, Petrus said, 'Thanks, Sam. You and Melissa speak for all the lodges and rangers. I'm sure you'll head up the World Wildlife Fund one day.'

As they climbed into bed, Melissa asked quietly, 'Sam, what do you want to say and discuss.'

'I love you, Mel, and that's a problem.'

Mel smiled, 'I know. You said you loved me in the lounge, in front of all those people, so I have witnesses. Why's it a problem?'

Sam looked at her. She could see he was serious, 'Mel, you said when we had dinner at Ranzi with our friends that there are places where people belong. I think that's true, and I know that you belong here, in Botswana, just as the San, the elephants, and all the game do. Belonging brings happiness. I feel I do, too. I know because I was unhappy when I didn't belong to any place until I came to Africa. I want to marry you, but that will bring a problem in the future.'

'Sam, I want to marry you too. Where's the problem?'

'We'll have children, Mel.'

At least he didn't say we might *have children; he's determined.* 'Why's that a problem?'

'I've been thinking about it, Mel.'

Melissa felt relief and happiness. *So that's why he seemed distant these last days.* 'Tell me.'

'Mel, you know I'm an orphan. I can't help feeling that, except for an accident, I want to be a father to my children all my life, especially during their first twenty years. I'm sure it would destroy me if I had to live my life far from my young children. I must be sure they don't experience the destructive feelings of loneliness and isolation I did. But I also know I cannot live where I don't belong, such as in a city. Children need schooling. I don't want to lose them and you before they grow up.'

'Sam, Annelie will start a school for the kids at her lodge. We could do the same.'

'That only puts it off for eleven years. Coenraad owns that lodge, and Annelie can do what she wants. I'm only a ranger, although I like to believe I'm a good one. I cannot offer you anything except a ranger's life.'

'I'm sure you'll be the lodge manager soon, but we'll both think about it. A team that can save a baby elephant can do anything if we work together. Now cuddle and kiss me, and we'll sleep.' *I'll look for a lodge to buy.*

The mokoro was waiting for them after breakfast. The boatman stood on a platform at the rear end of the shallow canoe with a long punting pole. A large box of food and drink in front of him, with a folding table and two chairs in the bow. Sam had his camera bag, and in shorts and a blouse, Melissa carried two wide-brimmed hats. Cushions arranged in the centre welcomed them.

Seeing the mokoro with the reclining cushions reminded Melissa of several movies she'd watched years before. It had been the period when she dreamed of love and a handsome prince, and the films were all love stories. Some had included a scene where a boy takes a girl for a punt ride on a river, usually the Cam or the Cherwell in Oxford, where other young men wearing straw boater hats had to manage the poles inexpertly. The funniest films must have appealed to many, where the boys either fell overboard or ended their passionate quest hanging from the stick while the punt with the girl on board drifted down the river. Usually, she remembered, the girl was saved by an even more handsome hero. Melissa had found the funniest those where the girl had ended up in the water. She had two favourites. In one, the boy had proposed marriage, and without putting the ring on, the girl had thrown herself at him to kiss him, unbalancing the boat and tumbling overboard. She remembered the girl surfacing, holding the ring in the air and crying, 'I saved it!'

The second, after the boy had said the crucial words, 'Will you marry me?' the girl had spread her arms wide. She said, 'Of course, James.' The boy had tried to stand and step forward, slipped, and fell on his backside. The ring had spun through the air, in slow motion, naturally, and had fallen into the river, followed rapidly by the girl.

Melissa laughed at the memory.

'Mel, what are you laughing at?'

'Movies I remember. This mokoro reminds me of punting on the river Cam.'

'Did you go punting?'

'No, I never went to Cambridge. I was laughing at the movie.'

She told him about the second one. Sam laughed and asked, 'Did she find the ring?'

Melissa could hardly contain her laughter. 'I don't know. The funniest part came next: the boy looked where she'd gone into the water, shrugged his shoulders, and then poled the punt down the river.'

When they stopped laughing, Sam said, 'Well, I can't propose like that. I don't have a ring. You wouldn't let me buy one.'

'I know, a ring doesn't matter.'

Sam handed her into the mokoro and said, 'Sit in front, looking forward. I'll be behind you.' As he stepped in, he added, 'Much as I would like to spend hours looking at your adorable face, this is a guided trip. You must look forward, seeing things, but you can lean back against me.'

It took Sam several seconds to work out how she did it in the confined space, but seconds later, she was facing him. *She lifted her knees to her face and spun on her bum!*

'No, Sam, it's not a guided trip. I'm a fellow ranger. You said you would make me a famous author and would find me experiences to write about, remember?'

'To make me happy, help me write my book, not look at hippos.'

'Okay. As soon as we arrive at Likesedi, you can start work, and I'll help you every day.'

She spun back, leaned on him, and asked, 'Sam, where are we going?'

'This time, I can't tell you. All I know is that we'll try to see hippo, which should be easy but a little dangerous, then two rarer species: the lechwe and the sitatunga. As we float slowly past the islands that rise above the reeds, we might see leopards or lions; usually, they will be in a tree here.'

As the hours passed, and during the lunch break on a small island, Sam and Melissa sensed it happening: the happiness they had felt at dinner the night before leaked out to nowhere as the end of the trip grew closer.

35

· · · · ·

ONCE BREAKFAST WAS OVER AND THE LANDY LOADED, SAM said, 'Mel, this is the last two-hundred-kilometre stretch of our trip to Likesedi. Do you want to split it and spend a night at the Savuti River? We can camp, find a tented lodge or one with cottages.'

'Sam, what is there to see?'

'Not much. The game would be the same as we've seen, so nothing new. The second hundred, or rather the last seventy-five, would be the most interesting, where the elephants congregate in the dry season, near the Chobe River.'

'How long will it take us to Likesedi?'

'Between six and eight hours, say seven to nine hours with stops.'

'That's 4 to 5 pm. I said yesterday, Sam, the guiding is over. I can't work on the move, and you are due back at work. I know you'll be the new manager soon, and I won't be responsible if you lose that job. Let's drive through to Likesedi.'

'Okay.'

Melissa drifted into her dreamworld, where the continuous engine noise blanked out everything, and she could play her memories of the trip with Sam day by day. The gap when she spent three weeks in England became a ten-minute stop to take a leak and did not interrupt the string of days, as if she and Sam had spent a single night at Ranzi on the way north. She reached the end at 2 pm when Sam pulled off the road for lunch.

Sam had driven without noticing much. His mind was reeling,

slamming back and forth like a tennis ball, trying to find a solution.

He almost drove past the planned 2 pm lunch break.

They ate lunch in semi-silence.

Melissa recognised the situation. *We're both in question-and-answer mode again; he won't speak unless I ask. I wish I knew the answer to the problem.*

Sam had different but similar thoughts.

'Mel, let's pack up. We can reach Likesedi before dark.'

They hadn't spoken for the last fifty kilometres, each lost in their thoughts. The looming arrival and the end of the journey through Botswana appeared to her as an empty void into which the Landy would plunge, carrying them both into the unknown.

Sam stopped in front of his cottage and descended. He stretched, feeling flat. It should have been euphoric as the journey had passed without severe problems, but he felt an emptiness; the problem seemed unsolvable.

Melissa climbed out the other side, still saying nothing. The burden of an unknown future weighed heavily.

Peter arrived from the office. 'Hello, Sam. Hello, Melissa. I'm glad you made it. I've been looking forward to your arrival.'

Melissa replied first, a quiet, expressionless hello. Then Sam said, 'No problems, Peter. A scorpion stung me, but Melissa nursed me through it.'

Peter turned to Melissa. 'Melissa, I did tell you there's only one cottage available for three days: it's number four. We have a full house for the next two months.'

'I remember. That's okay. I don't need it. I'll stay with Sam.'

'Sam, I'm short two rangers, but they'll return in two days. I'm glad you're here. Could you do some game drives? I'll leave you to sort out your gear.'

Peter left, and Melissa said, 'We'll unload the Landy and put everything away, and then we have something to discuss.'

Melissa had decided to return to London and put some space between her and Sam to allow for reflection. She could visit her aunt and see the lawyer to discover if she could buy a lodge. She also had piles of notebooks she needed to complete her book, and she could refer to them and write at home.

'Sam, we have a serious decision to make. It would be best to put some space between us while we think about it. I need my notebooks in London, there's a pile of them, to finish my book, and you have work to do here. We should sign off my tourist visit, so we're free of it. Tomorrow afternoon you can drive me to Victoria Falls. I want to see them, so please show me and stay the night. You can return after leaving me at the airport the next day. I'll book a flight to Johannesburg at 10 am. Ask Peter to book a hotel for us.'

She sat at a different table that night and answered questions from the clients and rangers about saving the baby elephant but did so without cheerful descriptions. Sam did the same, feeling lost and lonely.

Sam took a group on a morning game drive at 5 am, so he didn't see Melissa for breakfast. He returned at 10 am.

He couldn't tell whether she was forcing herself to be distant or had already left him. 'Good morning, Sam. My bags are in the lounge.'

They drove to Victoria Falls in silence – a silence filled with despair – intense feelings and tension felt by both. Sam felt the same pain he'd felt when he went to boarding school. Melissa felt a different pain. She was not only leaving Sam, but all the people she'd met who loved her, and she thought, *people I love*. She turned away from Sam to look out the side window and hide the tears that dripped steadily onto her lap. *Why must we go through this agony?*

They reached Victoria Falls in time for a late lunch. Sam was in agony. *I should have let Benjy bring her. I'm an embarrassment, and she doesn't know what to say.*

Melissa dried her eyes with a tissue and thought much the same, *I should have asked Benjy to bring me. Sam hates being here.*

'Sam, what are you going to show me after lunch.'

'The standard tour of the Zimbabwe side.' Sam perked up a bit. 'Livingstone's statue, Devils Cataract, and a walk along the gorge's edge in the rain forest. I have plastic ponchos and rain hats. Then you'll return to the Landy, cross into Zambia and visit the opposite side. Our hotel is on the Zambian bank, much quieter, and once the moon rises, I'll take you to my favourite spot. It's a climb down steps to a shelf near the bottom at one end of the gorge.'

'Why's it a favourite?'

'I don't know. I love it, and seeing the rainbow in the moonlight is magic, but if you don't want to come, I'll go alone and commune with the spirits.'

Melissa didn't want to go, but she sensed Sam needed to go for some reason and felt that refusing would hurt. 'I'll come, Sam.'

As they walked through the forest by the edge of the gorge on the Zimbabwe side of the falls, Sam said, 'Don't take your hat off in the rainforest. If you look up, you'll see dozens of vervet monkeys. The tourists feed them even though the notices say don't, and monkeys poo whenever necessary. I brought a couple here once, and the wife received a dollop of monkey poo in her hair. It stinks terribly. She had to wash her hair three times before it stopped stinking.'

At dinner, the restaurant tables lined the Zambesi River's edge a metre from the river as the rippling water slid silently towards the fall into the gorge. The candlelit hotel dinner would, in other circumstances, have been romantic. Both Melissa and Sam thought so and felt it was a waste. It didn't help the conversation, for they said nothing.

As dinner ended, Sam said, 'The moon is bright and will be high enough to light up the gorge in a few minutes. We'll drive down to the car park and then go down the steps. Do you have a jacket?'

'I'll fetch it. You fetch the Landy. I'll meet you outside.'

Fifteen minutes later, with the thunder of the falls filling the air around them, Sam took the first step, with Melissa behind him, holding his hand. She almost turned back; the noise was deafening.

At first, Melissa looked along the line of the falls with the continuous cascade of water pouring over the northern edge and falling a hundred metres to the bottom. The spray so visible in the day blotted out the stars, but the moonlight turned it into an eerie grey billowing cloud, and then she saw the rainbow. To Melissa, it seemed a rainbow of death, not the glorious colours of a daytime rainbow, but a muted yellow and grey with a tinge of brown. *It looks like a rainbow in hell would look.*

She didn't look again, for the steps, watered by the continuous spray, became slippery, and Sam stepped gingerly onto each one. They reached the ledge, and she stood beside Sam and gripped his arm. Melissa grabbed his hand again as fear began to build, a fear generated by the crescendo of sound. The power released by the water seemed palpable; she imagined it wanted to beat her to the ground, crushing her under its weight, then wash her away into the boiling maelstrom below.

Sam sensed her grip tighten, glanced at her face, and felt he was cruel. *She's in pain. I should not have brought her. She's terrified.*

Suddenly, Melissa's mind turned inwards. She was once again a child, assaulted by unbearable noise. She turned to Sam, wrapped her arms around him, and, shaking, buried her head in his chest to shut out the sound. Sam wrapped his arms around her and squeezed her tight. *I wanted to hold her again, but not because I terrified her.*

Then Melissa heard the rapid thumping of his heart, and she concentrated on it. The bellowing of the falls became a whisper, and all she could hear was Sam's heart.

Thumpity-thump, thumpity-thump, thumpity-thump, ...

Sam felt her terror fall away as she stopped shaking and relaxed. They stood there for five minutes.

Thumpity-thump, thumpity-thump, thumpity-thump, ...

Then Melissa let go. Sam released her and she turned to the steps. Sam followed behind her, ready to catch her if she slipped. At the top, she said nothing, just walked to the Landy.

Inside the Landy, with the windows closed, the sound of the falls fell to a level permitting speech without shouting. Sam didn't turn to look at her. He didn't want to see her reaction. He was sure she would tell him to leave at once, so looking straight through the windscreen at nothing at all, he said, 'I'm sorry, I didn't know it would be so frightening for you. I shouldn't have taken you down.'

Her reply initially didn't register. 'I'm glad you did. It's a terrifying spectacle, but if it frightens, it comes from within, not the falls. It took me back to my early childhood when a noise like that was unbearable. I learnt that I can now stand up to it.'

Wonderingly, Sam turned to her and asked, 'So you're not mad at me?'

'Not at all, because I learnt something fundamental there. Now tell me why you like to go there.'

Sam, carried away by her forgiveness, said, 'The first times I went, I didn't understand, and then on a subsequent visit, I did. It's because down there, I feel the incredible force and power of nature that transcends anything people can do to me, and feel that if I can stand there, I can stand and face anything puny humans can try to do to me.'

Melissa looked tenderly at him. 'I understand, for I learnt that no matter how terrible things may appear – if I can put my head on your chest and listen to your heartbeat, they will go away. You can drive us back to Likesedi, and I won't leave until you throw me out.'

Sam said it slowly and carefully as if thinking of each word as he said it. 'Are you trying to tell me something?'

'Yes, sometimes you don't appear too bright.'

Sam didn't react to her dig at him; he focused on something else.

'Are you saying you want to marry me now?'

'It seems like you're getting there. Sam, we have a problem, and I've learnt the only decision we must make is to make decisions together; that way, we'll solve every problem we meet in our lifetimes.'

Sam suddenly felt euphoric, 'Darling, will you marry me?'

Melissa grinned. Sam thought it was the happiest grin he'd ever seen. Her eyes twinkled as she said, 'I will. There are conditions, though. You must finish your research and submit your thesis, and I must finish my book. Then we can go on a honeymoon.

'Do you remember saying you would make me a renowned author because you wanted a famous girlfriend?'

'Yes, I think I remember every word we have said to each other.'

'You had it wrong, my darling. I'm going to make you a famous zoologist because I deserve one.

'Now, let's return to the hotel.'

'Only after I've kissed you.'

36

WHEN MELISSA RETURNED WITH SAM, PETER ASKED, ALTHOUGH their smiles told him the answer.

'Melissa, I didn't expect you back. What happened?'

'It took an effort, Peter, but I managed to tie Sam down. He's agreed to marry me.'

'Then, congratulations to you both. I'll tell Sally.'

He did, and within two days, Martha and Annelie knew and called to congratulate them.

A week later, after lunch, Mel said, 'Sam, you told me once about your special spot, your favourite, when you told me about Karen. Take me there.'

Sam was thrilled. 'There's a bit of a climb, so boots or sports shoes. We'll leave in an hour. I'll fetch some gear and some drinks, and we should be back in time for dinner.'

'Okay.'

The climb, a bit more than halfway to the top of the rocky tree-spotted outcrop, was only a hundred metres, but it was steep. As they climbed, the vegetation became greener and thicker, and the chirrup of crickets died until the rocky shelf they reached gave a superb view over the Chobe to the plain of Zambia on the other side.

'Sam, this view is worth the climb; it's fantastic.'

'Now, I'll show you the best bit.' Sam led her to the far end of the ledge, through a cleft between two huge boulders, and stepped to one side. She stopped, amazed. The chimney in the middle of the rocky hill was fifteen metres in diameter, rising vertically to the blue sky above. On the sheer wall opposite, a trickle of water dribbled from a crack and fell, tinkling into a crystal-clear pool, with a small patch of a lichen-covered shelf on their side, no more than two double beds in size.

Melissa said, 'If the water's cool, I'll call it Yak Dar Behesht.'

'Yes, the water's pleasant and cool. But what does that name mean?'

'It's a Persian dessert, "Ice in Paradise".'

'It's my bit of paradise anyway. I come here for peace.'

'Do you swim?'

'Yes.'

'Then I'm going to swim.' Melissa stripped and stepped into the water. 'Come on, Sam.'

Sam did and swam to the side where the water trickled into the pool, looked up and let the water dribble into his gaping mouth.

'Are you drinking that water?'

'Yes, it's pure rock-filtered water and tastes great. Come here and try.'

Melissa swam over and held onto him while she tried to wriggle into the correct position, and Sam held her, conscious of a soft breast against him.

'Mel, I'm going to be busy. I'm going to see what I can do to improve Likesedi. If I can do so, it will increase my chance of becoming the manager.'

'Then I'll help, Sam, but I'll be busy too. I'm going to write the baby elephant story.'

'That's great. If you need help, ask me. I'm looking forward to hearing you read it to me.'

'I will, Sam. I promised. But do you remember I suggested you should employ a woman ranger and allow young children? You could even have a nanny and allow the under threes.'

'Would it work, Mel?'

'I'm sure it would. Plan out a short drive that includes dung beetles, antlions, and similar things, and find a woman. I would go for a young one. She might marry a ranger and stay.'

'Then we would have lodge kids and another problem.'

Melissa grinned, 'All the more reason for a school, Sam. Talk to Peter about it.'

Sam did, and Peter was enthusiastic. Sam worked out the logistics and costs of a creche and a kiddie's drive, and Peter estimated the number of such guests that would come. He was surprised at the replies he received after sending emails to every agent he knew asking for their opinion.

Sam saw the emails. Every agent replied positively, and several included a list of the enquiries they had turned down because of young children. Two said the turned-away queries were twenty-five to thirty-five per cent of their accepted bookings.

'I'm not surprised, Peter. If the agents can increase their commissions, they'll all be in favour.'

'Mel, I have a problem.'

Melissa looked up from her computer, 'What, my darling? Do you have another tick on your testicles?'

Sam smiled, 'No, that happens rarely. Not even yearly, and that time, it happened to be where I couldn't see it. Next time, I'll take it off myself.'

'Don't, Sam. It was fun. You squealed so much when I brought the tweezers near your manhood that I had trouble keeping my hand steady from laughing. Next time, grit your teeth.'

'The problem is: Where do we find a female ranger?'

'What qualifications have you written down?'

'A young and ravishing beauty who likes kids and knows a little about nature.'

'Leave out the beauty bit. We don't want the rangers following her with stars in their eyes. The answer is right in front of you, Sam.'

'Where, Mel? I can't see it.'

'A primary school teacher. One who teaches nature studies or has studied the subject. There are hundreds. And before you say getting one to leave school to come here is impossible, I'll add that there are three terms in a school year, and many of them easily manage a term or two off to have a child, so they could have a term off to spend at the lodge to further their knowledge of the wild. They would tell the other teachers how marvellous it is and how handsome the rangers are and in no time requests would flood in. Their salaries aren't excessive, so free travel, board and lodging and a salary will be attractive. Write out a spec, and let me check it.'

'You're a genius, darling. What I would do without you, I don't know.'

'Keep that thought, Sam.'

Sam met with Peter and explained what Melissa had said, and Peter replied, 'If Melissa's right, that solves the last problem. I think we have enough to justify a request to the owners. You do your part, and I'll do the rest. We'll need baby cots and small beds to put into parents' rooms.'

Peter sent in the request, and as he had no desire to spend the rest of his life as the lodge manager, he made sure that the proposal made it clear that Sam was the driving force behind it.

The directors approved it when a recruiting agent reported he would have no difficulty filling the required recruitment specification. Peter was hard-pressed to arrange the accommodation for the female ranger to be ready before she arrived, days before the start of the next school term.

Annelie called Melissa before breakfast. After an update on Annelie's pregnancy and activities, Annelie asked. 'Melissa, we've heard you are opening the lodge to children. Can you tell me more?'

Melissa did, and then Annelie surprised her. 'Could you and Sam buy shares in Likesedi if they were available?'

Melissa didn't hesitate. 'Annelie, if you know of some, please tell me.'

'We bought some Likesedi shares before Lion Sands came on the market. A shareholder who doesn't like the idea of a lodge with children called Coenraad last night and asked if we would like to buy his shares. He called us because he knows that his shares and ours make a majority. We can't buy them but have three days to tell him no.'

'Annelie, email me his name and contact details immediately. I'll forward that to my lawyer in England. You may have solved one of our problems. Thank you, and I'll call you in a few days and arrange to visit.'

Sam was determined to finish his research, for it was one of Melissa's conditions for marriage, but he decided the lodge could serve breakfasts for the clients at a high point in the reserve. He was surprised when he told Melissa.

'Sam, I've finished the baby elephant story, and I'm working on the one about you and the scorpion. After I add my account of the Hadza, I think it will be a book. I've enough time to help with the breakfasts. You must continue researching when possible. If they work, dinners beside the river will be next.'

'Okay, Mel, can you read me the baby elephant saga?'

'Tonight, Sam. In bed.'

Sam said nothing until Melissa finished reading the story. When she turned to look at him, he said before she spoke, 'Darling, I don't know what it is, but that story gives me the shivers.'

'What do you mean, Sam? Did it frighten you?'

'Not fright, darling. It took control of me. It was all happening again, but it was somehow wonderful. I don't think I can suggest anything to improve it. Send it to Amelia and continue with the scorpion.'

Amelia received it the next day but didn't read it. She took it home. As each story had arrived, she'd found it better than the last and had taken them home to read, where she could descend into the magical world the story took her to without interruption.

After reading the Mongoose cook story, because it was so good, Amelia shared it with one of the library clients, a retired teacher five years older than her. Amelia had met him when he asked if the library had a copy of a booklet of poetry by a renowned but long-dead poet. She didn't have one but had promised to ask the other libraries if they had it. He'd left his phone number for her to call if Amelia uncovered a copy. She'd found several things for him, and he'd asked her to tea on the third occasion. Amelia had discovered a sensitive man with a love of poetry, who had taught English literature and in retirement indulged in reading the poems he'd never had the time for when marking students' work. He lived in a small house in Twyford outside London, with a garden of roses, and had once asked her where she lived.

She'd called him when she received the mongoose story and asked, 'David, would you read a short story I recommend?'

'Why, Amelia?'

'Because although prose, I feel it's poetry.'

'Can you come for tea on Saturday, Amelia? If you wish, come early, and we'll walk along Twyford Brook if the weather's fine. Take the Elizabeth line from Ealing to Twyford and call me when you leave. I'll meet you at the station.'

She'd gone and he'd met her in his mini car, and they had walked along Twyford brook and back. Amelia learnt he'd been a widower for five years and lived alone. His only child, a daughter, was in Australia.

After he poured the tea, he read the story, and Amelia said nothing while he sat, staring out the window. Finally, she said. 'David, your tea's cold; I'll pour you another,' she took the cup to the kitchen to empty it.

When she returned and handed him the fresh tea, he said, 'Thank you, Amelia, both for the tea and the story.'

'So, what do you think of it?'

'I've learnt something today, something important. I've learnt that writing prose equal to the finest poets is possible. I must revise how I evaluate prose; most are insignificant compared to this story.'

'That's how I feel, David.'

'Is there more?'

'I hope so. The author, Melissa Grouwer, has promised to send me each episode.'

'Then you must come and have tea and bring them for me to read. I didn't realise you were such a sensitive person. What makes this story so good?'

Amelia replied, 'It's not the words or the phrasing, although they are outstanding. For me, what shines from each paragraph is love – love for the place, the mongoose, and Sam.'

'Is he married?'

'No, but they will marry unless Sam has a heart of stone.'

Amelia had visited with every story, and the accounts brought them together, two people who had not realised how lonely they were. The baby elephant story did something else. After David read it, the discussion was long because once Amelia said she would edit it, he asked if they could do it together.

They did, and then David looked at his watch. 'Amelia, it's late. I've whatever's necessary to make supper. Can I ask you to stay the night?'

Amelia was surprised, realised she wasn't shocked, and thought *Melissa would.*

'Yes, David. Can you lend me some pyjamas?'

SAM LEFT FOR KASANE AT 10 AM. HE HAD SUPPLIES TO COLLECT, a lodge safari vehicle that needed new tyres and alignment, and at 5 pm, a new client to collect from the incoming Francistown flight.

Melissa was working on her book in the lounge of their cottage. She and Sam were unaware that Karen McPherson had arrived on the early flight from Gaborone, and another ranger had collected her. Karen had booked a four-day stay and arrived at 10:30 am. A week earlier, she'd broken up with her boyfriend when she'd told him that her ratings were down, and he'd walked out. She remembered Sam.

Peter didn't know Karen had visited the lodge and hadn't yet mentioned the booking to any rangers. Peter met her, took her to a cottage, and left, inviting her to lunch.

Karen didn't unpack. She walked to Sam's cottage and knocked on the mosquito screen door.

When a woman opened the door and said, 'Hello, come in,' Karen stepped inside, surprised.

Melissa asked, 'Can I help?'

'I don't know. Is Sam here? I've just arrived.'

'No, he left for Kasane. He has things to do and will bring back a new client. He should be back this evening.'

Karen saw the papers, books, and notepad on the desk, the pile of folded clothes on a chair with women's underwear on top, and the row of three pairs of women's shoes by the door.

'Doesn't Sam live here anymore?'

Melissa could sense something. She was now sensitive to the body language of animals and people, and there was something in Karen's voice. 'He lives here. So do I. I'm his fiancée.'

Melissa sensed her disappointment. *She must be an ex-girlfriend. She's beautiful and vibrant.* 'Why do you want to see him?'

'I met him some months ago when I came on a visit. I'm Karen McPherson. He might have told you about me. I did a publicity drive for the lodge.'

'I'm Melissa. He mentioned you. I saw the pictures and videos you took, and they are marvellous. Have you checked in for a stay?'

'Just calling, Melissa. I'm going to Kasane and Gaborone tonight. Is Sam still doing a thesis?'

That's a relief. I've no idea what competition I might have. 'Yes, Sam's nearly finished, and I'm near the end of my book that Sam is helping me to write. We've planned our marriage when both are complete.'

'Then let me congratulate you and wish you many years of happiness. Sam's a great guy, and you're a lucky woman.'

'I know. Thank you.'

Karen left, went to the office, cancelled her booking, and asked for a reservation on the evening flight to Gaborone and the first available flight to Johannesburg. She told Peter, 'I'll have lunch, and someone can drive me in afterwards. I don't want to wait hours at the airport.'

The office confirmed both, and Peter had an idea. He called Sam.

'Hi, Sam. When will the tyres and service be finished?'

'About 3 pm.'

'And the shopping? Can you do that by then?'

'Sure, no problem. Why?'

'I have a client leaving urgently, so Benjy will drive her there. He can pick up your client, and you don't need to wait three hours.'

'That's great. Give Benjy the details. I must check out the garage service, so probably leave between 3 and 4 pm.'

Benjy left thirty minutes after Sam and the two met on the road. Of course, they stopped, side by side in the bush, and Sam looked over and said, 'Hi Benjy, everything okay?'

'Sure, Sam, lots of time. The flight has a fifteen-minute delay.'

Then Sam saw Karen, 'Karen! Where did you come from? Wait a moment.'

He drove off the road into the bush, then returned on foot to Karen's side. She climbed out to meet him.

'I came from Joburg to meet you again, Sam, but I met Melissa, so I'm returning.'

Sam could sense she was sad. 'That's a relief. I don't need to explain about her. But why did you come?'

'My boyfriend walked out on me. I learnt he was only interested in me because I was successful, and as I told you it would happen, my popularity is waning. After being depressed for a week, I decided to come here to see you. I'm sorry you aren't available.'

'Karen, it would never have worked. Your world and mine are far apart. Melissa is the only woman I've met who is ready to share mine, but don't despair. Your life isn't over.'

'If I can work out what to do, maybe not.'

'Karen, you have guts and energy and thousands of followers. Ask them what interests them, where they want you to go, and what they want you to do. You might be surprised. Also, you and Jenny make a talented team, start an agency and hire out to make TV ads, and start thinking of alternatives. This is your chance to branch out.'

Sam was sure she cheered up, so he added, 'Change your tactics, don't wait for clients to come to you. Take that campaign you did for

Likesedi, set it up as a demo, and go to every lodge owner you can identify, asking if you can do the same for them.'

'Sam, I never thought of it like that. Thanks. I must go if I'm to catch that plane.'

She lifted herself on her toes, kissed him, and climbed back into the safari vehicle.

When Sam reached the lodge, he went to see Melissa but didn't mention seeing Karen. 'Sam, you're early.'

'Yes, Benjy is fetching the client. The flight is late. How's the book?'

'Coming along. Can we go for a sundowner on the veranda?'

'Of course, let's go.' *Melissa has something to tell me.*

With a beer and Melissa's usual Appletiser, Melissa said, 'Sam, I need the notebooks I left in London to finish our book.'

'Then send for them.'

'There are dozens when all I need are one or two, but I can't tell Mrs Drew which ones. I don't remember. How about if I go to London for a month, finish the book, send it to a publisher and then return.'

'When?'

'Let's say a month before you must go to submit your thesis. Then we can meet in London, both free to go on a honeymoon.'

'Do you know where you'd like to go?'

'Yes, Sam. A retired gentleman in the care home looking after my mother, told me. I want to go to Lapland and see the aurora.'

Sam said, 'I estimate that will be two months. You would leave in a month. Is that right?'

'That will work fine. Let's go for dinner.'

Sam showered first, then slipped into bed as Melissa entered the bathroom. When he heard the bathroom door open, he turned to look at her. She didn't have her nightie on. Instead, she had a small bead apron hanging strategically from a string around her waist and a bead necklace with two decorated patches that covered her nipples. She stopped halfway to the bed. 'Sam, am I beautiful?'

Sam had a frog in his throat. It was hard to speak, so he gulped, 'The most beautiful woman I've ever seen. Am I your special man?'

'Yes, Sam. The Hadza women gave these to me.'

'Dior needs a lesson from the Hadza on how to dress a woman to be enticing; you're lovely.'

'When they told me to wear the costume for a special man, they said I must jump up and down like the Maasai do, like this.'

Melissa jumped, and Sam had a fleeting glimpse of everything hidden as the bead patches rose and fell.

'Do it again, but even better: jump like that to the bed.'

She did, then slipped into bed beside him, turned to him and said, 'Kiss me.'

A minute later, she whispered, 'You know what the bead costume means, Sam.'

'Yes, my darling, lie on top of me...'

'Mel, the Hadza are incredible couturiers.'

'Why?'

'Because these clothes don't get in the way, and....'

'Sam, oh, Sam. *More, please.... More!... .*'

'You've lost out, Sam.'

'What do you mean.'

'You've often said you wanted to eat me. Now I've eaten you.'

'Technically, I guess that's true. I surrender; eat me as often as you like.'

'That sounds like a sensible suggestion... '

'I could lie here like this forever. If only I had known, I would have eaten you long ago.'

'You can lie on me all night. Now go to sleep.'

Melissa woke in Sam's arms and looked at his face until he opened his eyes, and then she kissed him. She moved back and spoke.

'Karen was here yesterday, Sam.'

'I know. I met her on the road when our cars crossed. I told her I was always the wrong guy, for our lives were too far apart.'

'And ours aren't?'

'No, we're a perfect fit.'

Melissa grinned at him; Sam could *feel* her lascivious smile. 'Sam, I'm going to roll onto my back. Please prove we're a perfect fit... '

'You're quite something, Sam Daniels. Let's shower and go for breakfast. I've five kids to entertain this evening while their parents do a night drive. And the first opportunity you have, I want to return to Paradise. I want to christen it.'

'How will you do that?'

'With a sleeping bag to lie on and my Hadza clothes.'

'Mel, are we mated now?'

'Yes. And don't forget, foxes mate for life.'

A month later, Melissa packed her bag. 'Sam, don't forget to come to London. I'll be waiting.'

'I'll be there. That's one thing you can be sure will happen.'

The drive to Kasane seemed to fly by. When they arrived in town Melissa said, 'Call in at the pharmacy. I need some travel pills and Panadol.'

'Do you suffer from airsickness?'

'Sometimes I'm queasy. Having some with me is best.'

After checking in, they sat together on the concourse until they heard a call for passengers, and Sam kissed her thoroughly. 'It'll be a long month. I'll try and make it quicker.'

He watched her go through the passenger route, then fished his airport pass from a pocket. It would allow him into the restricted area where he could watch the plane leaving. He had to visit the toilet and reached the window to see a queue of passengers by the aircraft steps.

He couldn't see Melissa but assumed she'd already entered. He watched until the plane took off, and then, feeling low, he returned to his Landy. Fifty metres from it, he saw the shadow of a person in the front seat and burst into a run, for he thought, *Some bastard's trying to steal something.*

He threw open the door and was about to grab the person when he realised it was Melissa.

'Mel! What are you doing here? I thought you had gone.'

She was sitting, her hands folded in her lap, and staring at her hands. She didn't turn to look at him.

'I'm scared.'

'Why?'

She opened her hands and, still without looking at him, handed him a packet. 'I bought it in the pharmacy and used it in the departure lounge toilet.'

Dreading what he might learn, Sam looked down at the packet. It took him several seconds to understand. 'Is it positive?'

'Yes, I was too scared to go alone. I need you beside me.'

'Mel, it's the most wonderful gift any man can have. Come down. I want to kiss you...'

Melissa smiled, 'So you aren't mad at me?'

'Wait until we reach the lodge, and I'll prove it.'

'If these seat backs folded back flat, I'd ask you to prove it now!'

Sam replied as he started the engine. 'That's brilliant. You should tell Land Rover customer support. They might increase sales!'

Sam sent an email to Robbie's dad. He included the foreword he'd written, and Melissa had reworked it for her book. He'd based it on the speech he'd given at Mashatu.

> Dear Tom,
>
> Melissa has a collection of notebooks at the London address below. She needs them to finish the book. Can you arrange for someone to collect, pack, and send them to her at the lodge address below? You promised help, so I'm taking advantage.
>
> I have attached the foreword I wrote for Melissa's book. Melissa corrected it, but I suspect someone far more skilled than me can do a much better job. If you are still interested in publishing her book, you will receive the completed manuscript before anyone else in about four weeks.
>
> Regards from us both to you, your wife, and especially Robbie,
>
> Sam and Melissa.

The crate of notebooks arrived with a note by courier a week later. 'Waiting in anticipation for your manuscript.'

Epilogue

THERE IS A LONDON STREET OF THREE-STOREY GEORGIAN HOUSES with stone facades, once a gleaming pale cream and now fifty shades of grey – stolid, eternal, grudgingly lending but not giving status to the occupants. The gargoyles adorning the porticos that shield the heavy wooden doors have various expressions, but the doors are all identical. Closer examination will reveal that the massive, smiling, polished brass door knockers are all the same, except one.

It's new.

The little label beside the bell push reads, 'Dr and Mrs Sam Daniels.'

They are rarely there. Sam is usually elsewhere as head of the World Wildlife Fund, and Melissa is with him unless she's at Likesedi. Their son, Grant, who has degrees from Harper Adams, runs Likesedi Lodge, and their daughter, Savannah, runs something else.

Three kilometres from Likesedi Lodge, there is a clearing, five hectares in size. In it, surrounded by playing fields, is a primary school and a secondary school. The badge of the school uniform shows a human figure with a raised arm and open hand standing before an elephant.

There are three school badges: the primary school badge is smaller, with a child, and the other two are the same, except the girl's badge has a young woman, and the boy's badge has a young man. The school motto underneath them is common to all three. 'We are One'.

Savannah is the primary school principal. The high school head, Petrus Jacobus, called Jama by his family and friends, is Annelie's eldest son and Savannah's husband. Although the notice board at the school entrance announces the official school names, Likesedi Primary and Likesedi Secondary, ask any ranger in Botswana and many in the surrounding countries where they went to school. The reply will be *Melissa and Sam Daniels's*.